Inspired by a true story

Carol Cujec
Peyton Goddard

SHADOW
MOUNTAIN

*To all teachers who see their students
with possibilities instead of limitations.*

—CAROL CUJEC

*To all awed by feeling you are nothings,
know you are pertinent to the whole of creation.
Know you are real to God and me.*

—PEYTON GODDARD

Visit us at ShadowMountain.com

Characters and events in this book were inspired by the life of Peyton Goddard but are represented fictitiously.

Library of Congress Cataloging-in-Publication Data

Names: Cujec, Carol, author. | Goddard, Peyton, author.

Title: Real / Carol Cujec, Peyton Goddard.

Description: Salt Lake City : Shadow Mountain, [2020] | Audience: Grades 7–9. | Summary: Sometimes Charity cannot control her body and because she has low-functioning autism, Charity cannot communicate her thoughts to anyone else, even though she feels all of the frustrations, fears, and doubts of a typical thirteen-year-old.

Identifiers: LCCN 2020033163 | ISBN 9781629727899 (hardback)

Subjects: CYAC: Autism—Fiction. | Selective mutism—Fiction. | People with disabilities—Fiction. | Interpersonal relations—Fiction. | Schools—Fiction. | LCGFT: Fiction. | Bildungsromans.

Classification: LCC PZ7.1.C827 Re 2020 | DDC [Fic]—dc23

LC record available at https://lccn.loc.gov/2020033163

Printed in the United States of America

Lake Book Manufacturing, Inc., Melrose Park, IL

10 9 8 7 6 5 4 3 2 1

Real is being loved. It is the quest of all.

—PEYTON GODDARD

The R-Word

My name is Charity. I am thirteen years old plus eighty-seven days. I love sour gummies and pepperoni pizza. That last part no one knows because I have not spoken a sentence since I was born. Each dawning day, I live in terror of my unpredictable body that no one understands.

●●●

"Little surfer, little one . . ." Dad's music echoed from the bathroom. I watched steam escape under the door.

"Scrub all the sand out from between your toes!" Mom yelled to him from my bedroom across the hall. Then she stood me in front of the full-length mirror with a see-how-pretty-you-look grin. Her white teeth smiled for both of us. Her green eyes opened wide, hoping I would agree.

I did not.

My own face, minus expression, stared back at me. My mouth hung open like a sea bass. Some people think if I do not show emotion that means I do not feel any.

That is like saying if someone is asleep, they are dead.

Page 254: Giant sea bass can change color to warn
members of their group about potential danger.

*If I were a sea bass, my body would be blinking bright red
now.*

Mom smoothed my mousy-brown hair, braided into pig-
tails, and wrapped her arms around my shoulders. "Beautiful.
My precious girl."

People besides my mom have called me beautiful. Except
they say it with a frown, so that "beautiful" sounds like "what
a pity."

I begged for words to yell at Mom.

*What are you thinking? I look like a prissy pink cupcake
clown in this dress! Itchy lace is strangling my neck. And a giant
bow at my waist . . . Really? You think I am still five?*

Thoughts flooded my head, oozed from every pore. But
all that escaped my lips were noises with no meaning. I could
not complain like other teenagers. Only grunt like a horse. My
tongue stuck out of my mouth, my palms slapped my hips,
and my knees swayed apart-together, apart-together in those
pink, ridiculous knee socks. Mom planted a silk flower in my
hair—the cherry on top of a dog-poop sundae.

*You think if I look cute, people will forgive my weird behav-
ior?*

My knees swayed apart-together, apart-together.

Probability: low.

My whole life, I have lived with this brain/body disconnect. The Thinkers—the people with fancy initials after their
names—have examined, poked, analyzed me a million times.
After all the tests, I am labeled, like a strange species of toad

2

they have discovered. Most people see me only as that label, not as a real person.

If they stuck a nametag on my shirt, it would say: "Hello, my name is Autism."

My official diagnosis: *low-functioning autistic*. Nothing like setting high expectations.

Some call me *special*. Is that supposed to make me feel good?

And do not get me started on the R-word. I mean, think of a really disgusting food. For me, that's oatmeal. Hello? A luke-warm cereal that looks like barf? Even if Mom stirs in chopped apples and walnuts, then it's just chunky barf. Anyhow, that R-word, every time I hear it, tastes like oatmeal to my ears.

After taking so long to tug on my clothes and torture my hair, Mom had to get herself dressed in a flash. Not so hard, since her one and only dressy dress was a baggy peach thing that reminded me of a nightgown. Mom is so pretty and grace-ful she managed to look beautiful in it anyway.

Dad shuffled into the room, stiff as a soldier, wearing his cream-colored suit and sky-blue tie. He hated wearing long pants any day of the year. Since he owned a surf shop on the pier, he did not have to suffer too often.

One look at my ridiculous outfit and he said, "Gadzooks, Gail! What have you done to her?"

That's why I love my dad.

I wish people could see inside my head. It's amazing in here. First of all, my memory is infinite. Scenes from my past play back like high-def IMAX films with surround sound. I can hear a melody once and know it forever.

This can be irritating too, like when that Tubby Trash Bag commercial gets stuck on repeat in my brain.

Na na na na—icky, yucky, stinky mess!
Na na na na—Tubby Trash Bags are the best!

Everything I read, my mind archives in color-coded folders tucked into alphabetized filing cabinets. That's how I imagine it, anyway. Since forever, Mom gave me books to keep my hands busy. My favorite book—the one I still take everywhere, even with its well-worn cardboard cover and silver duct-taped spine—is *The Amazing Kids' Animal Encyclopedia.* People think I like looking at the glossy pictures. They do not realize I have memorized all the animal facts—*all* of them—a total of 327. My mind flashes back to these facts like a prayer, especially when I get jittery nervous.

Numbers, too. My mind soaks them in like thirsty paper towels mop up my spilled oatmeal. (Mom does not get why my oatmeal bowl keeps falling on the floor.)

Na na na na—icky, yucky, stinky mess!

I can keep track of how much money our grocery cart will cost with each item Mom puts in. I want to scream when she weighs the organic, steel-cut oatmeal from the bulk bin: *Do NOT buy $6.49 worth of that barf. You could get a whole POUND of gummy worms for that price.*

Could I solve a Rubik's Cube in less than thirty seconds? In my head? Probability: high. Getting my hands to cooperate in making all the turns? Probability: zero.

In the car, Dad strapped on my seatbelt, and Mom handed

me my sippy cup. Yes, a sippy cup of watered-down apple juice
. . . for a thirteen-year-old.

Could I get a caramel frappuccino JUST ONCE?

Even worse, she covered my lap with the fluffy Barbie princess blankie I've had since I was three, in case I spill.

Did I mention I *am thirteen*?

"You're going to see your cousin Mason today, sweetheart. Can you believe it? How long has it been?"

Eight years, fifteen days and five hours, to be exact. It was the one thing that made this day bearable. My long-lost cousin was moving back to our town. At last, a friend for Charity.

Then Mom handed me my animal encyclopedia and turned on a Disney CD, probably so I could not hear them talking. It played "When You Wish upon a Star" from my least-favorite movie, *Pinocchio*, about the puppet who wants to be a real boy. I sang a different song inside my head and flapped my fingers in front of my eyes to make the sunlight dance.

Flap, flap, flap.

If my brain moves like lightning, my body sometimes moves like it's been invaded by aliens. For no apparent reason, I might jump, flap my arms, clap my hands, shrug my shoulders, squish my lips out like a duck face. Sometimes I am in control of my body, sometimes I am not. Even I do not understand how my body works. And no one can imagine how scary that feels.

My cousin Mason is one of the only kids who never looked at me weird. That's because cousin = friend. It's a rule.

Adults are even worse than kids. They just shake their

heads and whisper that disgusting R-word. They think that because I cannot talk, I do not understand what they say. They think I cannot see the such-a-tragedy look on their faces.

Fact: my senses work *great*—maybe too well. My five senses notice everything. Except sometimes the input gets jumbled, or becomes so growling and intense, I feel I will explode.

I have a sixth sense, too. I can often sense the emotions of people around me. They flow through me and pound on my heart. A painful talent for someone who most people consider brainless.

Mom's prickly anxiety in the car, for example, hit me hard.

Mom fastened her pearl earrings in the mirror. "Steve, we have to make this work." She flashed me a smile in the back seat. I noted a dribble of sweat running down her neck.

Luckily, Mom's constant code-red worry is balanced by Dad's aloha cool. Their competing emotions rumble in my chest—Dad's spring rain usually drenches Mom's forest fires.

"It'll be fine, Gail. Cherry and I will take a walk when she gets fidgety."

Cherry, that's Dad's nickname for me. One of many.

Wherever we go, Dad takes me for little strolls to calm my restless body. We sashay, gallop, and skip all over town. For me it's scary to stay still for too long. My body begs to move most of the time—dart, turn, tap, jump, flap, rock. My hands beg to touch things around me—books on shelves, pebbles on the ground, people's faces, or lint on their clothes.

In second grade, a boy screamed when he saw me reaching for his throat. I only wanted to feel the silver, shiny buttons on his coat.

"Fishface tried to strangle me!" That was his nickname for me—Fishface. How come *I* was the one sent home for the rest of the day?

Dad parked the car across from a white church overlooking the ocean and unbuckled me. "Hang in there, princess," he whispered. "I stashed our favorite T-shirts and shorts in the trunk. We won't have to suffer too long."

He helped me out of the car, and I breathed the salty, fresh air. My body hopped, and Dad hopped along with me while Mom finished painting her lipstick on perfectly.

Hop. Hop. Hop. Hop.

"Hey, remember our first trip to that beach?" Dad pointed to a ribbon of sand below the cliff.

Of course I remembered that day: July 30th. I was five years old. Dad promised to take me to the beach, and I was expecting the usual splashing and bobbing in my crab floatie. Instead, Dad zipped me into a small wetsuit and strapped an orange life vest around my chest. Then he walked me toward the water, holding his surfboard under one arm. "This is the day Princess Charity gets her mermaid tail."

I had watched *The Little Mermaid* eight times, and I knew she did not ride a surfboard. Dad was goofy to think *I* could.

Goofy Dad did not give me time to panic. Once in the water, he laid me belly down on the board in front of him and paddled us out toward the waves. I clung tight with both hands and squinted my eyes almost closed. I tried to calm myself by imagining manta rays swimming below, the rubbery ocean bats we once pet at SeaWorld. Maybe they would scoop me up if I sank too deep. But after a few minutes of feeling the rhythm of the ocean, the lightness of floating up and down on the waves, I felt I was one of them—a manta ray, gliding through the water on my fishy wings.

Dad eyed the horizon and turned the surfboard to face the shore. "We're gonna stand up on the count of three." He said it calmly, as if we did this every day. Sure enough, in one . . . two . . . three . . . Dad pulled me *up* and held on to me as we rode the breaking wave all the way back to the beach. I giggled and grinned bigger than a spotted hyena.

Dad and I caught dozens more waves that day, and, with each one, my muscles slowly learned the pattern. Near sunset, he looked at his watch and realized Mom was probably going to kill us for being so late. "Don't let anyone tell you what you can't do, Cherry Girl," he said to me as he tied his board onto the roof of the car. "Life's an adventure. Dive in!"

••

"We'd better get in there." Mom smoothed my hair for the tenth time that day and poofed out the skirt on my prissy princess dress.

Where is a fairy godmother when you need one?

Then she fastened my hand to hers like superglue to cross the street. She always worried I might dart into traffic.

She was right to worry. My body had done that before—darting into the street to the sound of screams and screeching tires.

We walked through a giant wooden doorway into the church entrance hall. As soon as people saw me, whispers buzzed in my ears. Everyone was probably wondering the same thing: *Would Charity have one of her famous freak-outs?*

I could make a prediction. An hour-long service . . . with a hundred people watching . . . including all my family . . . and all their friends.

Pressure: high. That is a bad start.

> Page 30: The Madagascar chameleon can change
> its skin color to blend into its surroundings.

My dumb pink dress was doing the opposite for me.
Maybe Mason can help me.

My eyes scanned the room for my cousin's grin, stained with grape Kool-Aid the last time I saw him. Would he grab me in a monkey hug like when we were five?

My nose drifted toward a smell. Lilac hand cream. The next second, I felt Grammy's warm cheek on my ear.

"Pretty as a September peach. 'Bout time your mother bought you some nice clothes."

She said that last part with a wink to Mom. Gram grew up a true Southern lady before she moved here with Pops. The wild water's edge, she called it.

Next, I caught a whiff of black cherry, flavor of the week at Pops' ice cream shop.

"There's my chipmunk!" Pops offered his hand for a fist bump—I am good at those—then bent down for a whisper. "Bet you can't wait to get out of that silly getup they put you in."

I tried to nod and smile, but I think all I did was wiggle a little.

Pops was royally right. I just hoped I would not rip my dress off in the middle of the ceremony.

Mom turned me around. "Charity, you remember your cousin Mason?"

Thank goodness.

My eyes searched. Mom pointed to a boy in a navy blazer wearing gold, glossy sunglasses.

Could it be him? Who wears sunglasses inside?

This was not the monkey boy I used to splash in the kiddie pool. Now he looked like one of the surfer boys at Dad's shop, the kind who say *dude* and *gnarly*.

His mom, my Aunt Kiki, pushed him in my direction. "Mason, sweetie, go hug your cousin."

My heart wanted him to squeeze me like toothpaste. But he just stood there. The corners of my mouth melted down.

Mason tilted his head and scanned me over the top of his sunglasses. My lips puckered in a duck face. He took a step back.

"What the flip is wrong with her?" he whispered to his mom.

Aunt Kiki pretended not to hear as she shoved Mason into the church.

Just keep smiling and pretend everything is fine. That's how my Aunt Kiki handles problems. I guess she never told Mason what a disaster I had become.

Chances of friendship: zero.

Page 197: Ocelots are territorial and solitary.
Because of their small size, they often
fall prey to large cats and snakes.

I swallowed hard.

The music started, and Mom pulled me to our seats. I sat between Mom and Dad, a worry-filled girl on a wooden bench, hoping against all probability that I could keep calm.

I am like Pinocchio sitting on the shelf. Will anyone ever know I have a real heart and can feel it break?

Charity Case

My eyes darted from wall to wall, noting all the details of the Chapel by the Sea. Light beamed through stained-glass windows, shining a kaleidoscope on the altar. Every color of dress and suit decorated the long oak benches. We sat near the back, in case we needed to make a speedy exit.

Mom was already sniffling at the idea of her little sister getting married. "I hope Elvi doesn't start crying when she walks down the aisle."

"Yeah," Dad whispered, "she's probably wearing a metric ton of mascara, so it wouldn't look pretty."

He barely escaped Mom's elbow in his ribs, but I noted the corners of her mouth trying not to smile.

My sixth sense told me Aunt Elvi felt more pity than love toward me. And it was hard to tell who she pitied more, me or Mom.

I noted Elvi's frown whenever Mom had to help me do something.

Sad to say, I need a lot of help. Many tasks that seem simple are like mountains I struggle to climb. I cannot cut my food or button my pants or go to the bathroom without support. A typical teenager would say my life s-u-c-k-e-d. I do not use that word, even in my head, because Gram does not like it. She sweetly scolds random teenagers whenever she visits Dad's surf shop. "Honey, we don't say something *sucks*. We say it *vacuums vigorously*." They do not understand the joke, so they usually stare at her like she is from another planet.

Me too. I do not understand things sometimes—for example, about Aunt Elvi. (1) Why does she listen to music that sounds like an owl screeching in a bowling alley during a thunderstorm? (2) Why does she bring a black lace parasol when she goes with us to a baseball game? If it rains, the lace will be useless to keep her dry. (3) Why do all her friends have so many skull tattoos?

I could go on.

But I understood why Aunt Elvi did not want me at her wedding. She was probably afraid I would mess it up with my icky, yucky, stinky autism. For weeks, she hinted this to my mom. Five days before the wedding, they had a faceoff in our kitchen.

"You don't get it! It's my big day, Gail. I want it to be perfect." Sitting at the kitchen table, Elvi blew her cat-black bangs out of her eyes, heavy with red eyeliner. She scrunched her mouth into a pucker. With her white-powdered face and blood-red lips, she looked like a vampire from one of Dad's favorite classic horror movies.

Elvi is Mom's youngest sister. I noted that with a slight rearrangement of letters, her name would be *Evil*.

Elvi kept complaining while Mom chopped onions for

chili. The smell attacked my nose, and my mouth complained with a loud "Arrghhhhhhhh."

"You want the fan on, honey?" Mom was pretty good at interpreting my noises.

My eyes followed the rhythm of the fan blades spinning round and round, round and round. Watching things spin fills my brain with peace.

My body stood and spun with the blades.

Spin-spin-spin-spin.

Even though she's an adult, Elvi could whine as high as the two-year-old next door when his popsicle dropped on the driveway. "I mean, geez, you're my big sister. You're supposed to be up there *with* me, not babysitting your kid in the audience." Her squeaky voice scratched my eardrums. I stopped spinning.

Mom flashed Elvi a look of warning. Her teeth smiled, but she was like a cobra ready to bite. Mom had told Elvi a total of eighteen times, "Don't talk about my kid right in front of my kid." Lots of adults do that, though.

Hypothesis: Because my mouth cannot speak words, people think my ears cannot hear them.

"We've discussed this," Mom said, smiling in my direction. "I can't be in the wedding because I need to be with Charity."

The fact that the bridesmaids' dresses were the color of an orange hazmat suit might have had something to do with it too.

Elvi kept complaining till her voice reached frequencies only dogs could hear. "But Gaaaaail, couldn't you just hire a dang sitter? I mean, even if she doesn't make a scene, I don't want Joel's relatives to feel uncomfortable. They don't have any . . . *retarded* people in their family."

And there it was. The R-word. Coming from my own aunt.

That's when Mom lost it.

"Listen to me, Elvi." She pointed the chef's knife toward her sister's face. "Don't you *EV-ER* call my daughter that. She has more smarts in her little finger than anyone I know. Charity is a member of this family, and she's been excluded from important occasions more times than I can count. From now on, it's *all* of us or *none* of us."

Mom stabbed the knife into the cutting board. "Your choice."

Elvi snatched her velvet black purse and marched away. When she reached the door, she turned and hissed, "Fine."

That's why I love my mom.

Knowing that Mom fought for me to come to the wedding, I felt more pressure to stay in control. Unfortunately, when I am nervous, my unpredictable body usually does the opposite of what I want. And when I am really nervous, my insides boil like hot water in a teakettle until I pop my top in a massive KETTLE EXPLOSION.

I put my hands on the wooden bench beneath me and felt it vibrate from the church organ playing Mozart, a song called "Ave Verum Corpus," which means *Hail, true body.* I first heard this on Mom's classical music station three years ago—May 4th, to be exact. The chords flowed around my own imperfect body like the swirling, bubbling water of Gram's whirlpool tub. For a few seconds at least, the music calmed me.

In front of us sat my cousin Mason and my stylish Aunt Kiki. A tiny purple hat was perched on top of her head. I watched its feathers dance in the air.

I noted Mason peering at me over his shoulder.

Apparently, this silly pink dress does not make me look NORMAL.

Dad handed me my lucky sea glass, made smooth and round by tumbling ocean waves. We found it on the beach last spring, the color of a blue crab among all the brown, boring stones. Rolling it in my fingers kept me from biting my knuckles.

Roll. Roll. Rolling my lucky sea glass.

One by one, neon orange bridesmaids drifted down the aisle.

"Should've brought our sunglasses," Dad whispered.

Roll. Roll. Rolling my lucky sea glass.

The music paused. The organist hammered the opening notes for the "Bridal Chorus." Pounding chords shook the whole church. I covered my ears.

Everyone looked back to see Elvi wearing a black wedding dress fitted tight to her tiny waist with a ball-gown skirt. I imagined how the silky fabric felt on her skin. Her dark hair was draped over her bare shoulders. A heavy silver necklace sparkled around her throat. She beamed as she marched down the aisle on Pops' arm.

She glanced at me for a nanosecond.

I held my breath.

I am the statue of a perfectly normal child.

Roll. Roll. Rolling my lucky sea glass.

My perfect pose was broken by a man in a frilly black pirate shirt who pushed into our row. His musky cologne made me want to barf my morning oats. Acid gurgled up into my throat as all my senses overloaded.

I did not want Dad to take me out already. I had to get through this so Mom could give Elvi the tiniest *I-told-you-so* look at the reception. I breathed through my mouth.

Stay strong, Charity.

Once Elvi arrived at the altar, the organ stopped. The whole church got quiet.

Pin-drop silent.

My stomach tightened.

Get me out of here.

Even after so many explosions over the years—in classrooms, movie theatres, grocery stores, restaurants—losing control here would be embarrassing beyond calculation. Elvi's big day. A hundred people sitting silently. In a church!

I can do this.

My body rocked back and forth, back and forth, and that silly *Pinocchio* song played on repeat in my head.

Rock. Rock. Rock. Rock.

Fact: Wishing upon a star does NOT work. I have tried. And, far as I know, NO one has a magic talking cricket.

Rock. Rock. Rock. Rock.

Keep a lid on the kettle.

Lots of times, I can stay in control. It's just so much harder when the pressure is high. My meltdown would ruin it for Mom and Dad too.

We would never be invited anywhere. Ever. Again!

My body rocked back and forth, back and forth.

> Page 259: The great white shark has sharp,
> triangular teeth to tear up flesh.

The lace on my collar bit into my neck. My hands shook. They begged to rip off this cupcake dress and run out the door in my underwear.

The pastor began with a prayer. His voice sounded like a lullaby. "Heavenly Father, we pray for your presence here as we gather to unite this man and woman in holy matrimony."

I prayed too. Or tried to. My silver sandals tap-danced on the stone floor.

Tap, tap, tap.

Mason peered at me again.

Stop! Not you too!

My mind wandered back to the sandbox, our faces smudged with peanut butter and blackberry jam. I scooped sand into buckets while Mason planned the castle layout. "Fill it higher, Charity. Right to the top. Then I'll put water in, and it'll be cement for our tower."

Cousin = friend. I thought that was the rule.

Tap. Tap. Tap. Tap.

Not anymore.

He looked back again. His eyes were hot laser beams. They shrank me to a puny guppy.

Stop staring!

I see all the pity-stares. I see them even when people think I am not looking.

Define *pity*: A poison offered to another person as if it were a gift of pure gold. People feel better about their own lives by looking down on mine. That's my definition, not *Webster's*.

"Are you okay, honey?" Mom asked.

Even she could not predict that I would not last five minutes. Pity poisons bubbled up inside me like steam rising in Gram's copper teakettle. My mind tried to turn off the heat, but my hopeless body continued to percolate past its boiling point . . . KETTLE EXPLOSION, coming fast.

Probability: HIGH.

The pastor's voice droned on and on. My thumping heart set off a tremor inside my chest. Stronger and stronger. A magnitude 8.6 earthquake.

Page 111: The heart rate of a blue-throated hummingbird can reach 1,200 beats per minute.

My hand squeezed the sea glass tight. My fists beat my shaking legs.

Stay still! Stay still!

I gulped hard.

You got this . . . you got this.

Dad's voice called from a million miles away. "Let's take a little walk, Cherry Girl."

Countdown to KETTLE EXPLOSION . . . 3 . . . 2 . . . 1 . . .

My hand yanked free from Dad's and hit Aunt Kiki in the head. Her feathered hat flew off like a tiny frisbee. She shrieked. Dad scrambled to pick it up.

When he moved, my body bolted into the aisle, jumping and clapping. My brain told my body to stop, but somewhere the wires short-circuited. My body did not obey.

Jump, clap, jump, clap.

I screamed at myself inside my head.

Stop now! Sit down! You are ruining everything!

For everyone!

Forever!

My legs jumped higher.

What a relief to move. I could jump to the clouds.

Misfire! Misfire! Why can't my neurons talk to my muscles?

Jump, clap, jump, clap.

Mason's eyes popped out of his head.

You wanted something to look at? How is this for you?

Mom tried to grab my elbow.

Hard to catch a moving target.

Jump, clap, jump, clap.

Page 83: A tree frog can jump 150 times its own length.

I begged my mouth to stay shut, but I could not breathe. I gripped my neck. Could not get air . . . into . . . my lungs. Then I breathed in sweet oxygen and exhaled . . . an ear-smacking scream.

AHHHHHHHHHHHHHHHHHHHHHH!

All eyes on me. Elvi's white face somehow now red as a baboon's butt.

I tumbled down the aisle. My pink underwear in full view.

Could this get any worse?

At last Dad scooped me off the floor and flew me out superhero style. My voice moaned like a humpback whale.

OOOOWWWWWWWWWOOOOOOOOAAAAAAAAAH!

Page 312: Whales communicate using a complex language that scientists cannot yet understand.

Mom ran out the door with us and turned to offer an "I'm sorry" nod to all the guests. I did not look at them, but I knew they were shaking their heads and whispering, "Those poor parents are saints."

My name is Charity, and I am a charity case, someone that other people pity.

It's right there in the name.

Bert and Ernie

My parents are as different as Bert and Ernie from *Sesame Street*.

Mom, she is Bert—a whopper worrier and as serious as long division. Her brown, flowing hair is always sensibly ponytailed, and by the end of her busy day, half-fallen in her face. Her green eyes focus like a four-eyed fish on her multiple tasks of helping me while still looking after Dad, our dog Hero, and the brick cottage we call home, exactly 0.3 miles from the bay.

Page 73: The four-eyed fish has large, bulbous eyes divided into two parts that allow it to see above and below the water surface at the same time.

No matter what the Thinkers said, Mom and Dad always believed I could learn. Mom was a second-grade teacher before I came along. She gave up her twenty-five students to focus all her energy on me, her class of one. The two hours before dinner she called homework time. I never got actual homework from school. They assumed I could not learn anything beyond

"Cows go moo! Pigs go oink!" Every afternoon, though, Mom sat next to me at the kitchen table, laying out supplies.

Crayons, pencils, flashcards, puzzles, books.

Then she would wrap a slender arm around my shoulder and steady my fingers to hold a pencil and draw letters. Our hands and arms worked in rhythm, like Olympic ice dancers.

"Keep going. Eyes on the page. You can do it."

Even when I just sat doing a puzzle, Mom played educational TV shows, science shows, math videos. Aunt Elvi always had her pity look when she saw me watching videos on decimals or atoms or volcanoes. "C'mon, Gail, what makes you think she gets any of this?"

Mom stared her flat in the eyeballs. "What makes you think she doesn't?"

Homework was not just for home. Wherever we went, Mom toted a beach-bag-size purse full of activities so we could play matching games or look at flashcards in waiting rooms, restaurants, or between therapy appointments. In the car, she played audiobooks, and my hungry brain took in the data as eagerly as our bulldog, Hero, gobbled up liver treats.

By age three, I could read, thanks to *Sesame Street* and Mom's daily homework sessions. Mom would have been properly proud if she knew. I read signs and labels, newspaper headlines, and every book I could wrap my tiny hands around. My fidgety fingers liked feeling the pages—and tearing them sometimes too. Sad to say, that made Mom put most books on a high shelf after reading them to me. *The Amazing Kids' Animal Encyclopedia* was the first book she let me keep all to myself.

I clung to it like a life preserver.

Mom did everything she could to teach me, even though she had no evidence that it was sticking in my head. Sitting right next to her, with no way to communicate, I felt we were a million miles apart.

Define *frustration*: Being told to do the same thing over and over and not being able to do it even though I really, really want to, even though I understand *how* to, even though I *did* it once last week—but getting my body to cooperate was like teaching a hippo to tap dance.

•••

Dad, he is like Ernie from *Sesame Street*. Happy and carefree. To him, I am just right.

"We could be twins," he jokes whenever our faces smush together for a selfie.

He was a little right. We both have blue eyes ringed with specks of grasshopper green. He calls me Princess Charity or his Super Cherry or Cherry Girl, and he never treats me like I am "special."

"There's no such thing as failure, only opportunities to learn." That's his annoying attitude even when my body is a jiggly mass of cherry Jell-O. "Don't give up! Let's try it a different way."

More than once, he has proved my messy body could learn. His lessons started when I was two.

According to the "Developmental Milestones Checklist" that Mom laminated and posted on the fridge, I was supposed to be able to throw a ball by age two. When I could not do it, she panicked. Big time.

That's when Dad became my coach.

Dad was a basketball star in high school. "You were born to play ball, Cherry Girl," he told me. "You're gonna be our little hoop master."

He started off by rolling a Nerf ball. I grabbed it and drooled on it, and Dad waited and waited . . . and waited some more until I finally rolled it back.

After a week of rolling, we moved on to throwing and catching. Starting off with our hands almost touching, he tossed me the ball. I watched it hit my belly and drop to the floor.

"C'mon, Super Cherry!" he cheered.

He placed my hands out in catching position.

"It's the fourth quarter and we're down by two. You gonna let 'em win?"

I probably lost about a thousand imaginary games before finally, he threw it, and I . . . caught it! Dad jumped and whooped all over the living room. Hero—he was just a puppy back then—barked in celebration.

When I was six, I was not able to take dance classes with other little girls, so Dad had the improbable idea to teach me ballet. My sixth sense told me he was trying to make up for the fact that I had almost no friends. Believe me when I say he is no dancer. Dad's dancing is all finger-pointing and shaking his hips like a hula girl.

He was serious about this.

He made foot-shaped cutouts in different colors and taped them to the garage floor so I could see how to stand for each of the five positions. Instead of surfing on Saturday mornings, he inserted a *Swan Lake* CD into an old boom box and, dressed in his usual Hawaiian shirt and flip-flops, practiced *pliés* and *relevés* with me—those are fancy ballet words for bending your knees and standing on your tiptoes.

The music's racing violins and crashing cymbals made me feel I could leap to the clouds. My jumps flew my feet more than five inches off the ground.

On warm days, when the garage door stood open, we got big smiles from passing neighbors, especially kind Dr. Singh, a gray-haired lady who walked her beagle, Sadie, up and down the block twice a day now that she was retired. "Good for you, young lady. I expect you will be a ballet star soon."

Coach Dad launched an even bolder plan when I was eight and way too big for my tricycle. "I'm gonna teach you to ride a bike, a genuine two-wheeler, Princess Charity," he announced one Saturday morning. "Every princess needs a stallion."

The Thinkers said I could never ride a bicycle.

Never say never to my dad.

He did not tell Mom about his plan, not right away. As Safety Sheriff of the house, she would have outlawed it. He waited for a day when Mom was shopping with Gram.

"Better to ask forgiveness than permission," he told me.

Turns out Dad was a decent Safety Deputy too. It took him twenty minutes to suit me up in a helmet, elbow pads, double knee pads, and a pillow duct-taped to my back. I bounced around like a multicolored marshmallow. When we got to the big, empty parking lot at the high school, he opened the trunk and pulled out a brand-new bike with a basket in front, purple metallic streamers on the handlebars, and twenty-eight silver, shiny spokes on each wheel.

"Your stallion, m'lady."

My heart jumped to the sky. My hands clapped.

He lifted me onto the seat and placed my hands and feet in position.

Then I looked down.

No training wheels?

"Let's begin with a slow trot." With one hand on the handlebar and one on the seat, he jogged the bike in a big circle. "Pedal your feet. You can do it, Cherry!"

Dad pushed me for more than an hour till his T-shirt was soaked in sweat. Little by little, my feet got the idea to push down on the pedals.

"You got it, Cherry. Keep going!"

He took his hand off the handlebar and ran alongside with a hand on the seat to keep me steady.

"Haha! I knew you could do it!"

I noted his face stretched tight with a grin, and my chest puffed up with pride.

On the next lap, my feet pedaled a little faster. Dad let go of the seat and pretended to gallop beside me.

"Careful, honey. Not too fast."

Then my bulldog impulse took over—that's the part of me that acts on instinct instead of logic. I love my bulldog, Hero, but he barks at his own reflection and attacks the vacuum cleaner on a regular basis.

My feet heard the word "fast" and shifted into hyperdrive. I started pushing the pedals quick as a cheetah chasing prey.

Push, push, push.

> Page 32: The fastest land animal, the cheetah
> can run up to 75 miles an hour in short bursts.

I sped along the black pavement, feeling the wind on my teeth because I could not stop smiling. For the first time in my life, I felt freedom, pure freedom.

Push, push, push.

"Squeeze the brakes, Cherry! Squeeze with your hands!" Dad's screaming reached my ears.

I guess braking should have been lesson one. My eyes focused forward. My mind screamed.

Danger! Thorny bushes ahead!

My hands could not grip the brakes. My brain hollered *STOP!*

Probability of crashing? Falling? Bleeding? HIGH!

I squeezed my eyes shut and held my breath.

A second later, I was on the ground. My shoulder stung from where it scraped branches.

Dad lifted me up, breathing hard, his eyes full of fear. "My poor Charity. My princess. It was all my fault. Are you okay, honey?"

He dusted the dirt and leaves off my jacket. His eyebrows scrunched together with worry. "Let's get you home and make sure you're okay."

I squirmed out of his arms and pulled my bike out of the bushes with Dad's help. I quickly scanned its parts—the purple streamers, the white basket, the raspberry-colored seat, twenty-eight silver, shiny spokes on each wheel . . . thank goodness it was still in one piece.

I grabbed the handlebars and swung my leg over.

Dad shook his head and wiped his forehead on his arm. "No, honey, I think it's . . ."

My feet tried to pedal, but he held the handlebars tight. I pushed my leg hard as I could and grunted like a wild boar. "Grrrrraaaaaaaa."

Dad's eyebrows jumped, and a grin lit up his face.

"That's my girl. Right back on the horse."

Yes, it did hurt, but I cannot stand pity.

Especially not from my dad.

Boredom Academy

The wedding disaster weekend was followed by the usual miserable Monday. Mom pulled up to the drop-off curb, and Miss Marcia poked her head into our car, wearing her same orange, saggy sweater. Her breath stank like a cigarette-smoking donkey, even with all the wintergreen mints she stashed in her cheeks like a squirrel. When she talked, she was a symphony of crunching and sucking sounds.

"Morning, Mrs. Wood [*crunch*]. Hope you packed more of Charity's extra clothes. She's been having lots of accidents lately [*suck*]."

Mom gave me a worried glance. "That's strange. She hardly ever has a problem with this at home."

Miss Marcia unbuckled my seatbelt. She yanked me out of the car with one hand and grabbed my Wonder Woman backpack with the other.

What a joke—a helpless girl with a superhero backpack.

Still, I sometimes imagined my body spinning round and round—I love to spin—and in a burst of smoke I would transform into Wonder Woman. Strong and powerful. Ready to kick butt.

"I put three dollars in Charity's front pocket so she can buy hot lunch today," Mom said.

Miss Marcia smiled sweetly, putting on her angel face, her *I-care-deeply-about-your-child* face that she wore in front of parents.

"Oh, I'll make sure she gets it," Miss Marcia sang. "Sloppy joes today. I know how much she loves those."

"And I packed some of her sixth-grade vocabulary flashcards we've been working on," Mom said. "Could you go over those with her as well?"

"Of course, Mrs. Wood."

As soon as Mom's car drove away, Miss Marcia's smile disappeared. She reached into my pocket, pulled out the three dollars, and stuffed them into her own pocket. I saw her do this to other kids too, and I knew I would not be eating sloppy joes today. I also knew the flashcards would never leave my backpack.

If I ever do become Wonder Woman, watch out, Miss Marcia. You are first on my kick-butt list.

Kids who cannot talk are easy targets for bullies. At Borden, I learned teachers can be bullies too.

Probably the only thing I ever learned at Borden.

•••

My first few years of school, I was passed around like a radioactive potato to special education classrooms at four different schools. Most teachers made up their mind about me the second I stumbled through the door. Only one teacher believed I could learn—Miss Amira in first grade.

Because she loved nature, Miss Amira took us on field trips to the park, the forest, and the beach. We sniffed wild sage, observed ground squirrels, learned about bird calls, and searched for roly-poly bugs under rocks. She helped us grow a vegetable garden in the school courtyard and taught us how to make a blade of grass sing by blowing on it through our fingers—well, she taught other students that. I still cannot blow out my birthday candles. She even hung picture books from the trees outside our classroom to create what she called our "reading forest." Most important, Miss Amira looked at me with possibilities instead of limitations. When she saw I liked animal books, she sat with me to read, and then asked, "What do you want to do when you grow up, Charity? Maybe you'd enjoy working with a vet . . . or in a zoo? Maybe even a vet in a zoo." She grinned wide, and I smiled inside thinking about how to take an elephant's pulse or diagnose a sick skunk without getting sprayed.

After first grade, school became more and more frustrating. I needed extra help, but the schools would not let Mom come with me. With no voice, no handwriting, and fidgety fingers that would not point to the answers my brain chose, I would think to myself *diagnosis: doomed*. If I colored outside the lines, I would grab an eraser, but couldn't stop my hands from rubbing a big hole into my paper . . . which would make me crumple the paper and throw it on the floor, howling. That's when I learned about "time-out." But the time-out jittered me even more, so one time-out led to another. And another.

By third grade, I was considered too *special* for public school. That's when the Thinkers pressured my parents to send me to a private institution.

Define *institution*: a place where people are separated from the world instead of included. Separate can never be equal.

Borden Academy was not a real school. Schools are places for learning. Borden was a prison camp for disabled kids, complete with an escape-proof, eight-foot-high chain-link fence. Even the staff called it "Boredom Academy."

When Miss Marcia pulled the three dollars from my pants, she left the inside of my pocket sticking out. I get flustered by things not in their place.

Great. That is going to bug me all day.

Miss Marcia was the teacher's aide for our class for three years straight. What grade were we in? What did it matter? Nothing ever changed from one wasted year to the next.

Miss Marcia led me through the front gate. This day, as on many days, my feet refused to move any farther. My hopeless body plopped onto the blacktop about twenty-five yards from the classroom.

"Oh, for Pete's sake!" Miss Marcia yelped.

My body rocked back and forth, back and forth. I knew what was coming.

"Charity, get up. *Charity, get up.* CHARITY, GET UP!"

I wanted to scream at her.

I cannot do it, and your yelling does not help me!

Back and forth, back and forth.

•••

The Thinkers say I "lack gross motor coordination." I call it motor madness. Sometimes I am a broken robot stuck on repeat, doing the same thing over and over and over and over. I tap-tap the table, squint-squint my eyes, rock back and forth back and forth, or flush flush flush the toilet. Other times, it's like someone hits the off switch. And. I. Freeze.

This happened at least once a week in the car when Mom pulled into our driveway. I knew I was supposed to get out, but my body became a marble statue. She tried to pull or push me in the right direction. Probability of my moving: zero.

Finally, she made the best of it and stashed a few books in the front seat so she could sit and read to me until the oh-so-sweet moment my on switch worked again, and . . . hooray . . . I could control my movement. She did not get mad. She seemed to understand I could not help it.

Miss Marcia, on the other hand, squawked like a peahen—that's a female peacock—when my body froze. Her approach was to control me, not help me learn to move independently.

"For the last time, *GET UP!*"

Page 211: A group of peahens is called a party.

A group of Miss Marcias? That's no party.

"Just sit there then," she said. "I could give a rat's rump."

She dragged her worn-out loafers into the classroom (which was actually a trailer) and left me sitting in the middle of the playground—the playground where no kids ever played. A couple times, she glanced out the window to see if I had "decided" to cooperate. Or maybe she wanted to make sure there were no visitors who might be walking through the courtyard.

Another set of eyes peeked outside when Miss Marcia left—Isabella, my one and only friend in this place. Her small, round face was topped with a mop of red curls. She knocked on the window and waved for me to come inside. She kept waving until someone pulled her away.

Sad to say, my legs still refused.

And so I sat.

And sat.

> Page 4: The albatross sits on its egg up
> to 80 days before the egg hatches.

If Mom did not coat me with SPF 70 sunscreen every day, I would resemble a cooked lobster.

> Page 159: Lobsters turn red when cooked, but in
> nature, they can be many colors, even blue.

A sharp pebble poked my bottom, but my butt was glued to the ground.

Move, legs, move!

I squinted my eyes from the bright sunlight until the world became blurry, and I imagined myself as a peaceful protester, like one of the brave people who fought for justice with Martin Luther King Jr. They sat down and refused to get up until they had equal rights.

Nobody was marching or sitting down for people like me.

Isabella poked her head in the window again and held up a book. She waved at me like a baseball coach waving a runner to home plate. That finally triggered my legs to stand, and I staggered into the classroom.

Mom and Dad only saw this place when it was scrubbed and decorated for parents' night once a year. If only they could get a peek any of the other 364 days—Mom would have a heart attack. One look at our chaos-filled, zero-education class-room, and Mom would know. She would just *know*.

And she would save me.

Isabella ran up and squealed my name. "Charity, Charity, Charity is here!" She grabbed my hand and pulled me over to the beanbag chairs. "Come with me to look at books!" Her freckled cheeks puffed up in a smile, and her blue eyes, slanted a little from her Down syndrome, sparkled. Even this rotten place could not squeeze all the joy from her heart.

Isabella could not read, and I so wished I could read to her. She deserved a chance to learn. Everyone here did.

She patted the green plastic beanbag chair, its holes covered with duct tape. I sat down, and Isabella held up a book about elephants for both of us to see. I wanted to tell her all the amazing facts about them.

Page 62: African elephants feel a wide range of emotions, like grief, happiness, and compassion.

Most people do not know that I feel these emotions, too.

Clever Isabella made up her own story about a mama elephant who wanted to take her baby elephant to the hair salon. Her copper curls bounced as she told her tale.

I tried to focus on her sweet smile and eyes that grew wide when she got to the exciting part of her story. But every cell in my body itched to get out of this place, this waiting room for hopeless cases. According to the Thinkers, we were all throw-away kids that did not deserve an education.

Kids in wheelchairs were parked in front of an ancient television in the back of the room, forced to watch *Barney* for the ten thousandth time.

I wanted to scream.

They have brains, you know! So do I!

My ears were drowning in the noise—shouting and moaning kids, silly singing blaring from the television. It was the singing that made me want to stuff these beanbag chairs into my ears. No escaping the horrible smell either—like a mixture of sweat socks, wet dog, and Miss Marcia's donkey breath. My brain overloaded.

Woodpeckers chipped at my skull.

> Page 320: The woodpecker's chisel-like bill
> pecks at a rate of twenty times each second.

I wondered what kids in a real school were learning today—maybe how to calculate the area of a circle, or what Shakespeare meant by "To be or not to be," or why rotten eggs smelled like farts.

Do those kids know how lucky they are?

Probability: low.

Miss Marcia patrolled the room like a prison guard, snapping at kids to "Knock it off!" or "Put a lid on it!" and threatening to banish them to the dreaded time-out closet. I lived in fear of it every moment. Each lockup chipped away at my already broken heart.

Could I escape it today?

My body felt restless. I got up and shook my hands and legs. Maybe I could shake off the hopelessness.

Shake, shake, shake.

My feet walked toward a boy named Jacob playing with Lego blocks. He could not talk either, but he built amazing structures from the sad, mismatched Lego collection kept in a plastic laundry basket. How could they not see his cleverness? He stacked his bricks in tall towers—seventeen blue, nineteen red, twenty-three green, twenty-nine yellow—all prime numbers.

I reached out to touch a soaring tower, and he screamed with full force.

That made me scream too.

Ahhhhhhhhhhhhhh!

"You will be okay, Charity. You will be okay."

Kind Isabella was there in a flash, patting my cheek.

Thank goodness. Her kindness helped my mouth to close and my body to settle. But my peace did not last long. Miss Marcia pulled me by the arm and sat me in the nearest chair. She plunked a jack-in-the-box on the table in front of me.

Behavior data reports were due every day, so it was time for me to fail another test.

"Turn the handle. Turn the handle. Turn the handle." She repeated the same words robotically.

I begged for words.

First of all, a jack-in-the-box is a toy for a four-year-old, not a thirteen-year-old. Second of all, I would not turn the handle if I could. I do not want to see that white clown face jump out with his creepy smile, yellow hair, and missing eye.

My arm knocked the rusty metal box to the floor.

"You're tap dancing on my last nerve, Missy." Miss Marcia sucked and crunched her mints while marking my failure on the useless chart that analyzed my daily progress for the Thinkers.

Progress? What a joke!

Then she picked up the jack-in-the-box, held it two inches from my nose, and twisted the silver, tiny handle.

"Here's how you're supposed to do it," muttering, "for the umpteenth time" under her breath.

Da-ding-da-ding-da-ding-da-ping-ping . . .

Each ding and ping slapped my ear. The smell of her donkey breath hit me in the nose.

Da-ding-da-ding-da-ding-ping . . .

My heart pounded faster. Every note turned up the heat on the boiling kettle inside me. I begged my body.

Please stay in control. Please stay in control.

Miss Marcia smiled. Like the creepy clown.

Da-ding-da-ding . . .

My bulldog impulse took over. My hands squeezed into fists. Firecrackers exploded in my toes.

Stop it! Stop it! Stop it!

Countdown to KETTLE EXPLOSION . . . 3 . . . 2 . . . 1 . . .

I jumped up—knocking the toy to the floor—and screeched like a bat *on fire*.

Ahhhhhhhhhhhhhh!

**Page 15: Bats can produce sounds
louder than a rock concert.**

Isabella appeared by my side and jumped with me, clapping her hands.

Oh no! Too late.

Miss Marcia pushed Isabella away and grabbed my arm. I knew what was coming.

Nooooooooo!

Ahhhhhhhhhhhhhh!

Miss Marcia dragged me. Across the room. Opened the closet door.

Nooooooooo!

Ahhhhhhhhhhhhhh!

My mouth moaned. My fingers gripped the door frame.

Miss Marcia peeled my fingers off.

One.

By.

One.

Slam! Click.

Time-out closet. Cave-dark except for the ray of light peeking under the door.

Page 15: Bats use sound waves to navigate in the dark.

My body screamed and jumped.

Ahhhhhhhhhhhhhh! Ahhhhhhhhhhhhhh!

Locked up like a beast. They lock me away instead of trying to understand me . . . trying to help me.

Ahhhhhhhhhhhhhh!

I'm worthless . . . moldy bread . . . a spit-out piece of gum in the gutter.

After a few minutes, my mouth stopped screaming. I puffed air to catch my breath. There was nothing to do in here, nothing to sit on, even. I lay on the floor and peered beneath the door. Isabella's purple sneakers paced back and forth, back and forth. I could hear her crying. She was loyal like that.

Time stopped, and I squeezed my eyes shut.

I am valuable. I am precious. I deserve a real life.

If only I could believe it.

I felt a nudge on my shoulder and a wet nose on my arm. A gray wolf gently licked my cheek. I opened my eyes. Large as an IMAX film, the amazing animals from my kids' encyclopedia surrounded me and formed a protective circle, one that Miss Marcia could never get through.

I am valuable. I am precious. I deserve a real life.

Music rang in my mind. What song was it? Tubby Trash Bags? No, one of our favorites—Beethoven's "Ode to Joy." My animals swayed to the powerful chords of the organ (the ones with feet did, anyway). Around and around they circled, swaying, almost dancing. I danced with them.

Spin, sway, twirl, spin. Spin, sway, twirl, spin.

I spun and I spun and I spun . . . and . . . I . . . spun . . . until . . .

POOF!

In a burst of smoke, my IMAX film changed scenes. I looked down at my golden lasso, my tall red boots. I was Wonder Woman.

My superhero cape flew behind me as I kicked open the closet door.

KABLAM!

Miss Marcia froze when she saw me and lifted her top lip

in a sneer, showing her brown, crooked teeth. She rolled up her sleeves, ready to fight.

She stared at me.

I stared at her.

She laughed her evil laugh.

BWAHH HA HA!

She did not scare me anymore.

Time to KICK BUTT!

Miss Marcia shot Legos at me so fast they were just colored streaks of light.

POW! POW! POW!

I deflected them with my metal bracelets.

PING! PING! PING!

I jumped straight in the air . . . CHOOM! . . . and landed on the desk in front of the room.

Miss Marcia let out a shriek . . . ZOINKS! . . . and ran for the door.

That's when I twirled my lasso of truth . . . WHOOSH! WHOOSH! WHOOSH! . . . and wrangled Miss Marcia.

KABOOSH!

All the kids cheered. My animals roared, brayed, chirped, and squawked their approval.

Captured in the lasso of truth, Miss Marcia confessed everything: "I hate children! I steal their lunch money! I haven't washed my socks in three months! And I have donkey breath!" She laughed her evil laugh. "BWAHH HA HA!"

Everyone cheered again when I locked Miss Marcia in the time-out closet.

KABLAM!

Then I loaded all the kids into my invisible jet, and we soared far away from Borden. Forever.

Forever.

Forever. I have been locked in here forever.

How many more minutes until I would be released from this prison? Would it matter? My mind would never escape the prison of my broken body.

It was a life sentence.

Long Walk off a Short Pier

Pops offered me a fist bump when he saw us at the door. "How's my chipmunk today?" He has called me his chipmunk ever since I was a chubby-cheeked baby.

Slapping Dad on the back, Pops said, "Come on in, Steve, and we'll chew the fat a little. Hehehe."

Sunday dinners with the family were a happy tradition—until now. At least I would not have to face Elvi. She was still in Hawaii on her honeymoon. But Mason, my cousin who thinks I am a disease? Probability: high. Aunt Kiki and Mason had moved back to town after the divorce and were living with Gram and Pops for a while.

Aunt Kiki greeted Mom with a celebrity kiss. Her cheek grazed Mom's as she kissed the air.

"Who wears a silk shirt to a barbecue?" Mom teased. "One drop of hamburger grease and you're done."

"You know my motto, Gail," she put her hands on her hips and puckered her glossy lips, "Fashion doesn't take a break for the weekend."

Mom and Kiki sat on the faded flowered sofa and launched

into a hushed conversation. The word *divorce*—like the word *retarded*—was always whispered in our family.

I parked myself on the floor and pulled Gram's coffee table book of San Francisco onto my lap. A photo of Alcatraz jumped out at me—the prison built on a tiny island in San Francisco Bay. No prisoner had ever escaped. I stared at a picture. Concrete, gloomy cells with iron bars.

Not so different from my prison at Borden. At least those prisoners had a nice view.

Aunt Kiki stared at me, pressing her lips together like she might cry. "Gail, I remember Charity and Mason running around together at family barbecues when they were little. They jumped on the trampoline and chased each other around the house." She shook her head with a *what-happened-to-her* frown.

Mom reached for my arms and pulled me onto the sofa next to her. "She's not herself these days. Are you, sweetheart?" She jiggled me for a response.

I chewed my knuckles.

Mom pulled my hand out of my mouth. "You must be thirsty. Let me get you some apple juice."

When Mom left, Mason drifted into the living room wearing a Hang Ten T-shirt and flip-flops. He achieved a perfect imitation of a surfer dude, even though he had spent the last eight years in Milwaukee, approximately 900 miles from the ocean.

"S'up?" he said to no one in particular. He popped open a can of lemon-lime soda and took a swallow.

Aunt Kiki's eyes lit up. "Mason, sweetie, why don't you play with your cousin Charity?"

Mason stared at her as if she were speaking Chinese. I would have done the same if I could.

Play with me? Does everyone think I am still five?

He looked back and forth between me and his mom. My knees swayed apart-together, apart-together.

"Does she even understand what we're saying?" he asked.

Aunt Kiki patted the sofa next to me. "Come sit down, Mason sweetie. I'm sure Charity can push the buttons on a video game controller."

My knees swayed apart-together, apart-together.

Mason waded over as if he were moving through waist-deep water.

"Come on, sweetie." Aunt Kiki lowered her voice. "She probably doesn't have many friends."

Her hypothesis was correct.

Breaking news: Kids like me rarely have friends.

I used to think of Mason as my friend, even when he was gone. Now I see that was a miscalculation.

The largest number with a name is called a googolplex. My calculation was off by one googolplex.

After Mason moved away, I did have one other friend before Isabella. An actual come-to-my-house, run-around-the-backyard, hold-hands-hopping friend.

Grace.

She had long, golden hair the color of honey and thirteen freckles on her cheeks, which got darker whenever we spent the day outside. We met in preschool, where we played in the pretend kitchen mixing invisible batters. "What did you girls whip up today?" our teacher would ask.

Grace would shout "chocolate cake!" or "peanut butter cookies!" and I jumped and clapped in agreement.

Mom invited Grace over to our house for playdates every single week for almost three years. We dressed dolls and swam in our pool—one of the few places my body felt at peace, wrapped in the warm water. We baked cookies with Mom in our kitchen, both of us standing on stools wearing too-big aprons. Sometimes we put on princess gowns and ran around the yard trying to escape the dragon—my dog, Hero—who chased us and barked. We screamed with wild joy.

Once I started at Borden, our worlds drifted apart. Grace became busy with dance classes and soccer—and I was busy with therapy and doctor appointments. Still today, I imagine what my life would be like if we had stayed friends. She would braid my hair with beads, and we would talk about our forever crushes on pop stars.

I mean, if I were a normal girl.

••••

Aunt Kiki handed me a video game controller and talked to me in a loud voice, like maybe I was hard of hearing. "Push *here* to move your car *forward*." She put her purple manicured thumb on mine to demonstrate.

Mason set up the game—a car race with New York City as the background—and sat on the arm of the sofa. The screen flashed 3 . . . 2 . . . 1 . . . START.

Aunt Kiki yelled, "Okay, Charity, now go! Push the button like I showed you! GO! The race has started!"

Aunt Kiki meant well, but I wanted to strangle her.

I moved my thumb forward, and my car drove for about two seconds before it crashed into a wall and blew up in front of the Empire State Building.

Aunt Kiki cheered as if I won the Indy 500. I crashed and burned five more times until my uncooperative hand dropped the controller on the floor.

"Can I go now?" asked Mason. The tone of his voice suggested this was a complete waste of time.

I agreed.

I spared him the pain of playing with me by getting up and moving to the kitchen. Mom stood at the counter, holding my sippy cup. "Sorry, honey, I was on my way to give this to you." She put the cup in my hands and led it to my lips.

Bleh—warm apple juice. No one older than four should drink this.

Gram stood over a steaming pot wearing her stained apron. "Never trust a skinny cook or one with a clean apron," she always said.

I sniffed the air.

Maple syrup?

"My darling girl is here." Gram swung around to plant a kiss on my cheek, still stirring the pot with one hand. She folded my hand around the wooden spoon and guided it in a circle to stir the orange, creamy mixture.

Butternut squash soup.

"Now that my assistant chef is here, I can take a break."

Gram pointed her finger at Mom. "Gail, this girl is getting thinner and thinner." She squished my cheeks with her warm hand and examined my face. "Honey, where's that sparkle in your eyes?"

Mom sat down with a big exhale. "She hasn't been sleeping well, either."

"How's she doing at school?" asked Gram.

"Well, I've called them a few times and they say she's the same as always. I'm at my wits' end here." Mom pulled me toward her and brushed the stray hair from my eyes. "But I'm trying to get an appointment with a specialist . . ."

Gram cut her off. "Fiddlesticks. Charity, honey, you just need some hearty food and some chamomile tea at bedtime, maybe with a drop of whiskey." She winked at Mom.

Gram and Pops always acted as though I was a regular kid. Gram taught me the secrets of her kitchen. Pops let me help him at the ice cream shop and took me and Dad fishing at the pier on Sundays.

My unpredictable body sometimes caused trouble, like the time Gram's two-layer cake became a one-layer cake after I knocked a pan onto the floor. If she was upset, she did not show it. Instead, she shrugged her shoulders and said, "You're right, honey, I don't need *that* many calories traveling to my hips tonight, now do I?"

Gram yelled out to the patio, where Pops and Dad were talking. "Bob, it'll be a good hour till supper. You and Steve take this young lady for a little walk. She's in dire need of fresh air."

Mason strolled into the kitchen and dug into a bowl of chips.

"And take Mason with you," Gram added.

Mason stood there, a chip hanging out of his mouth. I felt sorry for him. He could not escape the torture of being around me.

Pops drove us to the pier in his 1968 GTO convertible with the top down. I lifted my face to the sky to be brushed by the wind.

"Too much air, Mason old boy? I can roll up the window if you like." Pops tried to get a grin out of Mason. It was not working.

Dad glanced back at the frowning boy, who had squished himself to the side—as far away from me as possible.

Seeing him squirm made me more anxious. My hands slapped my cheeks.

Slap-slap-slap.

"How do you like your new school?" Dad asked him.

Mason looked at Dad and blew air through his lips like a horse. "Full of suck-ups and phonies." Under his breath he added, "Now I'm one of 'em."

Boo-hoo, Mason. You have no idea how lucky you are.

My hands slapped my knees now. Slap-slap-slap.

Mason examined me a few seconds and asked, "What's wrong with her? My mom never told me anything."

Dad shot him a look with an eyebrow raised.

"No disrespect or anything, but, I mean, why does she act like that?"

I went back to slapping my face. Slap-slap-slap.

Dad puckered his lips in thought for a second. "Well, I think Charity sometimes dances to music only she can hear."

"Does she talk?"

"Not like you and me, but she communicates in different ways. Problem is, her body speaks a different language. So, for example, just because she's not looking at us doesn't mean she's not listening. Just because she jumps up and down doesn't mean she's happy."

That's right, Dad. Most people do not get that.

"So how do you know what she's feeling?" Mason asked.

"A lot of times, I can see it in her eyes. Sometimes even I'm at a loss, though." Dad reached back and squeezed my knee. "I know you'd really love to talk if you could, wouldn't you, Cherry?"

More than you know, Dad. More than you could possibly know.

Mason brushed his nose with his hand. "Yeah. That sucks."

Pops piped in. "It doesn't 'suck,' young man. It *vacuums vigorously*. Hehehehe."

A sea of cars greeted us at the parking lot. "Pesky tourists think they can elbow us off our own pier," Pops complained.

He crammed the car into a tiny parking space, and Dad helped me out so the passenger door did not hit the next car. Dad and I strolled next to Pops, while Mason trailed behind like he wasn't with us.

I remembered the new rule: Cousin ≠ friend.

This place usually calmed me, but today it was a war zone to my senses. Screaming seagulls dive-bombed French fries on picnic tables while a polka band sang out of tune, "In heaven there is no beer, that's why we drink it here . . ." Every boom of the bass drum hammered my head.

Each step became harder. I could almost feel the pieces of my broken heart clinking inside my chest.

Clink, clink, clink.

I numbered the hurts. Borden. Miss Marcia, Mason, Elvi.

Panic grew in my belly. My toes pranced on the wood planks like they were hot lava. I envied the gulls' freedom to fly away.

Hop, hop, hop.

Dad squeezed my hand tighter. "Easy, honey. We'll be in our peaceful fishing spot in a minute and you'll be fine."

Fine? Look at my life. Probability of peace: zero.

A thundering voice shot in our direction. "Bob, you ol' son of a gun. Howsit goin'?" A guy in a fishing cap greeted Pops with a bear hug. A battle of fishing stories began. Their voices became fuzzier as panic screamed inside my skull.

"A ten-pound sand bass, I swear on my honor."

"That's nothin' compared to the one we hauled in last week, is it, Steve?"

Where was Mason? Leaning on the pier, earbuds in both ears, looking everywhere *except* our direction.

Another piece of my heart chipped off and clinked inside my chest.

That's when my bulldog impulse took over.

I yanked free from Dad's hand and launched myself.

Page 5: Antelope have acute senses of hearing
and smell to detect danger in the open.

To where? I was not sure.

My legs flew me through the crowd.

**Page 5: The pronghorn antelope sprints
at speeds of 60 miles per hour.**

My pink sneakers sprinted over sticky wooden planks.

Get out of my way!

I dodged strollers, knocked into a bench, leapt past a kettle corn cart.

Run, run, dodge, leap, dodge, crash, turn, run.

My eyes spotted a ramp down the side of the pier, away from the chaos. I ran toward it. Then my feet froze. A chain blocked my path. The sign said, "Closed to the Public."

Keep going, keep moving!

I ducked under the chain and stumbled down the wooden planks toward the docked boats, bobbing up and down, eighteen of them in two rows of nine. Between each boat was a patch of water, dark and shiny as glass.

Fact: I cannot walk on water.

Still, my feet wanted to step onto the glass. Feel the ocean fold around me like a blanket. Water covering my legs and arms, my neck and face, quieting my frantic body.

Keep going. You can do it.

I could easily drop into the water and disappear without a sound. My legs led me to the edge, and my foot reached out above the water. The noise from the polka band seemed miles away. The sun reflected off the black, polished hull of a boat named *The Great Escape*.

I can escape.

A seagull landed next to me and perched on the wooden post. He stared into the distance.

I am hungry for peace.

My shoelace touched the water. I closed my eyes as my body tilted forward.

A hand grabbed my elbow and pulled me from the edge. A deep voice said, "Whoa! Hold on, my sister." I turned to see a man with a leathery face and long, gray hair braided behind his back. The sun glinted off a silver dolphin pendant hanging on a cord around his neck. He squinted his wrinkled eyes and smiled at me. "We each have a path and a purpose. Seek yours, my sister."

In two giant leaps, Dad bounded toward us, breathing hard. He grabbed me with both hands and looked into my face. "Are you okay, Charity? Are you safe? How did you run so fast?" He wrapped me in a tight squeeze. I felt his whole body shaking.

Pops ran up, huffing and puffing. He bent over, hands on his knees, to catch his breath. "Well, Chipmunk, if you didn't like the smell of stinky sausages, I couldn't say I blame you." He chuckled as he looked up at me.

Mason hurdled over the chain rope and ran up behind Pops. "What happened? Where was she going?"

I turned around to search for my guardian angel, the one who called me his sister.

He had disappeared.

Flavor of the Week: Freedom

"Okay, Chipmunk. Tell me what's what."

Thursdays were my favorite. On Thursdays, Dad picked me up from school and took me to Pops' ice cream shop. Today, as usual, Pops held out three small spoons with blobs of ice cream on them. Perched on a stool at the counter, I took the pale blue sample first and slid the creamy spoonful into my mouth while Pops looked on.

Pops turned to Dad. "Root beer bubble gum. Don't think that one's a winner. I can tell from her eyes. Try another, Chipmunk."

Pops could read my face about as well as Dad could. Why would *anyone* ever put those two flavors together?

I took the next spoon and let the frosty bite slide onto my tongue.

"Even worse than the last," Pops said, wiping his forehead with a napkin. "So, chocolate avocado is a definite NO."

He held out the last spoon. I bit and swallowed. This one had a nutty and cinnamon flavor, like Gram's pumpkin pie.

Pops nodded.

"Whew, there it is—sweet potato-walnut. That's gonna be our new flavor of the week. This girl can always pick 'em."

At Pops' ice cream shop, I felt like one of those celebrity chefs at a cooking competition. The unspoken rule was *no one tells Mom they're spoiling my dinner*.

I looked up to see Aunt Kiki emerge from the back room. "Will that be a cup or a cone, sweetie?" She wore a lace blouse under her blue-striped apron. This was her new job while she adjusted to her new life.

"She'll have a small shake," Dad said. "Less chance of spilling any evidence on her shirt." He winked at me.

Aunt Kiki struggled to scoop the ice cream, her gold bangle bracelets not making it easy. Then she fumbled getting the scoop into the shiny metal mixing cup. I watched the ice cream drop to the floor.

"Oops. There goes another one." She shrugged and then so did I.

Shrug. Shrug. Shrug.

Pops raised both eyebrows and whispered to Dad and me, "Third time today." Then he turned to Kiki. "You need some help, dear?"

Kiki smiled, "No, no. How will I learn if I don't practice?"

After slurping down every drop of my shake, I rose from the counter and wandered into the back room.

"Can I help you get something, sweetie?" Aunt Kiki looked nervous, but I knew what to do. I picked up a big package of napkins and brought them to the counter next to Dad. While Dad and Pops chattered, I lined up the napkin dispensers on the counter, all ten of them in a row like an army of silver, rectangular robots. I stuffed just the right number of napkins in each one. Not so much that the napkins stuck out and made the robot too fat. The right amount. Then I put all the dispensers back on the tables where they went. The whole time, Aunt Kiki stared at me in amazement, like I was an Olympic ice dancer doing back flips and camel spins.

"What in the world? How did she learn to do that?" Kiki asked Pops.

Pops seemed surprised by the question. "I taught her how. She's a smart cookie, you know." He put his hand on one of my robots. "Filling napkin holders, that's nothing. Last week, she helped me sort coins to take to the bank. She arranged them in piles faster than I could count."

"But I thought . . . I thought . . ." Aunt Kiki's eyebrows squished together so tightly that a line appeared on her forehead.

Pops put his hand on her shoulder. "Well, dear, you thought *wrong*."

The bell on the door chimed, and Mom stumbled in with teary eyes, walking like she were in a dream. She rushed toward me and wrapped me in a tight hug, a mommy cocoon. "I'm so sorry!"

My sixth sense felt a surge of sorrow churning inside her.

Dad put an arm around her shoulder. "Gail, what's wrong?" He led her to a stool.

Mom sat at the counter, and Aunt Kiki brought her a glass of water. Mom took a sip with shaky hands and swallowed hard. She looked at me. "I went to Borden after school today to talk to your teacher, Mr. Toll."

Mr. Toll was officially my teacher, but he never spent much time in the classroom. He was always off doing "administrative duties," which must be code for reading the paper and eating powdered donuts in the lounge, which is what I saw him doing every time I walked by.

I squeezed my fists tight, fearing the worst. Did he tell her I was a failure? List all the dumb "assessments" I could not pass? Did he describe my "uncooperative behavior"? I was 100 percent sure he did NOT tell Mom about Miss Marcia stealing my lunch money or locking me in the time-out closet or leaving me to sit outside on the blacktop for hours at a time. Anything Mr. Toll had to say about me would be *diagnosis: disaster.*

Pops' sweet potato-walnut shake churned in my stomach.

"I didn't have an appointment," Mom continued.

She spoke like a person in shock, like someone who had just witnessed Bigfoot battling the Abominable Snowman in the middle of Main Street.

Did Mr. Toll say I was too special even for Borden? What could be worse than Borden? Maximum security prison?

My body shivered.

"I wanted to talk to Mr. Toll . . . ask about Charity's behavior in school . . . tell him about her mood changes."

My heartbeat doubled.

He LIED to you! They are hiding the TRUTH!

The ice cream shake flip-flopped in my stomach. I pressed my lips together and willed it to stay down.

"When I got to the school, no one was at the front desk, so I walked directly to the classroom."

What? Did they stop you? Did you make it past the NO-PARENT zone?

Everyone gathered closer to hear Mom's words.

Mom continued. "The classroom that is always so spotless and cheerful every year for parents' night . . ."

Did you SEE it? DID YOU SMELL IT?

Mom snapped her head toward Dad and spit out her words rapid-fire. "Steve, I tell you it was a pigpen—filthy, stinking, full of broken toys and . . . and . . . not a place of learning at all. Nothing but scribbles on the chalkboard. Puzzles with missing pieces—wooden baby puzzles—were scattered on the floor along with mismatched Legos . . . and . . . and shoeboxes of broken crayons and dried-out markers. And a closet . . . a storage closet . . . labeled 'TIME OUT' in big, red letters." She shook her head. "I couldn't believe it."

Dad's face turned white, Mom's red.

"It made me so *angry*!" She pounded her fist on the counter.

SHE KNOWS? SHE FINALLY KNOWS?

Now I was the one in shock.

Big tears welled in Mom's eyes. "I took out my phone to take pictures of this so-called classroom. That's when Miss Marcia burst in and started yelling at me. She said I wasn't allowed to be there. That I had no right to take pictures. Then Mr. Toll came in and threatened to report me to the police for trespassing. So I yelled back at them. 'What kind of classroom is this? How could you possibly lock kids in storage closets for time-outs? I should call the police on *you*!' And Miss Marcia said, she actually said, and I quote, 'You don't *get* it, do you?

These kids are lost causes. Your kid was sent here because no other school *wants* her.'"

Mom put her head in her hands and inhaled like she was catching her breath. Aunt Kiki handed her a napkin from the dispenser. Mom blew her nose and continued. "Well, I don't want to tell you how I responded, it may have included a few four-letter, pardon-my-French words, but the last thing I said was 'Charity will *never* set foot in Borden Academy again. Just you wait until I tell the district what kind of school you're running here.'"

Mom dabbed the tears on her cheek and squeezed me tight again.

Even without a red cape, Mom did a pretty good job of kicking butt.

In my mind, I heard the squeak of an iron jail cell door opening wide.

Freedom? Is it possible?

My mind could hardly soak it in.

A tidal wave of emotion crashed inside my chest, and my entire ice cream shake spewed onto the floor.

Barbecued

Mason slinked into Gram's kitchen and stacked four cheese-loaded crackers into his palm, probably hoping to make a quick getaway before someone spoke to him.

"Good news, Mason." Mom put her arm around his shoulder. "Charity might be going to your school in a few weeks."

Mason's pale face turned even whiter, but he just stared straight ahead and said, "K."

Page 239: Startled rabbits freeze to
assess the danger then run away.

"That will be fun, won't it, sweetie?" Aunt Kiki, in a teal pantsuit, smiled big. "You two could eat lunch together."

Poor Mason. Hard enough being the new kid at his school. Having me there would be like *diagnosis: explosive diarrhea.*

Mason glanced toward me. I sat at the table tapping my fingers to the song in my head—Beethoven's Fifth Symphony—and munching my cracker in rhythm.

Tap, munch, tap, munch.

He ended the conversation by ducking outside.

"Public school?" Aunt Elvi stood in the doorway making her pity face. "Seriously, Gail, how's this gonna make any difference?"

Aunt Kiki whispered, "Come on, Elvi, be sensitive."

Mom clenched her jaw. "Don't start with me, Elvi. I've tutored Charity at grade level since she was three. She'll be able to understand. I know she will."

Elvi shook her head. "When are you gonna wake up, Gail?"

"Stop talking like that in front of her," Mom hissed.

Elvi put her hand on her hips. "Get real, Gail, what makes you think she understands a word we're saying? I wish she did. I wish to heck she did, but she doesn't." Elvi turned to me and smiled. "Charity, honey, blink twice if you understand what I'm saying. Just blink twice."

Everyone stared at me.

Of course, my eyelids did not obey.

Elvi went up to Mom and held both her hands. "Look at me, Gail. This isn't gonna work. You've been killing yourself for years and nothing works. Not only are you wasting your life, you're torturing the poor kid."

Mom looked her in the eyes. "You don't understand because you're not a mother yet, Elvi. Just wait. There's nothing you won't do for your child."

Elvi huffed a big sigh and held up her hands. "You're killing me, Gail. Literally killing me." She turned and walked away.

At least they were talking again.

"When will she start?" Aunt Kiki asked, smiling, as if the previous conversation never happened.

"Well, we're still not sure they'll accept her," Mom said. "If I could bribe someone, I would."

For the past two weeks, Mom argued with district administrators. They were the ones who kicked me out of public school in the first place and pressured my mom to put me in Borden. My mother, who could hardly bring herself to send back a bowl of soup with a fly swimming in it, roared into the phone every day.

"Ashamed, you should be ashamed! How can you call Borden a school? I can't believe you would let this abuse continue. You don't care what happens to these kids as long as they're hidden away where you can't see them."

I imagined Mom as a Marine drill instructor screaming at the top of her lungs. *Drop and give me fifty pushups, you useless maggot! You worthless pile of cat puke! You miserable excuse for a school administrator!*

"We are fully prepared to sue for damages unless our daughter is admitted to a public school. That is her legal right. And she needs a full-time aide to support her. Hiring an aide costs a fraction of the tuition that the district doled out to send her to that prison."

A real public school with actual learning? With actual teachers who teach? The idea excited me. It also terrified me. Equations filled my head.

Public school = learning.

Learning = hope.

Friendship potential = zero.

Embarrassment opportunities = infinite.

I imagined the jokes, the insults, the snickers every time my legs stumbled down the hall. At least at Borden our strangeness was shared.

And how could I move on with sweet Isabella still stuck at Borden?

Dad strolled into the kitchen. "Come on, Cherry. Let's get you a hot dog with extra grease."

After dinner, I wandered the garden counting ladybugs on Gram's bright yellow marigold flowers—there were eighteen last week. Elvi and her new husband, Joel, sat in the grass staring at the orange sky. I noted her dazed look, the look grownups get after a few adult beverages. The disaster of the wedding streamed in my mind, big as an IMAX film.

Elvi laid her head on the fresh-cut lawn, her tattooed arms folded behind her neck.

Joel smiled at me. "Hey, kiddo, what's up?" When I didn't answer, he turned to Elvi. "You think she understands anything we're saying?"

"Gail seems to think so, but just look at her. What do *you* think?"

Joel observed me hopscotching through the grass with flapping hands. "Geez, tough stuff."

Elvi kept talking to Joel like I was not even there. "If we have kids, babe, we gotta pray we don't get dealt a bad hand same as Gail and Steve, you know? I mean, I've been tellin' her for years—for yeeeeears—to put that poor girl in a home. Gail spends every minute of her life runnin' around takin' care of that kid. Of her life! When is she gonna face reality? I mean, would the kid know the difference?"

Pity poisons bubbled up inside me. I wanted to cry, but instead my body jumped and clapped.

I *begged* for words.

My ears work. My brain understands. Can't you see I am a REAL PERSON?

Jump, clap, jump, clap.

Aunt Elvi kept talking like I was invisible, like I was a five-foot-three fig tree. "I'm gonna talk to Gail about it again. Sooner or later, she's gonna have to face facts. I mean, now that Gail took her outta school, this would be the perfect time."

The Interview

"He just wants to meet you and say hello."

Mom tried to sound calm, but she was dusting the same cabinet for the third time, so I knew this was more than saying hello. The principal of Lincoln Junior High was coming to check me out.

Translation: He wanted to see how big a mess I was, maybe hoping to get rid of me before I set foot in a classroom.

I have spent my entire life being tested. After every test, the Thinkers put another label on me, and their conclusion is always the same. *Diagnosis: idiot.* Except they use more technical terms.

Their labels do not define me. They only limit me.

Mom sat me at the dining room table to work on one of my 200-piece puzzles—a flock of red cardinals perched in a snowy birch tree. Maybe she thought this would impress our visitor.

Probability: low.

Dad was in his usual aloha mood, cracking pistachios and

handing me a few at a time. I munched the salty seeds while separating red puzzle pieces into a pile.

1, 2, 3, 4 . . .

I liked following a certain order based on colors and patterns. For this puzzle, mostly red pieces, then mostly blue, then mostly white—birds, then sky, then snowy birch tree.

5, 6 . . . this one has equal red and white . . . it goes in its own pile . . .

Mom glared at Dad as she swept pistachio shells into her hand.

43 shells, 86 half shells . . . 7, 8, 9 . . .

"Can we keep this room clean for five minutes?"

Dad exhaled, preparing for Mom's eruption. "Relax, Gail. You're only making everyone more nervous." He shot me a goofy smile.

"Charity's suffered enough, Steve. They *have* to let her in." Mom polished the television screen with a lint-free rag. "Charity, you deserve the same opportunities as every other student."

Yes, but other students can talk and have bodies they can control . . . 35, 36, 37 . . .

"All we can do is hope for the best," Dad said. "And if it doesn't work out . . ."

Mom threw the rag on the floor. "If it doesn't work out, then that's it." Her voice got higher. "The next stop is . . ." She paused and looked at Dad like she might throw up. "PV," she whispered.

I knew exactly what she meant. Pine Valley Developmental Center.

The last time we went there, I almost did not come home. The thought made me want to throw up too.

• • •

I was eight years and fifty-three days old. My parents had fought to get an appointment with some superstar neurologist after a nightmare week of my body going berserk and me not sleeping.

When I do not sleep, nobody sleeps.

We walked in looking like zombies and were led to a refrigerator-cold exam room, where we waited for twenty-four minutes. Mom and Dad did not speak. The buzzing fluorescent lights grew louder every minute. My worried legs kicked the metal exam table beneath me.

Bang-bang, bang-bang.

Dad helped me down and held hands to jump with me, singing a peppy Beach Boys tune. "And we'll have fun, fun, fun . . ."

Hop-hop right foot, hop-hop left foot.

We were still jumping when Superdoc burst through the door without knocking. He raised one eyebrow, and Dad lifted me back onto the table. No time for chitchat. Same as all the Thinkers before him, he treated me as if I were a dog that could not be trained. He adjusted his glasses and started giving commands. I'm not sure what he had for lunch, but his breath smelled of stinky garlic and every few minutes, he let out a low burp.

"Stack these cups." [Burp.]

There were six cups in bright colors, and I knew how he

wanted me to stack them—so that they nested one inside the other, same as the beautiful Russian dolls Gram kept in her dining room cabinet. But my hands decided to line them up alphabetically, according to the name of each color: blue, green, orange, purple, red, yellow. He marked his clipboard. From his standpoint, I was sure that was a failure.

"Come on, Charity. You can do this, sweetheart. Like you do at home all the time," Mom said, rubbing my back.

"Please do not assist your daughter, Mrs. Wood." [Burp.]

He pointed to the chair. That was his command to Mom.

He turned back to me. "Jump," he ordered.

You saw me jumping a minute ago. You know I can jump . . . just not on command.

"Touch your nose."

How does touching my nose prove anything? It does not show what's inside my head.

With each failed task, he marked his clipboard. My heart beat faster. My feet begged to run, but he was blocking the door. Nowhere to escape. I was a laboratory rat too dumb to get through its maze.

"She's actually very coordinated when she plays with her dolls." Mom sounded desperate now. "She can comb their hair and dress them and put on their tiny socks and shoes."

The doctor poked and tapped me with his little rubber hammer.

Page 240: Rats have strong teeth that can chew through cinderblock, glass, wire, and lead.

I wish I were a rat so I could chew through these walls.

"She can put together 200-piece puzzles all by herself,"

Mom added as the doctor pinged a tuning fork and twirled it around my head.

My head did not turn toward the sound. Failure.

"Draw a circle," he said, holding out a crayon. [Burp.]

Great. Some days my hands are as coordinated as lobster claws. This was one of those days.

My right hand reached.

Got it.

My fingers gripped the thin cylinder. This was the hardest of all his orders. I thought maybe if I could draw this circle for him then it would cancel out the other failures. This puny crayon, this three-inch stick of bright orange wax could determine my future.

My beating heart knocked on my chest.

Mom had spent hours practicing letters with me. This was just an "O." The letter "O." O as in Octopus. An animal so much smarter than anyone could guess by looking at it.

Page 198: Highly intelligent, the octopus
can navigate through mazes, open jars, and
use coconut shells to create shelters.

He held out a small notepad. Holding on tight with my fist, I lifted the crayon. The orange—burnt sienna, actually—wax touched the page. Mom and Dad held their breath.

A tiny line.

I can do this.

An arc.

Keep going!

Then CRACK.

The sound of the crayon breaking in my grip was like a

piano falling from a tall building and smashing onto a concrete sidewalk. I opened my hand and watched the pieces fall in slow motion onto the floor.

Countdown to KETTLE EXPLOSION . . . 3 . . . 2 . . . 1.

Ahhhhhhhhhhhhh!

My swinging hands struck the doctor's arm and knocked his clipboard to the floor.

He backed up to the wall as if I were some rabid dog. Dad put his arms around me and held me. He pulled me gently onto his lap and Mom stroked my hair.

"Charity, you're okay, sweetheart," she chanted. "You're okay, you're okay. We are here with you."

I sucked in air and puffed it out through my lips.

Suck, puff, suck, puff.

The doctor bent down to pick up his papers. Then he scribbled his diagnosis on the clipboard right in front of me.

Moderate to Severe Intellectual Disability

"Mr. and Mrs. Wood, based on her files and my observations, Charity needs the type of support offered by a residential facility before her outbursts end up hurting herself or others." He rubbed his arm where I had hit him.

Residential facility? He wanted to take me away from my family? Make me live in an institution?

I breathed harder because I knew he was right. I lived in terror every day that I would hurt myself or someone else. I hoped Mom and Dad were not remembering the times I darted into the street. Or the time I knocked down Gram when she was helping me put on shoes. Or the times I poked, pushed, or grabbed one of my classmates. I was only trying to play with them. I never wanted to hurt anyone.

Suck, puff, suck, puff.

The doctor's voice sounded grandfatherly now. "I can only imagine how difficult it is for you to give round-the-clock care to a child who can hardly feed or dress herself."

Mom stared into space.

I could not believe my parents were listening to this Thinker talk about sending me away.

"Believe me, Mrs. Wood, you've lasted longer than most parents in your situation. You are only two people. At Pine Valley, we have a regular staff of twelve to supervise the residents, help them participate in recreational activities, and look after their every need."

Mom's eyes overflowed and leaked onto my cheek. Dad clasped her hand. The doctor was wearing them down. My worst nightmare was about to come true.

"Fortunately, we have an opening. She can be admitted this afternoon."

I dug deep into my spirit and begged the universe for help.

Please, God. Please, please, please let me go home with my parents today. I will owe you TIMES GOOGOLPLEX. I will spend my LIFE trying to repay you. Please, please, PLEASE do not let them take me away.

What happened next, I cannot explain.

I had heard stories of kids with no voice who, maybe once every ten years, opened their mouths and uttered a clear and complete sentence.

That's not what I did.

Reaching deep into my soul, I felt a spark of electricity in my toes. It traveled up my legs to my stomach, my chest, my neck, and at last my lips.

Not a whole sentence.

Just one word, one whispered word escaped.

If anyone had been talking or making noise, my one word would have been lost.

My voice breathed, "No."

Mom jumped up. "Steve, did you hear it?"

"I'm sure it was a random vocalization," the doctor said. "Our medical staff can . . ."

Dad bolted up with me still in his arms. "Enough! We've heard *enough*. We are going home now . . . *with* our daughter."

I wanted to shout for joy. I saw that leaving me was their worst nightmare too.

When we got home, I fell asleep—we all did—for twelve hours straight.

● ● ●

But now, five years later, Pine Valley threatened me again. I had an IOU with God, but that was a losing bet coming from a helpless girl like me.

If the public school rejected me, the district would send me to school at Pine Valley. That's where they send the most hopeless cases. School? Ha! It was even more of a prison than Borden.

The doorbell made us all jump, except for Hero, who ran toward it as usual, his stubby, brown bulldog tail wagging.

Dad opened the door to reveal a man and woman who did not look like they belonged together at all.

"Hello, I'm Celia Diaz, the special education coordinator."

She had long, crazy-curly hair and a leather jacket with eight zippers. I wanted to zip and unzip them all.

She bent down to scratch Hero's belly, which made his back leg thump, thump, thump. "Well hello, *chiquito*."

Her happy energy contrasted with the sour look of the school principal beside her, Mr. Edward Jergen. He smiled a *wish-I-did-not-have-to-be-here* smile. Wearing a gray suit, his hair stuck in place with gel, he looked more like a lawyer than a junior high principal.

Ms. Diaz—"Call me Celia," she insisted—hugged both my parents and came over to the table where I sat. She bent down to examine my puzzle.

"Look at this beautiful creation." Her hair smelled like cinnamon, and her curls tickled my cheek.

Mom invited them to sit on our leather sofa.

"Mr. and Mrs. Wood, as you know, we're here to assess your daughter's placement," Mr. Jergen said, pushing Hero away. I suppose he did not like drool on his shiny shoes.

"We want her to be in a school that best fits her, a school with appropriate resources for children with her . . . challenges."

"Sounds as though you've already made up your mind." Dad folded his arms.

"Well, given her difficulties at Borden, Mr. Wood, I'm skeptical of her ability to . . . benefit from our program."

Working on my puzzle—blue pieces now—I caught Celia smiling at me. Observing me?

122 . . . 123 . . . 124 . . . 76 more pieces to go.

Mom, ready for battle, pulled out her most recent notebook and listed all the problems with Borden—from uncertified teachers to unsanitary conditions to inhumane treatment of students. Mr. Jergen fought back by pulling *my* file from his briefcase and listing all my documented failures at that school. After a few minutes of back and forth, Mr. Jergen's voice got louder.

"Mrs. Wood, please forgive me, but if your daughter can't even pick up a pencil, I don't see how she can benefit from our school."

He stood up, took a pencil, and plopped it on the table in front of me.

A dare.

My body froze.

Oh no.

I dropped the puzzle piece I was holding. My hands turned into lobster claws again.

I wanted to dare him right back.

How about this—I pick up the pencil with my lobster claws if you make a phone call with your feet.

Mr. Jergen lifted his shoulders in a half shrug. "It's the most basic of skills, Mrs. Wood, and time after time, your daughter has shown herself incapable of doing even this."

Mom's lips frowned hard, but I knew he was royally right. The stupid yellow pencil lay there like a snake ready to bite.

I knew my hand would not pick it up. Not with everyone watching. Not with him thinking I could not do it.

My muscles froze. My heart raced.

Page 261: The king cobra can inject large
amounts of poisonous venom in a single bite.

Mr. Jergen pulled out the wooden chair facing me, its legs screeching on the floor, and sat down. "Go ahead, Charity." He spoke a little softer but did not really look at me. "Pick up the pencil."

Three seconds ticked on the grandfather clock in the living room, and his fingers drummed lightly on the oak table.

Tap-tap-tap-tap-tap. Tap-tap-tap-tap-tap. Tap-tap-tap-tap-tap. Tap-tap-tap-tap-tap.

He repeated his command.

"Pick up the pencil . . . pick up the pencil . . . *pick up the pencil.*"

Tap-tap-tap-tap-tap. Tap-tap-tap-tap-tap. Tap-tap-tap-tap-tap. Tap-tap-tap-tap-tap.

Page 261: The venom causes severe pain, rapid
breathing, blurred vision, and paralysis.

Each time, his voice got louder, and his fingers sounded to my ears like bass drums pounding.

Tap-tap-tap-tap-tap. Tap-tap-tap-tap-tap. Tap-tap-tap-tap-tap. Tap-tap-tap-tap-tap.

I felt pity poisons gnawing at my stomach. I wished I could pick up the pencil and fling it at him. A KETTLE EXPLOSION was approaching, and at any moment these puzzle pieces would fly.

Fact: He would be the winner.

Tap-tap-tap-tap-tap. Tap-tap-tap-tap-tap. Tap-tap-tap-tap-tap. Tap-tap-tap-tap-tap.

Hello, Pine Valley.

The venom causes severe pain, rapid breathing . . .

I clenched both fists, all four adults and even Hero staring at me. I imagined life locked in a small room with no windows. No pictures on the walls. No family beyond the walls.

Mom's chest heaved a single sob.

The lamp above the table scorched my cheeks. Sweat dribbled down my neck onto the dumb pink blouse Mom made me wear.

Tap-tap-tap-tap-tap-tap-tap-tap-tap-tap-tap-tap-tap.

The venom causes blurred vision . . . paralysis . . .

My arms started pushing puzzle pieces on the floor.

Tap-tap-tap-tap-tap-tap-tap-tap-tap-tap-tap-tap-tap.

Death soon follows.

Countdown to KETTLE EXPLOSION . . . 3 . . . 2 . . .

Celia leaned over and stopped Mr. Jergen's tapping fingers. She spoke softly into my ear. "Charity, *querida*, could you please pick up that pencil for me?"

I knew that word—*querida*. In Spanish, it meant *dear*.

Without thinking, my hand grasped the pencil.

"That's it, *querida*. Now draw a little something for me on my notepad, anything you like."

She touched my elbow, and I lifted the pencil to her yellow pad.

I drew a perfect circle.

Mr. Jergen sat there for a few seconds with his mouth open.

"Well, Mr. J," Celia said, "how would *you* prefer to be asked?"

She turned to my parents. "I have a feeling this is a very bright girl. Why don't you tell us more about her strengths?"

Wow. None of the Thinkers ever asked that before. Mom was the one hugging Celia this time. Then Mom threw open her notebook labeled *Accomplishments* and scribbled some notes, grinning widely.

By the time they left, Mr. Jergen could only say, "I will let you know the district's decision soon."

Three days later, we got a message on our voicemail that made Mom and Dad jump up and down. I could attend Lincoln on a trial basis for one month. Mr. Jergen used the phrase "trial basis" five times.

I was excited too.

Then I realized the torture I could face as possibly the strangest mammal ever to enter their doors.

I braced myself for the longest month of my life.

Chance of Snow in Mexico

Do most kids look forward to the first day of school? Nervous butterflies were ready to explode through my chest like an alien in Dad's late-night movies.

On Aunt Kiki's advice, Mom dressed me in actual teenager clothes—jeans and a T-shirt with a sparkly violet heart on it. Mom French-braided my hair to keep it out of my face and painted my fingernails bright pink. When my pink fingers went into my mouth, Mom gave me my animal flashcards hooked together on a key ring to keep my hands busy. I flipped them one by one.

Aardvark, flip, badger, flip, cobra, flip.

"You look maaaarvelous," she said.

Yeah, I thought . . . *I could almost pass as a real girl.*

"I don't think a backpack is supposed to weigh twenty pounds, Gail," Dad said, breezing into the kitchen for breakfast.

He poured himself a cup of coffee before planting a kiss on my cheek. "You'll do great, Super Cherry. I'll whip up my sunrise special to give you megawatts of energy."

Mom packed and repacked my backpack—zebra-striped instead of Wonder Woman, thank goodness—as Dad dished up his yummy avocado tofu scramble with salsa. I needed extra help eating because my body was already energized with too many megawatts.

After breakfast, Dad helped us to the car, and at 7:12 A.M., I took my first steps into Lincoln Junior High.

One foot at a time. Do not let the humiliation start on day one.

My legs shook like a newborn giraffe.

> Page 87: Newborn giraffes are about six
> feet tall and weigh 150 pounds.

Sun from skylights dotted colorful murals on the walls. I drank in the blues, yellows, greens, and reds until the images came into focus—portraits of Abraham Lincoln and other famous people. I paused at a portrait of Thomas Jefferson and stared into his gray-wolf eyes. In gold letters below his face were painted his famous words, "All men are created equal."

I wondered when those words would apply to me. When would "all" really mean *all*?

Other heroes of liberty lined the halls—Frederick Douglass, Susan B. Anthony, Gandhi, Martin Luther King Jr., Rosa Parks, Cesar Chavez, Nelson Mandela. The last one was a portrait of Malala, the young woman from Pakistan fighting for girls' education.

Malala's brown eyes looked into mine. I inched closer until my nose touched the dimpled concrete. My eyes swam in the rose and orange brushstrokes of her headscarf.

Giggles erupted behind me from a group of girls.

"Time to go, sweetheart." Mom turned me around.

How long was I standing there?

The girls laughed at something on their phones.

At least they were not laughing at me.

Were they?

The tallest girl wore her pink hair—*pink* hair?—in a sloppy bun. Another girl stared straight at me, holding her sparkling emerald fingernails over her mouth, ready to burst.

"Celia told us room 129," Mom said, pulling me forward.

We continued past the cafeteria—*pepperoni pizza cooking*—to a long hallway lined with brown, steel lockers.

BEEEEEEEEEEEEEEEP.

I covered my ears at the sound of the morning bell. The high-pitched sound stung my brain.

Ouuuuuuuuuuch!

The hall flooded with students rushing to homeroom—a sea of denim and multicolored backpacks. Mom tugged on my hand.

Move, feet, move!

"Come on, Charity. Celia is expecting us."

Rubber soles squeaked on the waxed floor. Smells of perfume, shampoo, and stinky armpits hit my nose. Too much too fast.

Mom's voice urged, "Keep going, sweetheart. Almost there."

My feet stuck to the tiles.

> Page 86: Geckos use microscopic hairs on
> their toes to stick to smooth surfaces.

Someone bumped my shoulder. My hands clamped into tight fists. Jergen's trial basis might end on day one.

My knees bent up and down.

UP-down-UP-down-UP-down.

Countdown to KETTLE EXPLOSION . . . 3 . . . 2 . . .

"My newest addition is here."

I heard Celia's voice behind me, felt her curly cinnamon hair on my cheek, and my feet obeyed her hand guiding my back.

"*Querida*, all will be well," she whispered in my ear.

She led us into her office and shut the door. Once I escaped the roar of the hallway, my heartbeat slowed.

"Please sit down, ladies. I'm so glad to see you."

No leather jacket today, but a tangerine tunic with a silver cross around her neck.

Photos and artwork filled the top of her desk, and my hands wanted to touch everything. Celia pulled up a chair next to us and handed me a plastic snow globe.

"Look at this, Charity. From my trip to Acapulco, Mexico, last summer."

I smiled inside, thinking of a snow globe from a city where it never snowed. Shaking the globe sent flakes swirling around a white cathedral with a sea-blue dome. I held it to my eyes.

Shake, swirl, shake, swirl.

Celia went over my schedule for the day, actually speaking *to* me instead of *about* me. Talking to me like I was thirteen instead of three.

"Charity, you will spend the first few weeks working with your aide to improve motor control."

At least I will not have to watch Barney.

"What happens after that?" asked Mom.

"As much as possible, I want to support her full participation in regular classes."

Wait. What?

Mom looked confused, but Celia kept talking.

"I believe in my heart—and research supports this too—that all students benefit from learning together. With the help of key faculty members willing to work with us, we have been successful so far."

I loved what she was saying. But did this woman really think I could join in a math or science class . . . with no words and a body I cannot always control?

Mom's face lit up. "That would be incredible. This is just what she needs."

Shake, swirl, shake, swirl.

"But there is something else I want you to know." Celia took the snow globe from me and placed it back on her desk. "Lincoln is heavily supported by donations from families. Our computers, science lab, the entire performing arts auditorium were funded through parent donations. These parents are pressuring Mr. Jergen to place greater focus on advanced curriculum."

"What does this have to do with Charity?" Mom pulled my hand out of my mouth and handed me my animal flashcards.

Llama, flip, manatee, flip, orangutan, flip.

"Well, some parents are worried that having special-needs students in regular classrooms lowers standards and distracts other students." She looked at me. "Charity, the administration is keeping a close eye on us . . . on you."

Translation: Jergen wants to get rid of me. I knew it.

Mom gasped. "Why in the world would you tell her that?"

"Charity is a big girl. She should know the truth."

Celia took both my hands in hers. Her dark eyes stared into mine. "I believe you *do* belong here, *querida*."

For a few seconds, my eyes met hers.

"We will support you to be all you can be. And your success will open doors for other students."

Thoughts swirled in my head like snowflakes in the globe. Celia's words echoed in my mind—*your success will open doors.* My hands flapped.

Flap-flap, flap-flap.

I made an IOU with God at Pine Valley. Maybe this could repay my debt. Maybe I do have a purpose.

My body sprang out of the chair.

Jump, jump, jump. Flap-flap, flap-flap.

Maybe I am not so different from those heroes painted on the hallways of the school. Malala fights for girls' right to an education. I could fight too. Fight for kids like me. Fight for Isabella.

My tongue fluttered and chirped like a chipping sparrow.

Maybe one day schools like Borden can be closed. Boarded up. Bulldozed to the ground.

"I think Charity is eager to begin," Celia said with a huge smile.

Then I saw Mom's face full of worry, and I stopped. Her worry weighed me down.

What am I thinking?

Joy turned to panic.

It would take a miracle for me to succeed. With my wild body and no voice, what chance did I have of being allowed to stay at Lincoln? Chances of snow in Acapulco were probably higher.

I sucked in air and puffed it out my lips.

Suck, puff, suck, puff.

Celia looked from me to Mom. "Mrs. Wood, time for you to go home. Let us take it from here."

Mom stood up and handed me my backpack. Then she squeezed me like an orange and backed out of the room as if I was boarding a rocket to Mars.

I knew Mom's stomach would sink every time the phone rang today.

Would I even make it to the next bell?

Humiliation Served Fresh

Celia swung open an olive-colored door with a gold, sparkly heart on it. "Welcome to the EPIC room," she said. "EPIC stands for Every Person Is Capable. Consider this your home base at Lincoln."

My eyes scanned the room.

Computer stations!

Shelves of books!

Real *art supplies!*

Compared to Borden, this place was Disneyland.

Was this a school where I would be treated as equal?

Define *equal*: Equal does *not* mean that everyone gets the same. It means each person gets what they need.

Probability: hopeful.

"Charity, meet Jazmine." Celia high-fived a small girl in a wheelchair. "She will show you the ropes. She is the EPIC room's official ambassador."

My first clue about Jazmine was the bumper sticker on the back of her wheelchair. It said, "I speak fluent sarcasm."

"Nice shirt," she said. "Much cooler than my dismal polo and khakis."

She twirled her chair to model her outfit and flipped back her brown hair supermodel-style. I wanted to poke all the buttons on her wheelchair.

"Just to let you know, I may look small, but I'm in seventh grade. Mighty Mouse is what Celia calls me. But you can call me Jaz."

I looked down at my animal flashcards.

Panda, flip, racoon, flip, salamander, flip.

"Oh, yeah. Celia said you can't talk yet, but don't worry. You'll still learn a lot."

Talk yet? YET?

"Hey, wouldn't it be great if we could trade places for the day?" asked Jaz. "I mean, I could have your legs to jump and run and ice skate. I've always wanted to ice skate. Twirl around in one of those silly tutus."

What makes you think I can ice skate?

"And you could have my flappy gums all day and finally tell everyone what you *really* think of them."

Wow. That would take more than a day. Just Miss Marcia alone.

Jazmine led me to a back table piled with gadgets in all shapes and textures—spiky balls, twisty plastic tubes, twirly spinners, squishy bean bags.

"We call these fidgets. Some kids hold them to keep their hands busy. It helps them pay attention better."

I dropped my animal flashcards and grabbed a bumpy, twisty, tangled tube fidget. My hands twisted and squeezed.

Twist, squeeze, twist-twist, squeeze.

"Have a seat." She pointed to a bright yellow stool that kind of resembled a turtle shell.

I sat down and felt it move and bounce with my busy body. I could actually move and sit at the same time.

"Or if you get tired of sitting, we have standing desks back there that some kids prefer."

At one of the desks, a tall boy with thick glasses and a puffy afro stood in front of a keyboard next to his aide. Jazmine led me over.

"Julian, this is Charity."

Julian looked up for a second. I saw kind eyes magnified in his glasses. Like me, eye contact was not his thing. Why do people make such a big deal about that anyway? I see you. I hear you. Why do I need to be staring straight into your pupils? For me, it feels too intense, like staring into the sun.

Twist, squeeze, twist-twist, squeeze.

"He doesn't talk with his voice," Jazmine explained to me, "but he can type what he wants to say. Maybe you could do that too."

Sorry, Jaz, that's where you're wrong.

I tried typing a hundred times with Mom and Dad. Each time was a failure. I mean, I knew what I wanted to say. I knew how to spell the words, but the signal got lost somewhere between my brain and my finger. I could reach for the letter *P* twenty times and miss it eighteen times.

Jaz looked up at Julian. "Do you want to say something to Charity on her first day?"

Julian smiled and started typing with one finger as his aide quietly encouraged him by his side.

"We just need to hold on a minute," Jazmine said.

We waited, me twisting my fidget as Julian pecked at the keyboard.

Twist, squeeze, twist-twist, squeeze.

After a few minutes, Julian pushed a button, and a mechanical voice spoke his words.

"POINTED TO PEACE, I ESTEEM YOU. YOU HAVE TREASURED QUALITIES THAT ALL MUST SEE."

His words . . . *I esteem you* . . . they rang in my ears. *You have treasured qualities that all must see.*

"That's beautiful, Julian," Jazmine said. "You're a poet. If I could just get you to write my English essays for me, ha ha."

Jazmine chuckled, and her laughter rang in my head in harmony with Julian's poetry. I stood in a trance until a girl with dark braids threw her arms around Jazmine.

"Don't break the merchandise, Skyler," Jaz said. "Meet Charity. This is her first day."

Skyler smiled big with shiny metal braces. Her braids bounced as she lunged to hug me too.

"The girl gives killer hugs," laughed Jaz. "Literally . . . she nearly strangles me every time."

Lots of people are afraid to touch me, but I like hugs, especially great big bear hugs like Pops and Gram give me. Skyler's tight hug felt as warm and homey as Dad's apple crumb cake.

"Charity is a beautiful name," Skyler said. "It sounds like cherry tree." She slapped her hands to her cheeks as if she had a great idea. "Let me make one for you!"

Skyler sat down at a table full of art supplies, grabbed a fistful of popsicle sticks from a bin and got to work.

I could see from Skyler's bright, slightly slanted eyes that she had Down syndrome like Isabella. Then I remembered Isabella stuck at Borden with broken crayons and dried-out glue sticks.

My spirit sank.

"This girl is an artistic genius," Jazmine said. "She did all those sculptures over there." Jazmine pointed to a bookshelf full of creations made of sticks and string, a vase made of shells, and a green toddler toilet seat transformed into a picture frame with fake jewels—twenty-nine of them—glued around it. The picture inside was of Celia dressed as a cat surrounded by a dozen kids in Halloween costumes munching orange popcorn and caramel apples.

They have actual parties at this school?

"My favorite is Alien Barbie over there."

Jaz pointed to a Barbie posed on a glitter-dusted pedestal, her arms lifted high. Her hair was green instead of blonde. Her skin was salmon-colored instead of milky white. No sparkly mini-dress for this Barbie. Her body was wrapped in brown twine, like a pudgy cocoon.

Jazmine laughed. "That should be the official uniform for all the snooty cheerleaders."

"Hey, you wanna hear a joke? You wanna hear a joke?" A boy appeared behind us with a huge smile and fast-blinking eyes. "Okay, okay, your mama is soooo fat. How fat is she? Well, she is soooo fat that you took a picture of her a month ago and it's still printing because she's so fat it uses a ton of paper. Ha!"

"Charity, this is Peter. He loves to tell jokes." Jaz rolled her eyes.

Peter told ten more jokes in a row without coming up for air—some knock-knocks, some about farts, some about why something crossed the road, and a few more about my mama being *sooooo* fat. Jazmine put her hand on his arm. "Thanks, Peter. I think Celia needs to talk to Charity now."

Jazmine held my hand and led me away, but my mind was already on overload. All the new faces . . . new sounds . . . new smells . . . everyone so kind . . . speaking to me as if I was a real human being . . . with a brain!

This place was 100 percent the opposite of Borden. So why was I panicking?

Twist, squeeze, twist-twist, squeeze.

Do I even belong here?

Twist, squeeze, twist-twist, squeeze.

My success will open doors for other students.

Twist, squeeze, twist-twist, squeeze.

But what if I do not succeed? My failure will close doors for other students.

Panic twisted and squeezed my chest.

Mom is royally right to worry. This will never work.

Twist, squeeze, twist-twist, squeeze.

"I think Ana will be your aide," Jaz said. "She's an awesome teacher."

Yes, but I am sure she cannot perform miracles.

CRASH.

I flung the fidget to the ground and fear flew from my throat.
OOOOWWWWWWWWWOOOOOOOAAAAAAAAH!

Kids covered their ears and stared in shock, but my voice
had to escape. My legs *had* to jump. My arms *had* to shake.

I.

Am.

Doomed.

Two slender hands wrapped around mine.

"You are safe here, Charity."

Velvety—that's how I would describe her voice—like the
tenor sax solos on Dad's jazz CDs. I looked into her face—a
sweet smile and caring, green eyes framed by short, black
bangs. Her words, spoken with a delicate accent, cast a spell.

"Let us slow down your breathing. Breathe in with me."

She closed her eyes, still holding my hands. My voice qui-
eted.

"Breathe in light."

I heard her inhale, long and slow, deep into her chest.

"Breathe out darkness . . . Shhhhhhhhhhh . . ." She released her breath through her lips.

"Breathe in joy. Breathe out fear. Shhhhhhhhhhhhhh . . .

"Breathe in peace. Breathe out anxiety. Shhhhhhhhhhhhhh
. . ."

My breath fell in line with hers, and my jumping-bean
heart calmed.

"I am Ana."

My fear, the panic I lived with every day, growled inside
my head, but her words tamed the beast.

How did she do that?

My sixth sense kicked in—I could feel her peace flow through my veins.

She stared into me and nodded. Could she hear my thoughts pounding inside their prison?

"We will find a way to let your mind express itself," she said.

Acceptance. Complete acceptance from the first minute. So different from how most new people react to me. They get stiff. They back away—like maybe I am contagious—and usually talk *about* me as if I am not there. Or they talk *to* me as if I am three years old.

Ana led me to a table. "Let's get started."

She helped me sit in a chair next to a wall, and she sat next to me.

Maybe my pounding body can settle here.

Next, she handed me a book. Not a picture book for first graders, an actual junior high history book with a map of the US on its cover. Her only command was, "Take a look at this, Charity."

What? You do not want me to touch my nose? Write the letter A? Try to tell a cow from a sailboat? If this is a test, I am not sure what I am supposed to do.

Automatic fail.

I patted the shiny cover and spread my hands to the four corners. I lifted the book to feel its weight. We never got our hands on books more than twenty pages long at Borden. I opened it and flipped through the pages, stopping to look at interesting pictures and read a paragraph or two. I had skimmed lots of history books at Gram and Pops' house (Pops is a big history buff). I could not read them cover to cover since my hands cannot turn pages very well, but I flipped and read, flipped and read enough times to read most every page.

Ana observed me as I examined the pages and ran my hands over the colorful pictures.

Flip.

The Jamestown Settlement.

Flip.

Gold in Sutter's Mill.

Flip.

The Battle of Gettysburg.

Flip.

The Great Depression.

I knew about all of these topics. But what did she expect me to do?

"I can tell by the way you are holding and touching the book that you are a tactile and visual learner. You prefer feeling things with your hands and observing with your eyes." Ana made a note on her pad.

For once it was not an F for fail.

"Which subject would you like to begin with in our tutoring sessions?"

She tore a small strip of paper from her notebook and ripped it into two squares. On one she wrote *history* and on the other *biology*. She placed the two pieces of paper on the table in front of me and repeated her question.

"Which subject would you like? History?" She tapped the piece of paper that said *history*. "Or biology?" She tapped the piece of paper that said *biology*.

I answered her in my mind.

Biology. I want to learn biology so I can try to understand my own unique brain.

How was I supposed to tell her?

BAM! I hit the table with both fists.

Ana reached over and held my left hand. "Tap your answer with your right hand. Either history," she tapped on *history*, "or biology." She tapped on *biology*, then tapped under my right wrist.

My left hand wanted to get away.

She repeated, "Tap your answer with your right hand. History or biology?" She tapped each piece of paper and then tapped my wrist.

Biology! It would be so much easier if you could just read my mind.

My right hand tapped one, then the other piece of paper. She repeated her question. "Tap your answer with your right hand. History or biology?"

This time my right hand reached toward her arm and *pinched* it.

What have I done?

She gently moved my arm back.

"I believe you have a preference, Charity. Please let me know. Tap the subject you prefer."

I saw the red mark where I pinched her. I felt terrible.

I do not think I can do this.

"You can do this, Charity. Tell me which one. Tap your answer with your right hand." All this time, her voice showed no sign of annoyance or impatience. I could tell she had no intention of giving up. I repeated to myself her original commands.

Breathe in light.

Breathe out darkness.

Breathe in joy.

Breathe out fear.

"Which one would you prefer? History or biology." She tapped both choices.

My hand tapped *biology*.

Finally.

"Just to confirm. You are choosing biology?"

Are you kidding me?

My hand tapped *history*.

More minutes of random tapping passed, my frustration growing with every unwanted tap. I slapped my hand hard on the table, and Ana put her hand on mine.

She spoke calmly. "We have much to learn from each other. From what I've observed today, Charity, it is clear you have sensory movement differences. You do not have full control over your body."

No kidding.

"But don't worry, Charity. From my studies, and my work with others, I've learned ways we can help you—at least a little—gain more control."

Breathe out relief.

She has not given up on me yet. Finally, someone who understands.

At lunchtime, Ana walked with me to the cafeteria. Jaz wheeled behind us, frowning.

"Many of the EPIC kids prefer to eat in the classroom," Ana said. "Personally, I think it is better to get out and see the world a little, don't you, Jazmine?"

Jaz answered in a half-whisper. "Sure, if you prefer your mystery meat served with a side of humiliation."

Ana loaded my tray with salad, blueberry yogurt, and a square piece of cheese pizza.

I wanted pepperoni.

From our corner table, we watched a small army of kids pour in. The noise level rose higher and higher. Even with so much chaos, Ana kept me focused on eating one bite at a time.

Jaz nibbled a ham sandwich, her head down and eyes scanning the room. My eyes scanned too.

There he is!

Mason strolled in, sweeping his surfer hair off his face as he walked by with his tray. He saw me. I know it because he jumped a little. Then he made his way to a long table in the center of the cafeteria. A few kids scooted over to make room.

My eyes followed him.

Jaz noticed where I was looking. "That's definitely the cool kids' table. Loaded with selfie-obsessed cheerleaders."

Hypothesis: Jaz is not a fan of cheerleaders.

I watched Mason for a few seconds. He looked cool, sat at the cool table with the cool kids, but I sensed he did not belong. Once in a while, he looked up and laughed at something someone said, but mostly he kept to himself.

Alone in a crowd. That's how I felt too.

The two giggling girls from this morning passed by our

table. Pink hair, green nail polish, and with them a girl with hair the color of . . . honey.

Could it be her?

And freckles on her cheeks . . .

Grace? My once-upon-a-time-a-long-time-ago best friend Grace?

GRACE?

On impulse, my body sprang out of my seat.

My brain hollered *stop!* But my feet ran to her. My legs jumped. My hands clapped.

Her face looked at me, horrified. She shrank backward as if I might bite.

She does not even remember me.

My heart snapped in two. That did not stop my stupid legs from jumping higher . . . my stupid hands from clapping harder.

Kids turned to look. They laughed. Grace covered her mouth. Her friend with green nails pulled her away as if she was a hero rescuing Grace from an oncoming train.

I am in hell.

Ana's hands on my shoulders turned me back toward our table. She sat me down, and kids went back to eating pizza and staring at their phones.

I tried to calm down.

My body rocked back and forth, back and forth.

Alone in a crowd. How is it possible to feel so alone in a cafeteria of two hundred kids?

Back and forth, back and forth.

Page 38: Cows have best friends and
become stressed when separated.

Jaz blew air out of her lips. "Sorry, kid. Like I said, a side of humiliation served fresh daily."

Back and forth, back and forth.

The three girls passed by again on their way out. Pink hair looked at me and leaned in toward her friends. "Can you imagine going through life like that? Hashtag tragic."

Green nails shook her head. "I'd rather die."

Grace kept walking.

So much for old friends.

A Warm Hornet Welcome

Dad hung up the phone with a giant grin. So annoying at times like this. "Congratulations, Charity, you're now officially a Hornet."

It was all Celia's fault.

She suggested I join some sort of extracurricular activity to interact more with what she called the neurotypical students. I love that word: *neurotypical*—as opposed to *normal*. It means they have typical brains that work in ways people expect. Me, on the other hand, Celia said I have a differently wired brain. Sounds so much better than abnormal, impaired, or worse: *that* word. Do people think Stephen Hawking had a typical brain? He could not control his body either, but he taught the world so much.

When Dad heard Celia's suggestion, he jumped into action. A friend of his is the coach of the girls' basketball team. With one phone call full of charm, I was on the team as an "unofficial participant."

Whatever that meant.

Even though Dad had taught me how to shoot a basketball,

I was in no way coordinated enough to play on a team. That did not stop Dad.

Nothing ever does.

Wednesday afternoon, Dad closed his surf shop early to take me to practice. The gym was a sea of bobbing ponytails and dribbling balls that made the whole room rumble in a nonstop earthquake.

Fifteen girls, fifteen balls, too many dribbles to count.

My feet pranced in nervous circles.

Jump-hop-leap-skip.

Dad strolled up to Coach George, his old surfing buddy, and slapped him on the back. Coach smiled with big, white teeth. He smiled a little less each time he looked over at me.

Hypothesis: Dad did not tell Coach about my unpredictable body.

I could not be angry. My dad was the only person in the world who thought I was perfect just as I was.

Jump-hop-leap-skip.

Then Coach slapped Dad on the back and called out, "Girls, this is Charity. She will be joining us as a very special member of the team."

There is that word: special. *How I hate that word. Charity, the charity case.*

"Her Dad was a legend on the court in his day."

Dad shook his head. "Yeah, about a thousand years ago, George."

Everyone laughed.

"He's being modest, girls," Coach said. "Anyhow, please give Charity a warm Hornet welcome."

Jump-hop-leap-skip.

That does not make sense. Hornets are not warm. Hornets STING.

> Page 101: Hornets release more venom in
> their sting than any other stinging insect.

A few girls clapped politely, but the look on everyone's faces said *Whaaaaaaat?*

Jump-hop-leap-skip.

"Let's get started, girls." Coach clapped his hands and began practice, leaving me to watch. Girls dribbled the ball through a zigzag of orange cones and shot free-throws.

I recognized a few of them, including Grace and her two friends. The girl with pink hair was called Lilly. The one with green nails was Darcy. They had already given me a Hornet welcome—I still felt the sting.

Dad kept looking at me and giving me thumbs up, but I sensed his growing frustration. After about fifteen minutes, he decided we should join in the drills with him as my partner.

The girls were working on passing, so we lined up with them, and he passed me the ball. It sailed past me and hit the coach.

"Sorry," Dad yelled.

Come on, Dad. What were you expecting?

We moved to the sideline to practice dribbling.

Bounce, bounce, bounce.

I liked dribbling the ball in one place.

Bounce, bounce, bounce.

I could do that all day.

Bounce, bounce, bounce.

Of course, Dad insisted I dribble and run *at the same time*.
Why must you torture me?

Every five seconds Dad had to fetch my runaway ball. A couple of the girls laughed at him after the third time.

This isn't working.

I walked in circles holding my hands over my ears.

Circle, circle, circle.

Their staring eyeballs pounded me like basketballs to my head.

Circle, circle, circle.

Countdown to KETTLE EXPLOSION . . . 3 . . . 2 . . . 1.

AHHHHHHHHHHHHHHHHHHHHHHH!

My scream echoed off the walls of the gym.

Balls stopped bouncing. Everyone stared. Darcy and Lilly giggled.

Dad led me to the bench. "Let's take a rest, Cherry Girl."

I breathed hard. Why could he not see how embarrassing this was? I stood to leave, but Dad pulled me back on the bench.

"Just a few more minutes, Cherry. When you're part of a team, you have to stick together."

I wanted to scream at him.

Can you not see I am not *part of this team?*

My body rocked back and forth, back and forth.

"Good work, girls. Form a circle." Coach waved his hand for the girls to come over.

He did not motion for me to join. Dad, of course, pulled me over anyway and a few girls made room—lots of room. As usual, my weirdness made them uncomfortable.

My body rocked back and forth, back and forth. Rock, rock, rock.

Everyone put their hands in for a closing cheer. My arm did not want to join. Thankfully, Dad did not force it.

"Goooooooooo Hornets!"

Girls dispersed to waiting parents, and Coach George patted Dad on the shoulder. "Hey, Charity did a great job today. She'll make a terrific team mascot."

Rock, rock, rock.

"Mascot?" Dad took a step back.

"Well, sure, Steve. I thought she could put on the hornet suit and do some funny moves on the court, make some silly faces like she's doing now. It'll crack everyone up."

Translation: I am a joke.

I was puckering my cheeks in a fishy face. Not helping Dad's point.

Rock, rock, rock.

Coach's smile faded when he saw Dad's expression. Dad did not get angry often, but when he did, watch out.

"We have a serious misunderstanding here, George." He pulled Coach aside, but my supersonic ears still picked it up. "We wanted Charity to play on the team, not be a clown."

"Well, exactly what did you have in mind? I'm sorry, Steve, but this isn't the Special Olympics."

Dad's face burned hot. "You corn-fed fool. You didn't even give her a chance!" He turned to me. "C'mon, Charity." Dad took my hand and pulled me toward the exit.

We stopped mid-court, and Dad turned around and hollered at Coach.

"Take a look at this, George."

Dad handed me a ball.

"Shoot, Cherry."

I launched the ball.

Swoosh.

It went in. Same as it usually does when we shoot hoops Saturday mornings. My arms automatically know what to do. If I stopped to think about it, I would probably not be able to do it. One of the few times my brain and body work together— like when I am biking or swimming.

Coach George stood frozen with his eyebrows scrunched together as we walked out.

Two points for Dad.

On the way home, Dad asked, "How 'bout a chocolate shake with extra whip to make us feel better?"

I smiled inside, and Dad pulled up to Pops' ice cream shop. As usual, Pops greeted me with a spoonful of my flavor of the month. Dad ordered the peanut butter-banana shake— Pops called it the Elvis—and got me my usual chocolate. I really preferred strawberry, not that I could tell anyone. The creamy, cold drink almost made me forget the embarrassment of basketball practice.

Almost.

The door jingled as a group of girls entered.

Grace and her two friends, Lilly and Darcy.

I choked on my shake, and Dad patted my back. "Whoa, slow down, honey."

Please do not let them see us.

My bad luck, Dad spotted them with their ice cream cones

looking for a table—how could anyone miss Lilly with her pink hair?

"Would you Hornets care to join us?"

Dad, how could you?

The girls stared at him for a second.

"Uh, sure," Darcy said.

They pulled up some chairs. Lilly grinned in our direction before turning to her friends and launching into a conversation about some pop star. Together but separate, same as at practice.

Dad heaved a sigh. Even his positive attitude was taking a hit tonight.

"Girls, Charity can't talk, but she can understand and maybe react to your conversation. Wanna give it a try?"

I wanted to cry. My jittery feet tapped the tile floor.

Tap-tap-tap-tap.

Dad, you cannot force kids to be my friends.

Darcy looked confused. "Uh, give what a try?"

Tap-tap-tap-tap.

"Try including her in your conversation. It would mean a lot to her to be included."

I wanted to crawl under the table. The girls all stared at the floor.

Tap-tap-tap-tap.

Grace looked at me and cleared her throat. "Charity, I'm sorry I didn't recognize you the other day in the cafeteria."

What's happening here?

Grace turned to her friends. "Charity and I were in the same preschool like a million years ago."

Dad smacked his forehead. "Well, diggity dog! You're little Gracie? You're the girl who used to come over and . . ."

"And make mud pies in the backyard . . . yes, nice to see you again, Mr. Wood."

Like me in the cafeteria, Dad could not contain his excitement. He jumped up and gave Grace a big hug.

Not only did she remember me, she admitted it in front of her friends.

Lilly and Darcy looked on in shock.

"You remember the princess costumes, Charity?" asked Grace.

I managed a smile and a nod. Lilly and Darcy gasped.

My chair scraped the floor. I needed to move, jump, *fly*.

Dad took my cue. "Well, girls. We'll have to continue the conversation later." He walked me to the door.

Grace called after us. "See ya tomorrow, Charity."

"Do you think she actually understands us?" whispered Lilly. "Hashtag totally tragic."

Lilly's words did not hurt me this time. My mind focused on Grace. She knew me. She *remembered* me.

And for a few seconds, I felt less alone.

Breathe in Hope

"Knock, knock!"

Peter was on his eleventh joke so far, and Jaz looked like she wanted to strangle him.

Or maybe she wanted to curse Ana, who insisted we eat lunch in the cafeteria again. This time Ana convinced Peter to join us.

"Knock, knock! Who's there? Wanda," Peter said.

"Peter, you're supposed to wait till we say, 'Who's there?'" Jaz rolled her eyes.

Peter was more than happy to have a captive audience.

Captive is the right word.

"Wanda hang out sometime? Ha!"

He ended each joke with a loud "Ha!" as if he just played a clever trick on us.

"I can't stand when food dribbles on my shirt when I'm eating," Jaz said. "I feel all eyes are on us—especially those dumb cheerleaders with their perfect white teeth and lip gloss and twirly cheer skirts."

You think the cheerleaders notice us? Probability: low.

Jaz tilted her head toward the cool kids' table. I noted Mason was not there today.

Ana did not sit with us today. Instead, she sat close by at the next table. "I'll give you kids your space," she said. That left me with knock-knock jokes on one side and complaints on the other.

Both conversations stopped mid-sentence when a fourth person joined us.

Mason.

Huh?

Mason put his tray on the table and nodded hello.

Jazmine and Peter's eyes grew wide.

Shoulders hunched, he crammed a bean burrito into his mouth in three bites, grabbed his milk carton and poured some milk into his already stuffed mouth—to help mush up the burrito I guess—picked up his tray, and left.

Nothing like a relaxing thirty-second lunch.

No one knew he was my cousin. I am sure Mason wanted to keep it that way. I am also sure that dear Aunt Kiki had told him to eat lunch with me. I imagined her saying, "Wouldn't it be lovely to have lunch with your cousin Charity, sweetie? You know she probably has no friends."

Now he could go home and report *mission accomplished*.

He was out of earshot—or at least pretended to be—by the time Peter thought to ask him, "Wanna hear a joke?"

Back in the EPIC room, Ana brought out the wobble board, which is curved on the bottom and flat on the top.

Here we go again.

The goal was for me to stand on it and balance as long as I

could without falling over. It reminded me of standing on the surfboard with Dad.

While standing on the wobble board, I had to beat a drum and rock in rhythm to the songs she strummed on a guitar. The first hundred times or so, I fell off after a few seconds. But with lots of practice, I got pretty good at it.

"Music therapy helps you with movement," Ana explained.

She was right. Now, when my body got stuck on freeze, she squeezed my arms or legs rhythmically, and that seemed to unstick me. What a relief.

After the wobble board, Ana dragged out the yoga mats.

"Yoga and mindfulness can help regulate your emotions. Let's start with downward dog," she said, tapping the mat.

I bent down, spread my fingers on the mat and lifted my hips up while trying to keep my heels on the floor. Same as Hero waking up from a nap—drool included.

A few poses later, we moved on to meditation. Ana told me to choose a mantra, a phrase I could repeat to myself over and over to stay focused.

"The most basic mantra is *Om*," she explained. "It simply means *It is*. But you could choose any phrase you want, like *I am at peace* or *I am stronger each day*."

The first few times, my fidgety body did not last thirty seconds. But after two weeks, we were up to as many as five minutes of breathing and sitting.

Sitting cross-legged on my purple mat, I struggled to tune out the voice inside that said I could not do it.

Breathe in friendship.

I am more than my body.

Breathe out loneliness.

I love and accept myself.

Mom and Dad practiced with me at home too. Our neighbor Dr. Singh did a double take when she saw me and Dad doing the tree pose in the front yard. He balanced on one leg and held his arms—his branches—in the air to feel the breeze.

"Are you two doing ballet again?" she asked. "I don't think that's one of the positions, Steve," she laughed.

Ana also helped me move better by tapping the body part that was supposed to react. When I got stuck sitting on the floor, for example, she tapped my leg and said, "Let's stand now." That simple touch usually reminded my legs what they were supposed to do.

After our yoga lesson, Ana helped me play games on an electronic tablet. She supported me gently, making it possible for my hand to tap and swipe.

One program taught me to draw letters with my finger.

"Good job, Charity. Now let's draw the letter C. Move your finger counterclockwise. There you go . . ."

"Breathe deeply."

I did not see her mark down any of my failures. For each new task, she gave me as much help as I needed and had faith that I would, eventually, learn it. Same as Mom when she taught me to read and Dad when he taught me to ride a bike and surf and ski. Why couldn't all teachers be like that?

When I finally drew the letter C with no support, she yelled "Whoopee!" and held up her hand for a fist bump.

Celia joined in for a triple bump, and Skyler did a victory dance. "You did it! We believe in you, Cherry Tree!"

My mind wandered again to Isabella, stuck in that smelly classroom at Borden, probably watching *Barney* season four, episode ten for the millionth time. How was it fair that I escaped and she had not?

After three weeks, Celia invited Mom to school for my first progress report. Finally, the word "progress" did not sound like a total joke.

"Charity has done a wonderful job adapting to a new and often chaotic environment," Celia said. "She should be very proud." Celia turned to me. "*Querida*, we feel you are ready to attend some mainstream classes starting next week."

What?

My body tensed up and started to rock.

Back and forth, back and forth.

Mom shook her head, "But things are going so well. Charity seems happier. She's eating and sleeping better. Couldn't we keep things as they are for now?"

Back and forth, back and forth.

"Mrs. Wood, Charity has already waited years to attend age-appropriate classes. She shouldn't waste any more time."

Ana put her hand on Mom's shoulder. "It will be all right. I will be there to support her, and the teachers and I have already discussed ways she might participate."

Mom smiled. She actually smiled. I sensed no worry hiding underneath it.

Maybe Ana really could perform miracles.

Down the Rabbit Hole

Mason's eyes popped when I stumbled into his math class the following Monday.

My stomach sent up a dribble of morning OJ into my mouth. My polo shirt wanted to strangle me after my nervous fingers had buttoned it all the way to the top. I tugged at the neck.

Ana squeezed my shoulder. "You will be all right, Charity." I focused on her soothing voice and tried not to look at the sixty-four eyeballs pointed in my direction.

Page 278: A turtle's upper shell is called a carapace. Its lower shell is a plastron.

If I were a turtle, I would hide in my shell.

Mason turned his eyes down to his notebook, as if he were deep in thought.

Do not worry, Mason. Your secret is safe with me.
Obviously.

Ana and I sat at the back table of Mr. Byrd's math class.

Jaz whizzed up next to me in her wheelchair. "You're gonna love this class, Charity. Mr. B is super cool."

I knew she was right when I saw his T-shirt with a picture of Einstein sticking out his tongue.

"Welcome, young Jedi knight," he said, bowing to me.

Still, I could not help gnawing on my knuckles for the first thirteen minutes.

I loved math. The logic and peacefulness of numbers. Sad to say, in all my classes at school, math lessons had never gone past counting to ten.

The teacher would command, "Pick up three blocks, pick up three blocks, pick up three blocks." When my hands grabbed one block or five blocks, the Thinkers concluded I had no understanding of numbers.

The aide at Borden would say the same thing over and over. "If Suzy has two pieces of bubble gum and Bobby gives her one more, how many pieces of bubble gum does Suzy have?" I prayed that Suzy would just choke on her stupid gum.

I watched Mr. Byrd scribble equations on the board and talk about monomials and binomials. My mind flashed to all of Mom's flashcards on multiplication and division. Algebra was the same but with Xs and Ys. Yes, it made sense to me, but with no way to communicate, I could only sit and listen. I started picking pieces of lint off Jazmine's sweater.

"Here is a fidget for you to spin." Ana handed me a blue spinner and my eyes drank in the perfect circle that formed each time I spun it. Round and round and round.

Mr. Byrd gave the class a problem to solve: $15x^2yx \div 5xy$.

Numbers and letters floated in my head.

Round and round and round.

The answer is $3x^2$.

Round and round and round.

No way to tell anyone, though.

Page 278: The leatherback sea turtle is the largest
species of turtle, some weighing more than 2000 pounds.

Round and round and round.

I dropped the spinner on the floor.

Mr. B walked over and handed me a Rubik's cube. "Maybe
you'd like to fix this for me, young Jedi."

I know he only gave it to me for fidgeting, but I so wished
my hands would cooperate in solving it just this once.

Fact: No one will ever know I have a brain.

Page 276: The Galápagos tortoise can
live for more than 200 years.

Twist, twist, twist, twist.

My mind could see the twenty-five or so turns that needed
to be made. Would my hands obey? To my amazement, they
did. I counted down the turns . . . 13 . . . 12 . . . 11 . . . Just ten
more turns, and I would have it. My body rocked with each
twist.

Rock, twist, rock, twist, rock.

My hands twisted the cube automatically.

Everyone will finally see what I can do.

Or not.

A noise scraped my ears. A bright light flashed above the
door.

CREECH . . . CREECH . . . CREECH . . . CREECH . . . CREECH . . . CREECH.

My hands dropped the cube and covered my ears.

Every blast hammered a stake into my brain cells.

"Let's exit in an orderly fashion, dudes and dudettes," Mr. B said.

My logical brain knew it was only a fire alarm. But my bulldog impulse acted on instinct.

My legs sprang up.

Run! Get away!

My feet sprinted out the door.

CREECH . . . CREECH . . . CREECH . . . CREECH . . . CREECH . . . CREECH.

Faster! Go!

Down the hall.

Move! Run!

The sound stabbed my ears.

Get out! Escape!

I crashed into kids, banged into walls, stumbled over backpacks.

CREECH . . . CREECH . . . CREECH . . . CREECH . . . CREECH . . . CREECH.

Run! MOVE!

My feet kept flying.

Away! NOW!

My sneakers scrambled like prey escaping a predator.

A flash of sunlight pulled me toward the end of a hallway, an emergency exit. I knew that beyond the exit was a sidewalk. Beyond the sidewalk was a busy street.

CREECH . . . CREECH . . . CREECH . . . CREECH . . . CREECH . . . CREECH.

My brain yelled at my feet: *Stop! Stop!* Two steps out that door, and I would be in the middle of the street.

My bulldog impulse commanded: *Keep going!*

The sun threw a spotlight on the door. A truck engine roared from the street outside. My brain hollered: *Freeze!*

My bulldog impulse commanded: *Get out NOW!*

CREECH . . . CREECH . . . CREECH . . . CREECH . . . CREECH . . . CREECH.

My arms rammed the door open.

I'm dead! I'm roadkill!

My left foot stepped outside, heading toward a massive garbage truck.

At that second, my body snapped back like a yo-yo. Someone had grabbed the back of my shirt. My throat choked on the collar. My arms swung around. My fist smashed a face.

Right in the nose.

Mason?

Mason breathed hard. He was hanging onto my shirt with one hand and covering his bloody nose with the other.

"What the crud, Charity."

How did you even keep up with me?

My feet froze. I stared in shock at the river of red dripping from his nose. He wiped blood onto his sweatshirt. Then he led me out the emergency exit and to the soccer field at the back of the school.

All the kids were standing in lines with their classes. In front of everyone, Mason held my hand and walked me to a frantic Celia, who was on the phone to a frantic Ana. "*Gracias a Dios!* Thank you for your help, young man!"

Mason nodded and left.

My heartbeat slowed as I watched Mason walk away, still wiping away blood.

Hypothesis: Cousin = friend.

•••

Even after my morning freak-out, Ana insisted on taking me to my new English class that afternoon. Walking down the hallway, I heard the whispers. I am sure they all knew about my five-hundred-yard dash that morning.

"That's the one who went ballistic . . . OMG, she almost mowed me down . . ."

I wanted to scream at them.

OMG, I have ears, you know!

Every giggle, every glare added a new bruise.

"That fire alarm was no drill," Ana said. "It was pulled by a student as a prank. For normal drills, we always lead our students outside before the alarm sounds since so many have sensitivity to loud noises."

My legs could barely take the next step, like they were plowing through frigid, knee-deep snow.

Ana squeezed my shoulders. "Do not let fear stop you, Charity. We conquer our fears by facing them head on."

When we arrived at English, more kids were staring.

Ana and Celia's little plan was not going so well.

Ana laid out a two-hundred-piece puzzle on the back table,

a sailboat gliding on an aquamarine sea. "This should keep your hands busy so your mind can focus."

My body rocked back and forth, back and forth.

"Breathe, Charity," she said. "Remember what we practiced."

Okay, I can do this. Focus on the puzzle. Look for blue pieces. Look for blue pieces.

I spotted Grace's friends, Lilly and Darcy.

Oh, great.

Back and forth, back and forth.

Blue pieces. Blue pieces . . . 7, 8, 9 . . .

The teacher, Ms. Beckett, came and put her hand over mine. "So nice to meet you, Charity. Welcome to our class."

I looked down at her fingers—dotted with age spots—and up at her face—wrinkled with wisdom. I felt welcome here.

Breathe in peace.

Wait a minute. Who's that?

Standing a few feet behind us was the principal, Mr. Jergen, wearing a frown. Next to him stood a large woman wearing a red blouse that tied in a bow at her neck. Her eyes pointed in my direction. She held a pen and notebook, and I could hear her nose whistle a little when she breathed.

Ana looked back at them and stiffened.

Breathe in peace?

Were they here because of me? Celia said the administration would keep a close eye on me.

My heartbeat multiplied by two.

Holy hippopotamus.

Blue pieces, blue pieces. How many did I have so far?

Ms. Beckett dove into a discussion about *Alice in Wonderland*. Her petite body bopped and boogied around the classroom as she described scenes from the story. The whole time her short gray hair never moved a millimeter.

Mom had read me the book when I was ten. As Ms. Beckett spoke, images of the blue caterpillar, grinning cat, and terrible Queen of Hearts floated in my mind. I could almost taste Alice's cake and tarts and tea. My brain felt like a dry sponge soaking in its first drops of water.

I can do this. Focus on the puzzle. Red pieces now . . . 1, 2, 3 . . .

I always felt close to Alice. She fell down a rabbit hole and found her body too small, then too large. The creatures in Wonderland considered her a freak, but, to her, *they* were the strange ones. Alice had a hard time living in Wonderland. Did the author Lewis Carroll feel out of place in his world? I filed that question away with a million others I would never get to ask.

Brown pieces now . . . 1, 2, 3 . . . Are Jergen and that lady still staring at me?

I peeked back. Jergen had left, but the whistle-breathing woman stayed. She reminded me of the Queen of Hearts. At any moment, I expected her to point and shout, "Off with her head!"

"Let's get in groups to discuss the questions on the board," Ms. Beckett said. "How about a few people form a group with Charity? Stuart, Alex, Lilly, Rachel, join her at the back table, please."

Lilly with pink hair? Oh, no. Hasn't she already called me tragic twice?

The kids pulled chairs up to my table, leaving miles of space between them and me.

Diagnosis: contagious.

Stuart was the only one who did not squirm at my strangeness. He opened his copy of *Alice in Wonderland*, crammed with yellow highlights and notes scribbled in the margin. His long legs barely fit under the table as he laid out his notebook and adjusted his glasses to examine Ms. Beckett's questions. I could guess he loved learning as much as I did.

"Okay, what does everyone think about question one?" he said. "What aspects of the story suggest that this is a dream?"

Ms. Beckett came up to Ana. "Can I ask you a few quick questions about our new student?"

"Of course," Ana said. "I'll be back in two minutes, Charity," she whispered.

My nervous body rocked back and forth.

Rock. Rock. Rock.

Rachel fiddled with her sparkly yellow bracelet and snapped her bubblegum—watermelon flavor, I think. Her head tilted toward me. "Is she supposed to participate?"

Maybe because I was not looking at her, she thought I could not hear her. I focused on my puzzle. Or at least tried to.

Rock. Rock. Rock.

"She *is* participating," Lilly said, twirling her pink hair. "Can't you see she's deep in thought?" A sneezelike giggle burst out of her nose. She and Rachel covered their faces.

My neck burned hot.

"Could we get back to the discussion?" Stuart sounded annoyed. "Alex, what do you think about question one?"

Alex, who was staring at me, turned to Stuart and scratched his arm. "Um, what was the question?"

Both girls crumpled into another giggle fit, and I realized my lips were scrunched into a duck face. By now, half the class stared. Lilly's friend Darcy, sitting across the room, mimicked my face and made the whole class laugh. My entire body burned. My hands hit the table.

Slap. Slap. Slap.

Keep it together.

Ana returned and put her hand on my back. "Breathe in, Charity."

Ms. Beckett marched over. "Lilly, Rachel, you need to come with me. *Now.*" She pointed to the door. The girls rolled their eyes and got up to leave.

Even with them gone, I trembled on overload.

Slap. Slap. Slap.

"Breathe, Charity," Ana said.

Too late.

Countdown to KETTLE EXPLOSION . . . 3 . . . 2 . . . 1.

My legs launched me from my chair. I knocked over the table, sending hundreds of puzzle pieces flying. A few kids screamed.

Ana pulled me out of the room, leaving behind a small disaster as the Queen of Hearts scribbled furiously in her notebook.

Off with her head!

•••

The phone rang five minutes after Mom and I got home from school. I heard only Mom's end of the conversation. I knew it was Jergen.

"Yes, but I assure you this was not violent behavior . . . but I find it difficult to believe that any student was injured . . . but you promised a one-month . . . but . . ."

Mom put the phone down and sat several minutes with no expression. I sensed she was trying to stay calm.

"Apparently, one of the students claimed they were injured by you today."

My mind flashed to Mason's bloody face.

How could he?

"A girl in your English class says she was struck by a falling table. Mr. Jergen will be discussing your placement with the superintendent tomorrow." She held my hand and kissed my forehead. "We will fight this, sweetheart. We won't give in so easily."

Her tiny voice made me think she already had.

My Rebirth Day

"Come on, Charity, let's get out of the car. Stand up, please." Mom touched my legs to unfreeze them like Ana taught her. I climbed out, slow as a sloth.

This is the last place I want to be.

Two days ago, practically no one knew who I was. Now that hurricane Charity had struck twice, I was legendary.

Not in a good way.

Once we got to the EPIC room, Celia pulled us into her office along with Ana and sat me in one of her red plastic chairs. Three adults stood over me. Their nervous energy flowed through me like electricity, with Mom emitting about a thousand kilowatts.

Celia knelt down eye to eye with me. "Charity, *querida*, what happened yesterday was part of your adjustment. You are getting used to a completely new environment. And from what I heard, your outburst in English class was provoked by some thoughtless girls."

"And I should not have left you," Ana said, leaning over Celia. "We know you are still struggling to control your body."

"Was a student injured? Who filed a complaint?" Mom asked. Her voice grew higher with each word and scraped my ears.

High pitch sounds = torture.

Celia sighed. "A girl named Darcy Warner. Her parents do a lot of fundraising for the school, so they have Mr. Jergen's full attention."

I could not believe it. Darcy was sitting in front of the room when I exploded. She could not have been hit by the table. Probability: ZERO.

I pounded my fist on Celia's desk.

Bam! Bam! Bam!

Words clogged my throat.

I want to tell you. I need to tell you.

Bam! Bam! Bam!

Mom put her jittery hand on my arm. "I know you're upset, sweetheart. But you *have* to stay calm." She was the last person to talk about staying calm. I wanted to scream.

Darcy is lying! She's lying!

Bam! Bam! Bam!

Let me talk this once. Just one sentence!

Ana's hands squeezed my jittery shoulders in a rhythmic pattern, and we began our breathing exercise.

"Focus, Charity. Reach into your spirit. You have the power to control your emotions."

Breathe in peace.

Why does she hate me?

Breathe out anger.

I never did anything to her.

Breathe in forgiveness.

Breathe out anger.

My thumping heart slowed.

"What happens now?" Mom asked.

Celia ran her fingers through her cinnamon hair. "Short term, Mr. Jergen may attempt to suspend Charity. His assistant, Rose, is probably filling out the paperwork as we speak. Apparently, she witnessed the event from the back of the classroom."

Rose—the Queen of Hearts!

"Long term, he'll request another placement for Charity, like—dare I say it—Pine Valley."

Gulp.

My hands flapped in frustration.

Flap, flap, flap.

"Which means we don't have much time," Ana said.

"What can we do?" Mom's voice screeched at the pitch of a high G.

Flap, flap, flap.

"We'd like to try something that may help Charity communicate and allow her to participate in classes," Celia said. She looked at Ana, who nodded. "It's a support technique that may allow her to type like Julian does. We need to give Mr. Jergen some evidence that this school can benefit you."

"What are you talking about?" Mom looked confused.

"Charity, you know Julian, right? Julian has, over time, been able to learn how to type independently using a tablet and predictive text."

I thought of Julian's beautiful words to me. *I esteem you . . .*

You have treasured qualities. But I could never do what he does. It took me forever to tap a stupid piece of paper—biology or history.

Mom shook her head. "No, unfortunately Charity has never been able to type before. We've tried many times. She doesn't have enough control over her hands."

"Exactly," Celia said. "We've been working with Charity on that, but I've invited a former professor of mine, Dr. Sarah Peterman, to help us. She's taught me and other educators and speech therapists some techniques to help people like Charity gain more control."

Hypothesis: One more test for me to fail.

We spent the next hour hiding out in a library study room (where Jergen could not easily find us) waiting for this new Thinker to arrive. Celia ignored her buzzing phone.

"Mr. Jergen will need to sit tight," she said.

A tall woman burst through the door wearing a dress with a gold belt that reminded me of Wonder Woman. She hugged Celia, and in a laughing voice asked, "How's my favorite teacher?"

Celia whispered in her ear. "We don't have much time, Sarah. Mr. Jergen may come in at any moment with suspension papers."

Sometimes I wish my hearing was not so awesome.

Dr. Peterman sat beside me and laid her soft hand on mine. "I'm so happy to meet you, Charity," she said. Her kindness flowed through me. From her large bag, she took an iPad and propped it up on the table in front of us. Next came a keyboard.

"Now, Charity, I am going to sit here by your side and steady your right arm until I feel you point to the letter you want with your pointer finger."

An eager audience—Mom, Ana, and Celia—sat silently behind us.

"Just relax and take a deep breath, my dear," Dr. Peterman said.

Breathe in hope.

Breathe out fear.

She held the keyboard up with her right hand and steadied my jittery right arm with her left hand. "Let's start with something easy. What's your favorite food?"

I looked at the keyboard and spotted the letter I wanted to type. Words pounded inside my brain. Bright fluorescent lights buzzed overhead. My shirt tightened its grip on my throat.

Breathe in hope.

I lifted my arm and took aim.

Breathe out panic.

My pointing finger pushed forward to touch a key.

P

"What's next?"

P for panda.

I could sense Mom holding her breath. I tried to keep going.

P . . . P . . . P

This isn't working. I am stuck on the first letter.

"Keep going, Charity," Dr. Peterman said. "What's the next letter?"

Favorite food . . .

> Page 208: Pandas eat bamboo.

Her questions encouraged me to move to my next target.

I

One letter at a time.

Tick, tick, tick . . .

How many ticks of the clock would it take to type one letter?

Z . . . Z . . . Z

"Is there more?" she asked.

Breathe in hope.

Breathe out despair.

> Giant pandas can eat 600 bamboo stems in one day.

Tick, tick, tick . . .

At any moment Jergen might find us.

After what seemed like forever, I looked up at the screen and saw the letters my finger had typed.

PPPIZZZA

Dr. Peterman pressed a green button, and a mechanical voice spoke my messy word. My one word. My first word.

Mom gulped air as if she was coming up from drowning.

"Excellent," Dr. Peterman said. "Let's try another question. Do you have a pet? Y for yes, N for no."

I reached my finger.

Y

"What is your pet's name?"

Each letter seemed like an impossible target. But Dr. Peterman supported me, and I moved my finger to the different keys.

H . . . E . . . R . . . O

A sigh or maybe a sob escaped Mom's lips, but I forced my eyes to stay on the keyboard. After about four more questions and answers, my body still cooperated, but my hand was starting to shake.

"You've done an excellent job, Charity," Dr. Peterman said. "Is there anything else you want to tell us?"

A handful of typed words would not convince Jergen that I could handle this school. It was not enough to prove I was not brainless like people thought. If this was my only chance to stay, what I typed next would be the most important words of my life.

I knew what I wanted to say. My first words—at age thirteen—had to count. With each letter, tidal waves of emotion traveled from my brain, out through my right pointer finger—decorated coral pink with Mom's nail polish.

My forehead dripped sweat, as if I were running a marathon instead of typing slower than a snail on a keyboard. When I finished, everyone stood to look at the screen. Dr. Peterman read my words out loud.

I AM INTELLIGENT.

"Yes, Charity. Yes, you certainly are." Dr. Peterman nodded at the spectators.

I turned to see a fourth person had joined the audience, his mouth wide open.

Mr. Jergen.

He stared at my words. "Well, would you look at that."

Celia and Ana leapt up and tackled me with hugs and kisses.

Mom sat in her chair and let loose a sea of tears. After a few moments, she stumbled to her feet and wrapped me in her arms. "I can't believe it . . . my Charity, my precious Charity."

"Well, now," Jergen said, "given this new development, I will . . . speak with Darcy's parents and see if they will dismiss their complaint."

Translation—I am still a Lincoln student. For now, at least.

For the next hour, Dr. Peterman worked with Mom and Ana, showing them how to support me, how to keep me going, how to be patient while I chose the letters I would type.

Then Celia ordered us to go home and let it all soak in. "This changes everything, *querida*."

She was royally right. I smiled. At least I think I did—I am never sure without a mirror.

Today should be my new official birthday. My rebirth day.

First Words

"I can't believe it, Charity. All this time, we could have been communicating with you. I mean, really talking."

Mom and I drove straight from school to buy a portable keyboard to connect to her iPad so I could type my words at home.

Mom sniffled the whole way. "Oh, my goodness, I have so many things to ask you—so many things I'm sure you want to tell us too. When I think of the wasted years . . . the time you suffered at Borden . . ." She inhaled deeply. "My precious girl." She turned to look at me. "My sweet, smart girl." She reached over to squeeze my hand. "I guess we can't dwell on lost time. We can only be grateful you finally have a voice."

Is it possible to feel every emotion at once? That's how it felt inside my mind as I stared at passing cars. Joy, anger, relief, triumph, sadness.

Fear.

Would I finally be seen as a real person? Was I Alice waking up from her dream?

Mom did not call Dad to tell him the big news. When

we made it home, we got right to work practicing typing. My sixth sense felt my mom's jitters, which spilled over onto me. My finger hit more wrong keys.

Can I still do this?

Thank goodness, the technique actually worked. Sitting side by side on the sofa with Hero at our feet, Mom supported me as I typed a message for Dad. After a day full of excitement, each letter was a struggle, but I did not want to stop.

Dad strolled in at 5:25 P.M., as usual, smelling of fish and coconut sunscreen.

"Steve, Charity has something to tell you."

He took in the scene, and focused on the keyboard in our lap. Mom pressed a button, and it played my prepared message.

DAD, YOU ARE MY BEST FRIEND. THANK YOU FOR BELIEVING IN ME.

He looked confused. Then Mom held my right elbow as I typed the final line.

I LOVE YOU.

Dad shook his head and tears welled in his eyes. "Is this . . . is she . . . you mean she can finally . . ."

He ran a hand through his hair and let it sink in. Then he started blubbering. "Charity . . . Cherry Girl . . . holy crickets." He wrapped his arms around me and Mom. "This is a dream come true!"

I am supposed to feel happy too, right?

Googolplex words all crammed themselves at the door trying to shove their way out. Some of them were screaming mad.

I pushed those words back.

•••

In class next day, Jazmine, Peter, Julian, Skyler and the other EPIC kids crowded around to "hear" me talk with Ana supporting me.

Ana read my message to the group.

THANK YOU FOR ACCEPTING ME EVEN BEFORE I HAD WORDS.

Skyler gave me a mega-hug. "I knew you could do it, Cherry Tree," she said.

Julian typed me a message on his tablet.

"YOUR SOUL IS NOW FREED TO TELL ITS TRUTHS."

I envied how his aide did not have to support his arm anymore. Ana said his independent typing came after years of practice.

"Wow," Jaz said. "Compared to you typers, most of us talkers sound like mindless parrots."

Julian typed his response.

"FOR US, EACH WORD IS A GIFT."

Mr. Jergen came to see me type again.

Hypothesis: He wanted to make sure it was not a fluke.

"I am indeed sorry I misjudged you, young lady," he said. "I look forward to hearing more from you."

Sounded like he really meant it.

Pandora's Box

Mom tangoed into the kitchen Saturday morning all excited to ask, "What do you want for breakfast, sweetheart?"

Wow. No one ever asked that before. So many possibilities came to mind.

"How about some of my special power oatmeal?" She held the keyboard and steadied my eager hand to type.

I HATE OATMEAL.

Mom looked surprised. "What?" She laughed. "Well, I guess I owe you about a thousand apologies for that. What *would* you like?"

I typed the first thing that came to mind.

STRAWBERRY SHAKE.

Mom yelled toward the next room. "Steve, you need to run to the store for some ice cream!"

Dad strolled in, wiping his face with a towel. "Ice cream at 9 A.M.?"

"This girl wants a strawberry shake, and she's already waited thirteen years for it."

That morning, the three of us slurped shakes for breakfast with extra whip. The whole time, Mom and Dad grilled me with questions—favorite foods, books, clothes, TV shows—those million little things that families already know about each other.

"What's your favorite color?"

I LOVE ALL COLORS. BUT NEVER DRESS ME IN PINK AGAIN.

"Wow—you'll need a whole new wardrobe, then." Dad laughed.

"How about favorite music?" Mom asked. "You've been putting up with my corny country tunes for years now. Here's your chance to complain."

ALL MUSIC BRINGS JOY. EXCEPT FOR TUBBY TRASH BAG JINGLE.

My stomach churned back and forth with each question, like the time Mason and I rode the teacup ride at the fair when we were five. Violent waves of emotions pulled me in opposite directions and made me want to barf.

A wave of joy—Wheeeeeeeee!

Anger—Eeeeeeeeeeeeee!

Relief—Ahhhhhhhhhhhh!

Sadness—Ohhhhhhhhhhh!

Guilt—Whoaaaaaaaaa!

Typing had opened a crack in my heart, and a thousand gallons of emotion were ready to spill out.

"What are your feelings on pasta? Red or white sauce?" Mom asked.

I pushed away the keyboard.

"Charity? Are you okay, sweetheart?"

All my hurts piled against the dam ready to burst through. Years of being treated as a nobody. People calling me . . . *that word*. Years of abuse at Borden. The pain of all the kids left behind. Especially Isabella. And here my parents were asking if I preferred red or white pasta sauce?

These are not the important questions.

Pandora's box—my mind kept going back to that story from ancient Greece. A woman named Pandora is given a gift by the god Zeus—a box or a jar, depending on which version you read—but she is told not to open it. So really not a gift at all. Zeus had tricked her. He knew she could not resist. When she finally peeked inside, all the evils of humanity escaped into the world—sadness, anger, regret, fear, hate.

Push the pain back inside. Superglue the lid shut!

Too late.

The lid on my Pandora's box had been ripped off.

My mind flashed to Borden. Sitting there in the musty trailer that's supposed to be a classroom, being serenaded by ancient Barney videos. Being dragged to the time-out closet.

Page 268: Tasmanian devils fly into
a rage when threatened.

So many voiceless kids who will never be heard. So many lives wasting away.

Tasmanian devils growl and screech.

Everyone deserved to be included in the world, to be counted as worthy.

Devils bare their sharp teeth.

Isabella in tears.

They tear apart prey with their powerful jaws.

Frustration boiled in my belly and shot out through my arms, legs, throat.

They devour their prey, bones and all.

Our little celebration turned to disaster.

Countdown to KETTLE EXPLOSION . . . 3 . . . 2 . . . 1.

I dropped to the floor. My arms and legs kicked and swung. My voice howled.

GGGGGGAAAAAAAAAAAAHHHHHHHH!

"Charity, Charity," yelled Mom. "Please, type with me. Tell me what you're feeling."

Kick-kick-punch-kick-punch-punch-kick.

If only they could hear the screaming in my head.

It's not fair. It's not freaking fair.

Kick-kick-punch-kick-punch-punch-kick.

Dad got down on the floor with me. "Take some deep breaths, honey. You'll be okay. You'll be okay. We're here with you."

You do not understand. How could you possibly understand thirteen years of agony?

Kick-kick-punch-kick-punch-punch-kick.

"How can we help you?" Mom yelled over my screams.

Thirteen years in PRISON!

Kick-kick-punch-kick-punch-punch-kick.

At last, my arms and legs collapsed. My chest heaved up and down.

Hero waddled over and licked my ear. The tornado had passed. But the sadness was going nowhere.

Dad lifted me onto the sofa. Mom sat down to offer support. Holding up the keyboard, she pleaded, "Talk to us, *please*. Tell us what you're feeling. We're listening."

BORDEN I WANT TO GO TO BORDEN.

"But it's Saturday," Dad said. "Borden is closed today."

I WANT TO GO TO BORDEN.

Eighteen minutes later, we pulled up to the front office, its windows plastered with colorful cardboard tulips. I headed for the gate.

"I'm sure everything is locked tight," Mom said.

I pushed down on the handle, and the rusty gate squeaked open. I marched across the playground with its shiny swing set and slide where no kids actually *played*. The playground where I was abandoned for hours at a time.

My body led us to the classroom where three years of my life were wasted, 136 hours and seventeen minutes spent in time out. I charged the door like an angry bull.

KICK, POUND, SLAM, SLAM, POUND, KICK

One strike for every wasted day, every hour left sitting on the grimy blacktop, every hour locked in the time-out closet, every useless test I failed, every "progress" report that made me feel worthless. Every lost opportunity.

KICK, POUND, SLAM, SLAM, POUND, KICK

Mom tried to grab my hands. "Charity, Stop—you're going to hurt yourself!"

Dad pulled her back. "No, Gail, she has to let it out."

KICK, KICK, SLAM, POUND, POUND, KICK

"But, Steve . . ."

"Let her be. She needs to do this."

I beat the door until my hands were throbbing, then fell to my knees breathing hard.

Dad lifted me to stand. I thought he would lead me back to the car. But no. He began pounding too. Mom joined in, their eyes leaking tears. Six feet kicking. Six hands thudding.

We sat on the steps to catch our breath. Mom pulled the keyboard out of her bag and helped me speak my truth.

THREE YEARS OF PRISON.

"I know, sweetheart. I know that now."

YOU SENT ME HERE.

She wiped her eyes with her sleeve. "I know that too. I'm so sorry, so, so, so sorry . . ." Her voice trailed off and we sat in silence.

"All we can do is move forward," Dad said, "and we will forever try to make it up to you."

My emotions seethed and growled and gnashed their teeth. Ready to devour me.

Bones and all.

●●●

Celia came to our house that evening after Mom phoned her about my explosion. She wore a long, slim dress that almost touched the ground. Her cinnamon hair was swept up in a twist held with a golden clip.

"Thank you for coming," Dad said. "Hope we didn't wreck your night out."

"I am glad you called." Celia sat next to me on the sofa and wrapped me in a hug. My stiff body melted into her.

"*Querida*." She smelled of lilacs tonight. "Tell me what you are feeling."

Mom sat beside me so I could communicate. Dad and Celia watched the screen patiently while I pecked letter by letter.

MY BROKEN HEART IS FILLED WITH TOO MANY HURTS. ANGER BUBBLES TO THE SURFACE.

"You are right to be angry." Celia squeezed my hand. "After everything you have suffered, I would worry if you were not angry. But anger is easy. What do you do about it? That is the important question."

I knew the answer. Celia waited patiently as my fingers reached and tapped, reached and tapped each key. Dad read each sentence out loud as I typed.

I CANNOT HAVE PEACE UNTIL THE KIDS ARE SAFE. BORDEN CLOSED.

Seeing the words in writing felt freeing. My wish floated from my spirit into the world.

Celia nodded. "Then you have a mission. And it is an important one. I can help you craft a letter to the district superintendent about Borden Academy."

I have a mission.

I typed more. Reach, tap. Reach, tap. Reach, tap.

BUT WHO WILL LISTEN TO SOMEONE LIKE ME?

"*Querida*, most people who changed our way of thinking were not rich and powerful. Consider the heroes painted on the walls of our school—Gandhi, Rosa Parks, Malala. It was their message that had power. Speak from your heart and people will listen."

I have a mission.

Breathe in hope.

Breathe out fear.

Why is it so hard to breathe out fear?

Celia leaned closer. "What else can we do to help you heal?"

I thought a minute.

I WANT A REAL EDUCATION.

Celia held out her fist for a bump. "Then it is time you got one."

Coming Out Party

Gram and Pops insisted on it.

A party in honor of my first words. Instead of our usual Sunday barbecue, Gram put together a feast of all my favorite foods—French toast, mashed potatoes with gravy, carrot soup, pepperoni pizza, and strawberry shakes.

The appetizer—sour gummy worms.

Before we ate, I had to endure a half hour of people hugging and sniffling every time I typed a word.

I AM GRATEFUL FOR MY FAMILY.

"Thank the sweet Lord our precious girl has found her voice," Gram sang out as if she was in church.

Aunt Kiki smudged her coral lipstick all over my cheeks. "Sweetie, I just knew there was more, I just knew it. I could feel it, I tell you. Mason, can you believe it? Well, can you?"

Mason stood there watching me, his head jutting forward like a longnecked turtle. "Wow . . . I thought . . . I thought you were gone. But now . . . this is . . . wow." He sniffed and wiped his nose.

It was Aunt Elvi I was worried about. She sat there, a frozen statue with no expression. I noted her face, usually pale, but now white as an arctic fox.

Gram finally unfroze her. "Say something, Elvi!"

Gram's words unleashed a river of tears. Mom ran over and held her tight, but Elvi broke away.

"No, no, I don't deserve any hugs. I'm so stupid . . . how could I have been so stupid?"

Aunt Kiki grabbed a tissue to mop up the black mascara flowing down Elvi's cheeks.

Gram led Elvi to sit across from me. Elvi could barely look at my face.

"I'm so sorry, girl. I had it wrong all this time . . . and I was a total brat to you. All I can say is I'll try to do better." She wiped her nose on her velvet sleeve. "If you could give me another chance?"

Pain still boiled in my soul, but hearing Elvi ask for forgiveness released some of that pain into the air, like the steam rising off the pot of Gram's carrot soup. Mom supported me to speak as Elvi watched and sniffed.

REGRET WASTES PRECIOUS TIME. ONLY FORGIVENESS BRINGS PEACE. FORGIVE ME FOR THE WEDDING.

Elvi shook her head. "No, no. After everything I did, everything my dumb mouth said without thinking. I had it coming, girl. That and worse."

"Enough of this," Pops said. "Our chipmunk has had enough of you ladies blubbering. Time to eat."

Mason held out the bowl of gummy worms and my hungry hand dug in.

This Is Only a Test

Fact: I hate tests.

Imagine failing every test you ever took. Even when you knew all the answers. Even when the questions were ridiculously simple, like "What is 2 + 1?" or "What letter begins the word *alligator*?"

When I could not get the answers right, Thinkers assumed my mind was deficient. It never occurred to them my body was to blame.

I hate tests.

Ana set up my keyboard in a library study room for peace and quiet. Even with the door shut, my ears picked up whispers outside, and my nose detected fish sticks cooking in the cafeteria.

"All questions are multiple choice. There are four sections—math, reading, history, and science," Celia explained. "I will display each question on the monitor and read it to you out loud."

My body shifted in the hard plastic chair.

Did Mom put sandpaper in my shirt today?

I scratched my neck.

Scratch-scratch, scratch-scratch.

"*Querida*, relax. This is just to determine if you need tutoring in any subjects before we create your new schedule."

Probability of failing: unknown.

Scratch-scratch, scratch-scratch.

> Page 210: A parrot can use tools such as
> sticks and old feathers to scratch itself.

In my mind, I heard Pops delivering his favorite saying in that deep, crackling voice of his—"Better to keep your mouth shut and let people think you're a fool than open it and remove all doubt."

For me, keeping my mouth shut meant keeping my hands off the keyboard.

No. I have to do this.

Scratch-scratch, scratch-scratch.

Time for silence is ended.

I have a mission. I need to prove to Jergen that I can be included in real classes. That all kids can be included.

My hummingbird heartbeat raced when Celia read the first question.

"A water tank can hold fifty gallons. What flow rate, in gallons per second, is required to fill the tank in twenty seconds?" She read all the possible answers. "Now choose answer A, B, C, D or E."

My pupils zeroed in on the letter B. Ana held my elbow as I pushed my finger toward the target.

"B—is that the answer you would like?"

I typed Y for yes.

Their eyes—Ana's olive green and free of makeup, Celia's

dark and painted with teal eye shadow and mascara—gave no hint of whether my answers were correct or incorrect.

Darn them.

For each question, my mind searched my brain for a corresponding memory from the color-coded folder in my head. It flashed through years of homework with Mom, books read to me, television documentaries, radio interviews, scrolling news updates at the bottom of the TV screen, years of pulling books off shelves in Pops' study and hungrily flipping through pages.

"How did the reign of Alexander the Great most affect Greece?"

The answer is B.

B is for Baboon.

Baboons live in groups of up to one hundred members.

"At which location is Earth's magnetic field the strongest?"

C is for Camel.

Camels can survive seven months without drinking water.

"Which of the following factors would most likely cause a hurricane to decrease in strength?"

A is for aardvark.

Aardvarks have long, sticky tongues to catch insects.

"Which of the following is a property of CO_2 gas?"

E is for Emu.

The emu, Australia's largest bird, stands six feet tall.

"Let's take a short break," Ana said after the first hour. "Maybe get you something to eat or drink."

NO, KEEP GOING.

Each question left me hungry for the next one. My body worked best when the gears of my mind were turning at full throttle. I continued for a second hour, then, after a brief walk, a third hour until my pointer finger became stiff, and my eyes blurred.

"*Querida*, you are finished," Celia announced.

Worn out, I sank into the chair and went limp like a wet rag. Then I nudged Ana so I could type one more word.

TRASH

Ana ran for the trashcan, and I barfed up the entire egg and cheese omelet Dad made me for breakfast.

Back in the EPIC room, Skyler held my hand while Celia graded the test. "I'm sure you did awesome, Cherry Tree."

I watched Celia through her office window, silver glasses perched on her nose, checking each response sheet against the answer key. Check, check, check.

Is a check good or bad? Why is it taking so long?

After half an hour, she came out, shaking her head.

"I checked your answers twice, *querida*."

Skyler squeezed my hand tighter.

"You got a 96 percent. Let's get you a new schedule!" Celia and Ana whooped and jumped in the air.

Breathe in joy. Breathe in freedom.

"We will need to find the best way to support you in each class," Ana said, "but prepare to get your real education." She sat next to me and held the keyboard. "Tell us what you are feeling, Charity."

I wanted to say I was feeling joyful, but that was not true. Ana steadied my arm so my finger could type the truth.

I AM NERVOUS. I STILL CANNOT ALWAYS CONTROL MY BODY.

Celia smiled and took off her glasses. "*Querida*, did I ever tell you about my brother Marco?"

She put her hand on my arm and sighed deeply.

"Marco was born without the ability to use his muscles. I was eight years older, so I was a second mother to him."

Celia paused and closed her eyes for a few seconds. "We knew he had a short time with us, and my father always wanted to keep him at home where no harm would come to him. He thought Marco's life would be easier away from pitying eyes of neighbors and strangers on the street."

I UNDERSTAND. PITY SHRINKS ME INTO A PUNY TADPOLE.

Celia nodded and smiled with a faraway look. She was seeing into the past.

"It was my mother who insisted my brother go to school and do everything his little body could. She saw his eyes grow wide every time he spotted a dragonfly floating above our garden. She saw his lips smile every time he heard music."

Celia's voice became shaky. Ana put an arm around her shoulder.

"My Marco, *mi corazón*, he left us when he was only ten years old. My mother shed no tears, at least not in front of me. She said, 'He is in heaven now, telling everyone all the wonders of his tiny life.' It was Marco who led me to teaching. I thought if I could help all children experience learning with his same sense of wonder, well . . . my life would be well spent."

Celia peered into my eyes. "*Querida*, it is your choice

whether to fully participate in this school. I am certain you will learn from it, no matter what the outcome."

I reached for the keyboard and Ana supported me to type. With each exhale, I breathed out more fear.

I HAVE A MISSION. I WILL NOT WASTE MY CHANCE. FOR MARCO.

Slam Dunk

"How 'bout a strawberry shake for my star athlete?" Dad waltzed into the kitchen Saturday morning, his usual perky self. "You'll need your energy for shooting hoops at the park."

Hypothesis: Dad has lost his mind.

I stomped my foot as Mom sat down next to me with the keyboard.

WHAT'S THE POINT?

"Coach George called to apologize. He said he wants you on the team. As a player this time."

BUT I CANNOT DRIBBLE. I CANNOT PASS.

"Well, you can run, can't you? You can block. And most important, you can shoot."

He grabbed the ball and two water bottles and headed for the door.

Fact: Dad's positive attitude gets annoying sometimes.

At the park, I saw kids on tricycles, kids playing in the sandbox, everywhere kids together. I bounced the ball in place.

Bounce, bounce, bounce.

I thought about all the years where my only playmate was dear old Dad.

Bounce, bounce, bounce.

Ever since he taught me to throw a nerf ball, he's been my biggest cheerleader.

"Let's practice a few free throws." Dad pointed to the basket, and I threw.

"She shoots, she scores!" Dad yelled it every time I made a basket.

Passing was a different story though. A basketball is much bigger than a nerf ball.

Pass. Drop. Pass. Drop.

He throws it, she blows it!

A voice yelled from the sideline. "Try keeping your hands in position, Charity."

"I see our assistant coach has arrived," Dad said, wiping his forehead. I turned to see Mason standing there in black shorts and orange high-tops.

Mason nodded to Dad and came up to me. "Hey Chare. I meant to tell you the other day . . ." He looked down at the blacktop. "I'm real sorry about . . . you know . . . I was kind of a jerk to you before. I mean, Mom never told me anything and then seeing you again . . . felt like I didn't know you anymore or you didn't know me. Anyhow . . . I guess I was in shock."

I wanted to tell him sorry too.

Sorry I whacked you in the nose.

I do not think he told anyone about that. Aunt Kiki would have said something to Mom about it for sure.

For the next ninety-two minutes, Mason and Dad took turns throwing me passes and teaching me to dribble. Sorry to say, my arms and legs still did not cooperate.

Felt good, though, to get another playdate with my cousin after all this time.

Wednesday after school, Dad took me to Hornets practice, and I realized he was right. I had to stick with the team to show I could fit in at Lincoln. To prove that kids like me could contribute and did not have to sit on the sidelines and watch other kids have a real life.

Dad helped me as I typed a short message to the team. I tapped one letter at a time while the girls looked confused and a little bored.

Dad pressed "play" on the iPad and an electronic voice spoke my words.

I AM HAPPY TO BE A HORNET. THANK YOU FOR INCLUDING ME.

A few girls smiled, and Coach George gave me a fist bump. "Waaaaay to go, kid!"

Darcy whispered something to Lilly and Grace that made all three girls giggle.

When we were little, Grace called me her BFF—her best friend *forever*. I guess her definition of *forever* was not the same as mine.

For the first drill, I ran alongside the court since I still could not dribble. When my legs darted in the wrong direction, Dad took my hand and led me the right way.

Finally, we got to shooting baskets. Coach George handed me the ball.

Everyone looked at me. I searched inside for confidence.

I can do this. Just like at the park. Twelve times in a row.

My hands became lobster claws. My arms became jelly-fish tentacles. I tried to launch the ball from my chest, but it did not go above my head. It fell to the floor and rolled away, which made some girls crack up.

Guess which ones.

"Hornets!" Coach yelled, "that is not good sportsmanship. We're all here to help Charity participate and cheer her on."

Oh, great, cheer for the charity case.

"Shoot it again, kid. I saw what you did last time. You just need to warm up."

The girls chatted while I lobbed flop after flop nowhere near the basket. My face burned hot from embarrassment and exhaustion. My feet jumped like the floor was boiling lava. That did not help.

Dad kept tossing me balls. "You can do this, Super Cherry. Same as we did in practice."

I wanted to yell.

I can NOT do this. I told you this was a bad idea.

Dribble, jump, dribble, jump, dribble, jump.

Page 141: Kangaroos can jump 30 feet in a single bound.

"Is she gonna throw the ball or what?" Darcy shook her head and wandered over to the sideline, probably to sneak a few texts.

Get me out of here!

My heart hammered. I felt a KETTLE EXPLOSION approaching in 3 . . . 2 . . .

Then I heard Grace's voice. She started clapping and chanting.

154

We got the ball [clap].
Get outta the way [stomp].
C'mon, Charity [clap],
Let's score today [stomp]!

I froze.
Is this a joke?
Other girls joined in.

We got the ball [clap].
Get outta the way [stomp].
C'mon, Charity [clap],
LET'S SCORE TODAY [stomp]!

Now almost all the girls were clapping and cheering.
Almost all.

We got the ball [clap].
Get outta the way [stomp].
C'mon, Charity [clap],
LET'S SCORE TODAY [stomp]!

A surge of energy traveled from my toes to my chest and
into my tired arms. I launched the ball into the air. It flew
toward the basket . . . hit the backboard . . . rebounded like
BAM! . . . and knocked Darcy in the back. Darcy's phone flew
out of her hands and slid across the floor, stopping right in
front of Coach.
She shoots, she scores!
Everyone burst into laughter. Darcy's face turned red when
Coach took away her phone.

I made no baskets, but at the end of practice, a few girls came up to me.

"Good hustle, Charity."

"Keep trying, you'll get it."

Grace whispered, "Nice job prying Darcy's phone away. I thought that thing was superglued to her hands."

For a few seconds at least, I was not a charity case.

Then I caught Darcy glaring at me. She moved her finger across her neck.

Like a knife to the throat.

Hypothesis: I have an enemy.

Cool Genes

The science room reeked from jars filled with floating specimens—fish, frogs, snakes, a tiny pig, and what looked like a few autopsied aliens.

"Let's sit by the door in case you need to take a walk." Ana set up my puzzle on the front table.

On full display, same as the other strange specimens.

I organized puzzle pieces as the school's brainiest kids entered for advanced science.

Orange pieces, orange pieces, 19 . . . 20 . . . 21 . . .

Grace walked in with her friends, who were wearing their yellow and black cheerleader uniforms—short, pleated skirts and sweaters with a big L on the front. Lilly and Darcy were cheerleaders.

I am beginning to think Jaz is right about cheerleaders.

All three girls looked at me, confused.

Jaz wheeled in and gave me a thumbs-up before parking in the back row.

The teacher, stone-faced Mr. Harding, peered at me from his desk and squished his eyebrows together. My shoulders shrugged over and over as if to say I did not know what the heck I was doing here either.

Shrug, shrug, shrug.

33 . . . 34 . . . 35 . . .

Brilliant but tough—that's how Jaz described Mr. Harding. Her actual words were, "He makes some kids pee their pants when he calls them out in class."

This may hurt a little.

Shrug, shrug, shrug.

Mr. Harding approached and looked down at us from his six-foot-four altitude. If Pops were here, he might joke, "How's the air up there?"

Harding talked to Ana as if I were invisible.

"As I told Ms. Diaz, your student is welcome to join the class as long as she does not disrupt the learning."

Maybe this was a mistake.

"I heard there was an issue in Ms. Beckett's classroom," he continued. "You will find me less tolerant than she of class-room disturbances. I do not permit disruptions from my . . . shall we say . . . traditional students, and I will not permit them from students of . . . shall we say . . . *special* status. That being said, welcome to my class, Ms. Dupont."

"It is not me you should welcome, Mr. Harding."

He looked confused. Ana pointed to me.

"Her name is Charity, Charity Wood. And of all the classes at Lincoln, she was most eager to attend yours. She insisted on it, actually. Against our advice."

It was true. I wanted to understand biology—my own nutty neurons in particular. But all of it fascinated me—animals, plants, insects, right down to the one-celled protozoa.

"What do you mean she insisted?" Harding asked, lowering his glasses to the tip of his pointed nose. "She can talk?"

"As we explained in the file we provided you, she communicates through typing. I support her arm to give her the motor control to type with one finger. One letter at a time."

He raised his eyebrows and brushed his fingers on his chin.

"She learned to do this only a few weeks ago," Ana said.

"Fascinating." Harding said this to himself and observed me for the first time. He did not exactly smile—his lips formed a straight line—but I had a feeling that was as close as he got to smiling.

Harding approached the whiteboard, pointing his black marker toward the class like a sword. His deep voice echoed off the green walls.

"Class, let us continue our discussion of genetics. I assume everyone has carefully studied chapter six."

His voice a human megaphone.

Breathe in peace.

Shrug, shrug, shrug.

Blue pieces now, 1 . . . 2 . . . 3 . . .

He dove into a lecture on genes and chromosomes, the secret code contained in all our cells, a code that was passed down from all our ancestors. It controls so many things about who we are and what we look like. I understood now how I inherited Dad's blue eyes and Mom's dimples.

Breathe out fear.

My mind latched on. I listened in a trance, seeing DNA strands in my mind, zipping and unzipping in endless combinations.

Harding's wavy silver hair flopped up and down as he sketched diagrams of genetic crosses on the board. Mr. Harding talked about mistakes in the genetic code that gave people diseases.

"Albinism is a genetic mutation that results in the offspring completely lacking pigment in the skin, eyes, or hair. It is caused by a defect of the enzyme tyrosinase, which is involved in the production of melanin."

Just because there is an error in someone's genes does not mean that person is an error. Does it?

Ana's fingers sprinted across her laptop, typing pages of notes for me, but I knew I would remember everything. Having my brain challenged kept my body in control as my hands automatically arranged and attached puzzle pieces.

Red pieces, red pieces, 32 . . . 33 . . . 34 . . .

Mr. Harding's brown loafers paced the tile floor as he patrolled the classroom. He was a wolf stalking terrified rabbits. Kids jumped in their seat when he called their name.

"Stuart! How many genes in the human genome?" He pointed a bony finger at Stuart in the front row.

"Twenty-three." Stuart replied in a deep voice, maybe to sound more mature.

Harding raised an eyebrow, and the blood drained from Stuart's face.

"I mean twenty-three hundred, give or take."

Mr. Harding nodded and moved on. Stuart blew a puff of air out of his lips.

"Darcy! What is the chance of this genetic cross resulting in an albino child?" He pointed to a diagram on the board marked with letters in boxes representing different gene combinations.

Darcy's face had been looking down—probably at her phone again—but she flung her long, blonde hair off her shoulder, looking easy-breezy under pressure.

"Two in four will be a mutant, Mr. Harding." Her white teeth dazzled confidence.

Harding frowned. "That is incorrect."

She squinted at the board as though maybe she hadn't seen it correctly. Five seconds of Harding scowling at her must have seemed like five years.

"You should spend more time reading the chapter and less time reading your texts, young lady."

Her face dropped, and the air hissed with muffled snickers.

I lifted my eyes from my puzzle to see Harding's gray laser-beam eyes piercing me.

Page 315: A dominant wolf stands tall with ears pointing upward and teeth exposed.

"How about our new student? What is the chance of this genetic cross resulting in an albino child?"

Ana nodded and got into typing position with me.

Is he testing me?

Page 315: A submissive wolf crouches low, its head between its legs.

I knew what albino meant scientifically, but I also understood what it meant to a real person. In the park when Dad and I practiced hoops, we often saw a boy about five years old whose snowy white hair and skin peeked out under a floppy hat. He wore long pants and sleeves to protect him from the sun. He usually played alone, scooping sand into his bucket and pouring it back out.

I studied the diagram, and Ana supported my arm to type while Mr. Harding waited with folded arms. A few kids yawned.

Breathe in confidence.

The ticking clock grew louder each second.

Breathe out doubt.

Ana cleared her throat and read my reply.

THE ANSWER IS ONE IN FOUR.

Mr. Harding nodded. Ana held up her finger to signal that there was more.

THAT CHILD IS NO MUTANT BUT SHOULD BE AS VALUED AS THE OTHER THREE.

His eyebrows went up. "You are correct on both counts, Charity."

He actually said my name.

"I see some people in the class nodding their heads," Harding said. "Thank you for helping us remember the human side of genetics here."

The last half hour of class was reserved for lab work in small groups. Ana scanned the room to see where we could join.

Grace, Darcy, and Lilly set up their microscope beside us. Grace smiled. "I liked what you said, Charity. It's practically impossible to impress Mr. Harding. How about joining our group?"

Lilly's eyes got big and flashed Grace an *are-you-kidding-me* look.

I typed, **I WILL DO MY BEST.**

Ana eyed Lilly and Darcy, probably remembering what happened in English class.

Darcy's berry lip gloss lit up a sudden smile. "Hey, sorry if we got off on the wrong foot, Charity. Let's be friends. I can tell you're really smart."

Lilly nodded in agreement, snapping her spearmint gum.

Could I trust them? I noted the expression on Lilly's face: *Hashtag whatever.*

Grace read the instructions out loud. We were working with live fruit flies, some of them "wild type" and some "mutants" with red eyes. The mutants actually looked cuter . . . if a fruit fly can look cute.

Grace stuck a small wand soaked in a chemical into the jar of wild flies to put them to sleep. After two minutes, she tipped the jar to transfer the sleeping flies onto a plastic petri dish.

Ana steadied my head above the microscope so I could observe. Giant eyes and delicate, transparent wings—nature's perfection in a minuscule package.

Lilly lowered her eyes to the microscope as if it might bite. "Eeeeew . . . these things are *so* gross. Hashtag nasty!"

"Give me a break," Grace said. "Didn't you say you wanted to be a doctor?"

"Yeah," Darcy said, "but she meant a loooove doctor."

The three girls laughed. Grace pulled Lilly away from the scope so she could take over counting male versus female flies. Darcy marked the totals on our lab sheet.

When we finished, Lilly picked up the petri dish and wrinkled her nose. "Let's smush these bugs before they wake up."

Darcy grabbed the dish from her. "No, you ditz, we need to put them back in the jar. Like Charity said, every life has value."

I nodded and typed my agreement.

YES, AND TODAY THESE FLIES ARE OUR TEACHERS.

Darcy reached out her hand for a fist bump.

"Right on," Grace said. She gathered the supplies to put back on the shelf.

When the bell rang, Ana went to talk to Mr. Harding about how to adapt the homework for me. With help, I could type and I could point now, but I still could not hold a pen to diagram genetic crosses. I was sure Ana would find a way to include me.

Darcy turned to me, hand on her hip. "Hey, fun working with you today, Charity." She and Lilly smiled big.

I could not believe it. These girls who treated me like trash a few days ago stood in front of me, talking to me as if . . . I was . . . a friend.

Breathe in joy.

They smiled and stared at me a few more seconds.

Jaz was wrong about cheerleaders.

"Don't you have anything to say to us?" asked Darcy. "Go ahead and type."

She pointed to the keyboard, but my hands were useless without someone to support me. My shoulders started shrugging again.

Shrug, shrug, shrug.

Darcy rolled her eyes at Lilly. "Told you."

It was not until I got back to the EPIC room that I realized how stupid I was to think these girls might be my friends.

I opened my backpack, and a cloud of fruit flies zoomed out.

Homework Help

Our neighbor Dr. Singh was so excited to learn I could type, she brought us a plate of homemade pistachio cookies to celebrate. "I always knew you had a spark, young lady. I could see it in your pretty blue eyes."

She squeezed my cheeks the way old people do and patted my face. "I have learned so much by observing your progress through the years—and now that you can type . . . well, you can teach me even more." Dr. Singh turned to Mom. "What can I do to help? You will find I'm a good worker ant."

Mom and I were in the middle of our daily homework session. Since I could not turn pages very well, Dr. Singh volunteered to record my textbook readings so I could listen while riding in the car or eating breakfast—my very own audiobooks.

I could not believe all the other people who volunteered to support me now that they knew I had a brain. Must be how Scarecrow felt after visiting the Wizard of Oz.

Random kids at school helped Ana collect my puzzle pieces at the end of every class.

Aunt Kiki became our graphic artist. She made posters of charts and tables and poems from my textbooks and pasted them to my bedroom and bathroom walls so I could study while brushing my teeth or getting dressed. I stared at a poem by a famous writer named Emily Dickinson—"'Hope' is the thing with feathers— that perches in the soul"—every night before falling asleep.

But the biggest surprise had to be Aunt Elvi. She sat me and Mom down on Gram's flowered sofa at one of our Sunday barbecues and handed us a box the size of a board game.

She gazed into me with her cat eyes. "I just hope it's not too little too late."

I opened the box top, and Mom dropped her head to her chest like she had been knocked out. "Elvi, this must've been so expensive. You guys can't afford this," she protested.

Elvi blinked back tears. "No, no, no, it's the least we coulda done. Turns out we had some cash hanging around after returning a few lame wedding gifts."

She knelt down. "Girl, this should be useful for your school. I was never good at school myself. I'm already proud of you, and you didn't even graduate anything yet."

Mom reached into the box to pull out a brand-new iPad with a Bluetooth keyboard in a cardinal-red leather case.

"Try it out. I already charged it and all. Guy at the store downloaded an app that will speak everything you type." Elvi sat next to me and lifted the leather cover to reveal the smooth, glass screen. Her hand, wearing five silver rings, patted mine.

My sixth sense felt a strong emotion flowing through her.

Elvi—the name my mind always rearranged to spell Evil—now rang in my heart as LV—the two consonants in the word *love*.

Mom sat next to me and supported my arm. My words appeared on the glossy screen. I pushed the "talk" button, and the iPad spoke my sentence.

NO WORDS TO SAY THANK YOU.

"Awww, you do good in school and that's all the thanks I need."

Doing good in school was my goal. With Mom's help, I worked on Elvi's iPad till ten every night, reading, completing homework sheets, and writing essays letter by letter.

Typing with one finger—ugh, it's slow. My mind races ahead a million miles an hour. At the same time, I have to control a body that itches to scurry and jump like a kangaroo rat.

Mom's job was to keep me focused as I typed by giving me prompts, just as Dr. Peterman had taught her. "Is that the letter you want? Great—keep going. Are you done with your sentence or would you like to say more? I know your legs want to stand up. Try to finish your thought first."

Dad took me for walks when I needed to move. He also became my personal cheerleader. Every time I finished an assignment, he punched his fists in the air, "Go, Cherry, go! Get to the goal!" with Hero wagging his tail and barking along.

For my advanced science project, I asked Mr. Harding if I could write about Down syndrome, which my friends Isabella and Skyler live with. I wanted to know how one tiny error in someone's genetic code could bully its way into every part of a person's life. I wanted to know why these two beautiful girls with the most loving hearts also had heart conditions.

Mostly I wanted to know they would be okay.

Mom read from books we checked out of the library. She explained the "abnormal cell division" and "extra genetic material from the twenty-first chromosome." After a few minutes, I stopped her, and typed.

THE TEXTBOOK EXPLAINS THE SCIENCE, BUT I WANT TO KNOW HOW PEOPLE ARE TREATED.

Mom sighed and pulled out another book. This one showed old pictures of children with blank expressions locked in cages or curled up into a ball on the floor of institutions. Mom read to me about kids being starved, used as test subjects for medical experiments, children still today denied medical treatment.

After a few minutes, her voice broke. She closed the book and shook her head. "I can't read anymore."

My heart flooded with emotion. I tried to type a W, but my hand slammed into the keyboard and threw up an alphabet soup onto the screen. Mom reached out and steadied my arm, and I started to type.

WHEN WILL WE HEAR ABOUT MY LETTER TO SUPERINTENDENT? ALREADY 14 DAYS PASSED.

Mom grabbed a tissue and dabbed her eyes. "I'm so sorry, sweetheart. Celia called me yesterday with the bad news. I wasn't sure how to tell you." Mom put her arm around me. "The superintendent said ours was the only complaint they received about Borden. She promised to keep it in a file in case other complaints come in."

Just what I thought. Why would they listen to a kid? Especially one like me?

IF I CANNOT SHUT DOWN BORDEN, MAYBE I CAN STILL SAVE ISABELLA. CAN I TALK TO HER PARENTS?

She exhaled slowly. "Well, Charity, they obviously feel that Isabella is in the best place for her . . ."

I smacked my palm on the book. Mom supported my arm so I could type.

NO, NOT THE BEST PLACE FOR HER. NOTNOTNOT

Mom frowned. "I can tell you're determined, but it would be nearly impossible to contact her family. Borden would never give us their information."

TALK TO HER MOM BEFORE SCHOOL AT THE DROP-OFF LINE.

Mom smiled. "Like super-secret spies, huh? Well, I can't guarantee Borden won't call the police if they see us on their campus."

I WILL TAKE THAT CHANCE.

Operation Isabella

Mom nudged me awake.

"It's time."

A gray light peeked through the daisy-print curtains above my bed.

Even the sky is still asleep.

Mom helped me get dressed and into the car. At 6:15 A.M., we pulled up to a curb to wait. Mom sipped hot coffee. Blueberry smoothie for me, through a straw. No more sippy cups, thank goodness.

We knew that drop-off started at 6:30, but we had no idea what car to look for or what time Isabella might arrive.

A real-life stake-out.

Mom played her achy-breaky country music as we watched car after car drive by. A few pulled up to the school. I was not sure what Mom had in mind, but I was hoping it did not involve a two-car collision.

Mom hummed her "friends in low places" song, when I saw a flash of red hair in the mirror—a woman driving a mini-van. That had to be her mom. I slapped the seat.

"It's go time." Mom sounded like a cop on one of those police shows.

She zoomed into the street and pulled alongside the minivan at the stoplight before the school. She honked lightly a couple of times before a woman with wild red hair rolled down her window. Through the woman's annoyed expression, I noted her nose dotted with freckles, same as Isabella's.

"Hi, I'm Mrs. Wood. My daughter Charity used to be in class with your daughter."

Isabella's mom shook her head as if she had no idea what was going on. I pounded my window to get Isabella's attention in the back seat. Could she see me through the tinted windows? Probability: low.

When the light turned green, the minivan drove forward and entered the drop-off line.

Miss Marcia started shuffling over. The sight of her made me want to barf.

Mom pulled alongside Isabella's car again. "Please, please, my daughter wants to talk with you and Isabella. Here is our number. Please call us." Mom crumpled up the paper with our phone number and threw it through the open window of Isabella's car. The redheaded woman shrieked as if Mom had just tossed a dead rat.

This is not going well.

Miss Marcia pointed at us and started dialing a number on her cellphone. But Mom sped away with a tire screech and a wave.

The Welcome Table

PEPPERONI, NOT SOGGY CHEESE.

Tuesday was pizza day in the cafeteria, and now I could ask for my favorite kind.

Julian joined our little lunch group, bringing his iPad to add his voice to the conversation. He typed, gazing intently at the screen through thick glasses. His electronic voice spoke with an Australian accent today. "I'm gonna sit at the welcome table."

"Hey—that's the name of a song, isn't it?" asked Jaz.

Julian typed:

"YES, A GREAT OLD SPIRITUAL."

"I remember learning about this in English class," Jaz said. "People sang it during the civil rights movement when African Americans fought for equal rights."

I typed with Ana steadying my arm:

WORKS FOR OUR CAFETERIA TOO.

"Yeah," Jazmine's face lit up, and she sang with Skyler clapping along.

> *I'm gonna sit at the cool kids' table,*
> *I'm gonna sit at the cool kids' table one of these days,*
> *Hallelujah!*

Jaz scooped a spoonful of peach yogurt and spilled a drop on her shirt. "Geez, by the end of the day my shirt looks like a Jackson Pollock painting."

Peter muttered with a full mouth, "What the heck does that mean?"

"He's the artist who dribbled and dripped paint on the canvas." Jaz shook her head. "And today those paintings are worth millions."

Skyler perked up. "I will paint one for you and you will be rich." She meant it.

Julian typed:

"YOU CAN BUY A TURBO-CHARGED, WINDBLOWN-HAIR WHEEL-CHAIR."

Jaz laughed. I giggled inside too—the electronic voice did not ruin the joke.

"Room for one more?"

All eyes stared at the guy standing over us with three pieces of pizza piled on his plate. He flipped his surfer bangs out of his face and squeezed between me and Skyler.

Hypothesis: Aunt Kiki was forcing him to sit with me again.

"I'm Charity's cousin, Mason."

Wow. Cover blown.

His cool-kid status was dropping every second he sat here with us EPIC kids.

"I get it," Jaz said. "You're the guy who led the lost sheep back to her flock during that disastrous fire drill. I suspect some dumb girls pulled the alarm on purpose to freak us out."

"Dumb girls? Usually it's dumb *guys* who do stuff like that." Mason smiled, a slice of pepperoni hanging out of his mouth.

Jaz eyed the cool kids' table, Lilly and Darcy the loudest of the bunch. "It's a feeling I have." She scrunched her eyebrows and peered at Mason. "How do we know you're not a spy? You could be here to gather dirt on us for future torture."

Julian pounded his fist on the table and typed:

"THIS IS THE WELCOME TABLE!"

He pointed to the screen and Jaz nodded.

"Don't worry about that," Mason said. "My days hanging with the jocks and cheerleaders are over. Being the new kid, I thought I could remake my image. But you can't change who you are. From now on, I'm going back to my usual strategy for fitting in: Keep your head low."

Jaz laughed. "And we're about as low as you can get at this school."

"That's not what I meant. I mean, I just try not to stand out."

"Then you've come to the wrong table," she said. "We stick out wherever we go. You can tell that by the people staring and gawking." Jaz slurped her chocolate milk then pointed at Mason with a dramatic *gotcha* stare. "Tell us what really happened. Did they kick you out of the cool kids' club?"

REAL

"I think they finally realized I'm a geek at heart. Charity knows I spent the last eight years living in Milwaukee." He grabbed his surfer T-shirt and pointed at the logo. "I've never even been on a surfboard. And I'd rather spend a day playing video games than hanging at the beach."

"MINECRAFT OR WARCRAFT?" Julian typed.

"Warcraft, definitely, bro." Mason and Julian bumped fists.

"No way," Peter said. "You guys are crazy!"

While Jaz refereed the debate between Julian and Peter, Mason scooted closer. I noted the painful expression on his face, like he was about to have teeth pulled.

"I, uh, actually wanna give you a heads-up, Charity."

Uh-oh.

Fact: No one ever gives a heads-up for good news.

"The main reason I'm done with those jerks is . . . well . . . there's this app they have on their phones. It posts anonymous comments from people at our school."

He spoke softly, taking bites of pizza as he went.

"A kind of chatroom for all that *he-said-she-said* junior high bull."

Mason scanned the cafeteria to see if anyone was watching.

"Anyhow, there's a comment that appeared there today from someone called Sassygirl72. It's freaking ridiculous, and I don't want to show it to you, but you gotta know."

He pulled out his phone and slid it in front of me like a spy passing top-secret intelligence. I read it and felt my heart slip out of my chest and skid across the cold cafeteria floor.

It said: **No retards in advanced classes. Tell Jergen.**

My body rocked back and forth, back and forth.

I slid his phone back so no one else would see. It would not help me to have Mom ranting to Jergen—or worse—Jaz mowing down cheerleaders in the hallway.

My hands drummed on the table.

Slap-slap. Rock. Slap. Rock. Slap-slap. Rock. Slap.

"Everything alright here?" Ana popped her head into our discussion.

That's the problem with needing an aide to communicate. No privacy. She took hold of my typing hand. I pulled it away.

Mason stuffed his last bite of pizza in his face to avoid further questions.

Slap-slap. Rock. Slap. Rock. Slap-slap. Rock. Slap.

I closed my eyes and retreated to the world inside my mind. All the sounds and colors of the world, so beautiful and bright.

Charity is not home at the moment. Please leave a message after the beep.

I could hypothesize which cool kid posted the message. Was Jergen collecting complaints about me? If so, how many strikes before I was out?

Mission Improbable

When the doorbell rang, Mom and Hero hurried to answer it. I held my breath.

> Page 36: Mother cougars have been known to
> battle grizzly bears to protect their cubs.

Isabella zoomed right to me. We danced, our feet flying.

"Mommy, I told you she was my friend! I told you it was Charity!"

Isabella's mother stepped cautiously inside and gave Mom what Pops calls a dead-fish handshake. Her thin lips turned up in an almost-smile.

"Halloo." I noted a soft accent. "I'm Emily Moore."

Mom offered her a seat in our most comfy armchair. "I hope we didn't scare you at the drop-off line. I had no other way to contact you. We're not exactly welcome at Borden anymore."

Mrs. Moore accepted the cup of ginger tea Mom handed her.

"In truth, I thought Isabella had no friends at Borden," Mrs. Moore said. "She doesn't talk much about school."

She took one of Mom's snickerdoodle cookies and dipped it in her tea.

"Isabella got so excited seeing Charity in your car, I knew we had to pay a call."

Isabella pulled a colorful book off the coffee table and patted the sofa for me to sit beside her. Like she did at Borden, Isabella turned pages and pointed to each picture for me to follow along while our moms chatted.

After a few minutes, my body grew restless. I bounced up and down on the sofa.

Bounce, bounce, bounce, bounce.

My mind begged.

Let me speak.

Mom understood and settled next to me with my keyboard.

Mom explained, "Until a few months ago, my daughter was unable to communicate. Since Charity began typing, she's told us many things about her time at Borden and how fond she is of your daughter."

Mrs. Moore smiled—a true smile this time—and nodded at me.

Mom continued. "And because Charity cares so much about Isabella, she has an urgent message for you."

Mrs. Moore stopped chewing and put down her cup of tea. Without a word, she watched me type for the next few minutes.

My chest sucked in air faster as I tapped the keyboard. The truth begged to come out.

Please let her listen to me.

Isabella stared at me, clapping at every word I typed.

ISABELLA SUFFERS AT BORDEN.

"*Suffers* there? What are you saying?"

BORDEN HAS ZERO OPPORTUNITIES TO LEARN. SHE SHOULD TRANSFER TO LINCOLN.

Mrs. Moore smiled politely. I could sense prickly anger growing inside her.

"Well, good for you, my dear. You've moved on. My own daughter does not have that option."

"But she does, Mrs. Moore," Mom said. "By law, your daughter should be placed in the least restrictive environment. From what Charity tells us, Borden does not bother teaching the children anything . . ."

"With all due respect, Mrs. Wood, you don't know what the devil you're talking about." Mrs. Moore stood. "Come on, Isabella. Time for us to go."

My body shook. My hands flapped.

Flap, flap, flap, flap.

I wanted to shout.

No, please stay! Please listen!

Isabella clung to me. "No, Mommy. I want to play with Charity."

Mom pleaded, speaking faster. "Charity has told us about abuses there. She was slapped and kicked and locked in a time-out closet for hours at a time. They're not doing right by these kids."

Mrs. Moore's face turned red to match her hair. Her voice filled the room.

"My daughter will *never* be a normal child. I will *not* be throwing her to the wolves for your daughter's amusement, or whatever sick game this is."

Mrs. Moore grabbed Isabella's hand and yanked her away from me.

My voice hollered.

GAAAAAAAAAAAAAAAAAH! AHHHHHHHHGH!

Mrs. Moore bolted out the door, and all my hope sank into my sneakers.

Pep Rally Princess

"It's entirely lame."

Jaz complained nonstop about the football pep rally.

"I can't believe Celia is forcing us to make posters. As if we actually support this sort of chauvinistic anti-intellectualism."

She liked using big words when she was angry.

Pep rally. It sounded like a happy tradition. But I was *not* happy ever since Isabella's mom pulled my friend out the door. If only Mrs. Moore could see Skyler bouncing up and down, her paintbrush dabbing a giant yellow poster board.

"Here, Cherry Tree, you paint something purple." She handed me the paintbrush already dipped in paint, and I made a few angry squiggles on the canvas.

"Good job! You made a purple sky!"

"I mean, we're a junior high," Jaz said. "It's not like we're headed to the Super Bowl. Why does everyone take this so seriously?"

Skyler guided Jaz's brush to paint delicate poppies in a grassy meadow.

"Skyler, this poster is not exactly following the pep rally

theme," Jaz said. "But I like it even better. Let's paint some dog poop nuggets in the grass to show how much this whole tradition stinks."

Peter pointed to Jaz and laughed at her joke. "Poop nuggets . . . HA! Good one!"

Celia walked over with wide eyes. "Skyler, *querida*, you are such a wonderful artist. I am afraid you are wasting your talent on this cheap poster board. I will get you some canvas panels to paint on next week."

Skyler tackled Celia with her famous choke-hold hug.

"Wanna hear a joke? It's a good one." Peter jumped over to us. "What do vegetarian zombies eat? Broccoli brains. HA!" Next, he rattled off a story about a talking snail followed by five fart jokes.

Thank goodness Julian approached with a message for Jaz. His electronic voice spoke with a British accent today.

"YOUR HEART CRIES FOR BEING LEFT OUT."

"Left out? Give me a break. I don't want anything to do with this beauty pageant." Jaz angled her wheelchair toward me. "You'll see, Charity. Students vote for eight girls to be on the football team's Princess Court to smile and wave in front of everyone before the game, but the election is a total joke. I mean, they're supposed to be picked based on good character and academics, but it always turns into a popularity contest."

Jaz turned back to Julian.

"I suppose it's a coincidence that all the cheerleaders are the ones who get elected. Not to be mean, but a lot of them couldn't get through the first twelve pages of a Tolstoy novel, let alone the twelve *hundred* pages of *War and Peace* I read last summer."

Julian's iPad replied,

"THEN USE YOUR GOLDEN VOICE TO FIGHT INJUSTICE."

Jaz whispered. "Already done. I wrote an official complaint letter to Jergen, reminding him of the guidelines for electing the Princesses. Not that it will do any good."

Jaz twirled her chair and waved her hand like a queen. In a silly high voice, she said, "Who wouldn't want to be a princess? Greetings, my lowly subjects."

Peter grabbed his stomach and fell to the floor laughing.

Ana arrived to help me type my science lab report.

FIRST A NOTE TO JAZ, I typed.

Jaz wheeled closer.

SEE YOU AT THE POOP RALLY!

She burst out laughing, but not as hard as Peter, who rolled on the floor for the second time today.

• • •

At 1:45, all classes let out for the pep rally. Ana led me to a seat on the bleachers, handing me my animal flashcards on a key ring to keep my hands occupied. My hands flipped through them automatically.

Seahorse, flip, sloth, flip, toucan, flip.

Jazmine pulled up next to me. "Got your earplugs?"

She was not kidding—twelve rows of bleachers, about fifty kids per row. Six hundred voices screamed when the bouncy cheerleaders—Darcy and Lilly included—jumped and hollered.

"Let's make some noise!"

Their black and yellow hair ribbons waved in the air with each bounce.

"Hoo-rah-rye! Hornets fly! Hoo-rah-roop! Hornets swoop! Hoo-rah-ring! Hornets sting!"

"Will you listen to that pathetic rhyme," complained Jaz. "Shakespeare is weeping."

I continued to sulk and flip my flashcards. Sulk and flip, sulk and flip.

Tiger, flip, sea star, flip, beaver, flip.

Peter leaned over to us. "See the one with pink hair?" He pointed to Lilly. "She's my girlfriend."

"You're delusional," Jaz barked. "That girl wouldn't talk to you if her pink hair caught fire and you were holding a bucket of water."

Jaz could be heartless sometimes. Still, I hoped Peter stayed away from Lilly.

Meerkat, flip, zebra, flip, falcon, flip.

Even with all the chaos, my body stayed in control as the school band played. I saw the smart kid Stuart up there. His cheeks inflated like balloons as he honked his tuba, and his long legs bent in rhythm with the school's fight song.

Skyler held her poppy-field poster high as the whole auditorium sang along . . . or, rather, *shouted* along. "We will win this game, fighting for newfound fame. Our team will fight with all its might, the Hornet you can never tame!"

Gorilla, flip, giraffe, flip, rhino, flip.

Everyone cheered at jet-engine decibels when Coach

George announced the members of the football team. They all lined up in uniform behind him.

Coach held up his hands for silence. "*Now*, what you have all been waiting for . . . "

"Here we go again," Jaz whispered.

Coach turned in our direction, smiling and nodding.

Is he looking at us?

Skyler smiled and waved back at him.

"The members of this year's Lincoln Hornets' Princess Court." His big, white teeth flashed us again.

Why would he look at us?

My heart thumped louder.

Hypothesis: He is going to parade me up there—the charity case—maybe to feel less guilty about calling me a mascot.

Elephant, flip, flip, flip.

Oh, no.

Coach announced each girl to the sound of a drumroll. As Jaz predicted, all of them were wearing cheerleading uniforms . . . so far.

I prayed—*please do not call my name.*

Each princess did some cute cheer move like pumping her arms in the air or moving her hips side to side.

Please do not call my name.

"Lilly Carter!"

Lilly trotted toward coach and launched into a double handspring. The crowd roared.

Please do not call my name.

"Rachel Lenox!"

Rachel held both her hands on her cheeks as if she never expected this in a million years.

Please do not call my name.

"Darcy Warner!"

Darcy strutted forward and pumped her fist in the air. Then she held both hands to her ears for kids to cheer louder. Everyone stomped the bleachers and chanted her name, "*Dar-cy! Dar-cy! Dar-cy!*"

"And our final member of the Princess Court . . ."

I held my breath and prayed *hard*.

Please do not call my name.

"Erica Zimmerman!"

Whew!

Breathe in relief.

All eight girls stood there, each one a thousand volts of perkiness, smiling and waving at the crowd.

"What did I tell you?" Jaz said.

Coach George held up his hand again, wearing a big smile, like he'd already won the football game. "Hornets, Hornets, we're not done yet."

He looked over at me again.

"This year, we decided to choose one special student to be an honorary member of the Princess Court."

"Special" student? Please, no!

My body rocked back and forth, back and forth.

"This student has distinguished herself by overcoming countless obstacles to do things that most of us take for granted."

Please do not explode in front of the entire school.

I tried to freeze myself into a statue, but my body shook harder.

Page 51: Wet dogs can shake 75 percent of the water off their fur in less than five seconds.

Ana knelt down next to me. "Charity, are you okay?"

A KETTLE EXPLOSION was approaching fast.

Ana grabbed my hand and helped me up for a quick getaway.

Coach announced, "Please welcome our special princess . . . Jazmine Cooper!"

My feet stopped. I turned around.

Jaz looked like she was going to barf. Her face went white. Her small body shrank down into her wheelchair.

I would not wish this sort of honor on anyone. It was a pity prize.

Jaz sat frozen as the applause died down.

Coach George brushed his nose with his hand. "Uh . . . will Jazmine Cooper please join the members of the court up front?" He waved his hand for her to come.

Students applauded again . . . less loudly.

Jaz moved her hand to control her wheelchair. Instead of rolling forward, she rolled herself backward a little.

A few people laughed.

Skyler scrunched her nose, confused. "Go, Jazmine, go! You won. Coach called your name."

I wished Jazmine could fly like a bluebird into Skyler's field of poppies, where she did not have to be paraded like a strange specimen. Was this Jergen's idea of being nice? Or was he getting back at her for complaining about the Princess Court?

Celia knelt beside Jaz. They whispered to each other. Jaz shook her head.

My eyes were glued to the scene. I could not stop myself from gawking along with all the other gawkers. Then I realized something—my negative attitude stopped me from seeing it before.

Jaz had only one choice—*dare* to be included.

I jumped and clapped to get her attention. Jaz turned to me with a look of terror. I nodded at her.

I believe in you, Jaz.

She nodded back. Then with the look of a soldier going into battle, Jaz faced Coach. She inched her chair forward to join the other princesses. Then she picked up speed. In the middle of the gymnasium, she stopped to twirl her chair and wave like a queen. The gymnasium burst into applause. She put her hand up to her ear imitating what Darcy did. Kids screamed louder.

Darcy folded her arms, looking annoyed as Jaz made a tour around the circumference of the entire gym. The crowd roared and chanted her name—"*JAZ-MINE! JAZ-MINE! JAZ-MINE!*" Then she aimed her chair straight for the center of the princess lineup and raced forward. Darcy and Lilly leaped to the side to avoid getting run over.

More laughter and applause from the audience.

Coach George announced, "Ladies and gentlemen, please welcome this year's Princess Court!"

The EPIC kids jumped and clapped, seeing Jazmine in the middle of all those cheerleaders. I jumped too. Leave it to Jaz to make poppies out of poop nuggets.

Diagnosis: Delusional

Stuart tapped his pencil on the table and ran a hand through his messy, brown hair. "What experiment should we choose?"

My new science lab partners, Stuart and Rachel, were drama-free so far. Stuart was different than most kids—I mean that in a good way. He loved learning, and he treated me like a real person. A person with a brain.

No more messages from Sassygirl72 on the gossip app. Was I now accepted as a student at Lincoln?

Probability: uncertain.

"I think we should let you choose the project, Charity," Rachel said. "I mean, you were stuck in those boring classes for so long. Your brain must be bursting with brill ideas."

With her hazelnut hair woven in a side braid, Rachel was fashionable without being snooty about it.

Neither of them seemed to mind that at that moment I was stacking my puzzle pieces on top of each other and click-clicking my tongue in rhythm with music in my head.

10, 11, 12, 13 . . .

Click. Click-click. Click-click-click.

Rachel twisted the fake diamond bracelet on her wrist. "Something that makes us *look* super smart but isn't super hard."

Stuart nodded. "Okay, so something between exploding a bottle of soda with a mint and curing lung cancer."

26, 27, 28 . . .

Click. Click-click. Click-click-click.

Rachel snapped her fingers. "Hey, do you think Harding would *let* us explode soda bottles?"

Stuart smacked his forehead. "What do *you* think?"

I nudged Ana to help me.

WE COULD GENETICALLY ENGINEER A NEW SPECIES OF TO-MATO. ONE THAT TASTES LIKE SOUR CHERRY GUMMY WORMS.

"Oh yeah," Rachel said. "That would make me eat my vegetables for sure."

"Technically, tomatoes are a fruit," Stuart said.

32, 33, 34, 35 . . .

Click. Click-click. Click-click-click.

Rachel socked him gently in the arm. "You're totally earning your nerd reputation today, dude."

Stuart observed me. "Charity, does your autism make you sensitive to smells? We may want to avoid strong-smelling chemicals."

Rachel jerked her head back. "Stu, that's so rude. You don't talk about someone's . . . you know . . . affliction to their face."

I typed, with Ana's help.

BETTER TO TALK TO MY FACE THAN TALK BEHIND MY BACK.

"Gee, I guess you're right." Rachel scanned the room. "Not that I would ever do that, you know."

MY NOSE SHOULD BE OK, STU. THANKS FOR ASKING.

Right when I reached out my hand for a fist bump, a sound pierced my eardrums.

EEEEEEEEEEEEEEEEEEEEEEEEEEEEEEEEEEEEEEE

I swept my tower of puzzle pieces to the floor and slapped my ears with both hands.

EEEEEEEEEEEEEEEEEEEEEEEEEEEEEEEEEEEEEEE

Slap. Slap. Slap. Slap.

Rachel put a hand to her mouth and gasped. "OMG, is she hitting herself?"

Slap. Slap. Slap. Slap.

"What's wrong, Charity?" Ana pulled a hand away from my ear to type, but the sound penetrated like an electric eel. I pulled my hand away and pounded the black lab bench.

Pound. Pound. Pound. Pound.

What's happening? Another fire alarm?

EEEEEEEEEEEEEEEEEEEEEEEEEEEEEEEEEEEEEEE

No. All eyes were on me. I was the only one hearing it.

I slipped out of my chair. My knees hit the tile floor.

"Charity, walk with me." Ana's voice sounded as if it was under water.

I screamed. Ahhhhhhhhhhhhh!

How could no one else hear it?

EEEEEEEEEEEEEEEEEEEEEEEEEEEEEEEEEEEEEEE

A million miles away, I heard voices. My lungs screamed harder.

Ahhhhhhhhhhhhh!

"Is she breathing?"

Ahhhhhhhhhhhhh!

"Somebody call 911."

Ahhhhhhhhhhhhh!

Firecrackers in my brain.

Ahhhhhhhhhhhhh!

Then, nothing.

The noise was gone.

Ana's hands cradled my head. She wiped drool off my cheek with a tissue. I released the death grip on my ears and opened my eyes. Her face came into focus.

"Charity, can you hear me?"

The entire class was standing above Ana. Their expressions ranged from worried to disgusted. Mr. Harding pulled me to a stand. "Maybe it's best if she goes to the nurse's office."

Ana nodded and led me away. On the way out, I glimpsed two girls bent over laughing. Darcy and Lilly.

Mom drove me directly to the hospital's urgent care, where they performed a hearing test. Mom helped me type my responses, and the doctor ruled out a hearing problem.

Then the conversation got weird.

The doctor scrunched up his nose. He had about four strands of hair combed over the bald part of his head and glued in place with gel. Did he think that would cover it up?

"Was your daughter under any particular *stress* at the time?"

Even now that I could communicate, the Thinkers were still talking *about* me instead of talking *to* me.

Mom steadied my arm so I could answer.

ALWAYS STRESSFUL TO LIVE IN MY BODY.

"Does your daughter ever hear voices?" he asked Mom.

"Do you ever hear voices, sweetheart?" Mom repeated.

I typed:

YES. WHENEVER PEOPLE TALK.

"Charity, you know what the doctor means. When people *aren't* talking do you hear voices—that is what you mean, isn't it?" Mom looked at the doctor, a new wrinkle added to her forehead, thanks to me.

He turned to Mom. "Sounds like an auditory hallucination—she is hearing things that are not there. Hallucinations like this can indicate a serious psychological disorder. Has your daughter been *seeing* things that aren't there as well as *hearing* things?"

Honestly, some of these Thinkers are as sharp as bowling balls.

"Why are you saying she's having hallucinations at all? You didn't let her answer." As usual, Mom's voice got higher as she became more jittery.

She turned to me. "Charity, have you been seeing things . . . things that are not real, sweetheart?" She shook her head no, expecting that to be my answer. But I was not sure how to respond.

The guy who saved me at the pier. Was he real? Was he only a dream? Maybe my life here was the hallucination.

Diagnosis: delusional.

Hello, Pine Valley.

Mom held my hand up to the keyboard. I pulled it away and folded my arms over my chest.

My body rocked back and forth, back and forth.

They both stared at me a few seconds.

The doctor held a stubby finger up to his puffy face. He looked like a blowfish.

Page 19: One blowfish contains enough
toxin to kill twenty adults.

"We will need to do more tests for certain, but given the severity of her symptoms . . ."

What do you mean symptoms? *This is who I am. Why are people always trying to cure me?*

"I can prescribe a psychotropic medication to control the hallucinations. I can also recommend a facility that uses electrical stimulation devices to modify unwanted behaviors."

My heels kicked the metal examination table in a protest that echoed on the white brick walls.

BOOM. BOOM. BOOM. BOOM.

Mom's voice thundered above my noise. "What do you mean by electrical stimulation? Are you talking about shock therapy?"

My mind flashed to news reports I had seen about this on TV—kids wearing wires, strapped to a board, shocked over and over for things like flapping their hands. One autistic boy was shocked thirty times for not taking off his coat when he was ordered to. Shocked for having a mind-body disconnect. Shocked for screaming about being shocked.

Controlling someone is not the same as curing them!

My body rocked back and forth, back and forth.

Cold fear swept through my body.

The doctor wore a tight frown. "Electrical shock treatments have been performed safely since the 1940s, and I assure you . . ."

"Treatments? *Treatments?*" Mom's voice filled the room. "It's nothing less than *torture*! This can't even be legal for prisoners of war!"

She pointed her finger in his face and backed him to the wall. "How could you *dream* of subjecting my daughter to this cruelty?"

Mom pulled me out the door before the doctor could put together a sentence in his own defense.

▪▪▪

Back home, Mom poured me green tea with honey—*no more warm apple juice*—while she told Celia about Dr. Blowfish and his torture prescription. Celia sat with us at the kitchen table, munching one of Dad's famous cranberry-walnut cookies.

"I'm afraid I lost it with him," Mom said, "but I can't stand people who think Charity should be treated like a lab rat because she's different."

Mom balled her hands into tight fists as she described the shock therapy he recommended.

Celia nodded. "My grandmother never uttered a curse word her entire life, but at times such as this, I think they come in handy."

She turned to me with her usual *let-me-help-you* gaze. "Charity, *querida*, do you know what caused your outburst today? Is something upsetting you?"

That noise in class. I heard it so clearly. Was it my imagination? Were my emotions ringing a fire alarm in my head?

I typed to her about the worries that clawed at my mind.

MY HEART BREAKS FOR ISABELLA AND ALL THE KIDS LEFT

BEHIND AT BORDEN. I ESCAPED AND THEY ARE STILL SUFFERING. I FEEL HELPLESS.

"You are not helpless, not anymore." Celia's golden, dangly earrings shimmered in a finger of sunlight. "You have a voice now. Use it to lead."

BUT HOW? MY LETTER TO THE SUPERINTENDENT FAILED. ISABELLA'S MOM WILL NOT LISTEN. WHAT CAN I DO NOW?

Celia squeezed my hand. "You were born a leader, Charity. Just keep being who you are. You are already making a difference at Lincoln."

YOU REALLY THINK I AM A LEADER?

"Absolutely. In fact, I believe you carry the wisdom of many lifetimes."

THEN WHY IS GOD PUNISHING ME IN THIS LIFE?

Celia smiled. "We are all children of a perfect God. You were put on earth for a reason—and that reason you already know."

Math Knights

"You don't have to tell me the answer. Just tell me if I'm on the right track. Somewhere in the ballpark."

Mason spread out his scratch paper on the table in front of me. Numbers littered the page, like maybe a chicken wrote it.

Ana supported my arm.

CORRECT UP TO STEP THREE.

"Geez, okay. What is step three?"

With Ana's help, I pointed to the number with the missing exponent. "Hey, stop hogging the class brain." Grace stood behind him with her notebook in hand.

Celia's hypothesis about me being a leader seemed to be coming true. It all started last week when Mr. Byrd walked into class with a stack of papers—our graded chapter exams, my first actual junior high school test.

Jitters prickled my legs and arms.

My body rocked back and forth, back and forth.

Mom and I had worked on equations for hours at home. I did not expect an *A*, but I did not want to fail miserably either.

"As usual," Mr. Byrd announced, "I will invite the top three scorers to come up and take a bow. I also want the rest of you folks to know who you can go to for tutoring. You can all learn from one another."

With his usual nerdy style, Mr. Byrd called Stuart's name and tapped him on the shoulders with a toy light saber. He knighted Darcy next—she pumped her arms to whoops and hollers from Lilly and her other friends.

Before announcing the highest-scoring student, Mr. Byrd lowered the lights in the classroom and played the theme song for Darth Vader.

"And now, young Jedi knights. Meet your new master. With a top score of a hundred and five percent—I had to give a few bonus points because this Jedi master found an error in one of my equations—please come up, Charity Wood."

The whole room inhaled a gasp, and Darcy shot me a stare like Death Star laser beams.

Since that day, a bunch of kids started asking me about their math equations. With Ana's support, I could answer them.

"Hey, is it hard helping Charity type?" Mason asked Ana while Grace was correcting the multiplication error I pointed out.

"It requires training and a lot of patience to do correctly," she said, smiling. "It is also important that Charity know and trust the person supporting her."

Mason nodded. "Even better if that person is a favorite cousin?"

YES, FAVORITE AND ONLY COUSIN, I typed.

Ana lowered her round glasses to look Mason in the eye. "If

you are serious, and if Charity wants to, then I can arrange for you to be trained. It will take hours of training and practice."

Mason shrugged. "Good thing I turned down that movie deal with Emma Watson, then. I should have plenty of time."

Ana winked a green eye at me. "Charity, I suppose it would be good for you to speak to someone your own age without me or your parents always intruding on the conversation."

THANK YOU, MASON. HAPPY TO TALK TO YOU AFTER SO MANY YEARS.

Jaz wheeled up and gave me a fist bump. "Congrats, kid. I still can't believe you beat out that cheerleader zombie Darcy. If you keep this up, you could knock her off the top of the honor roll. She would loooooove that!"

WHAT IS AN HONOR ROLL?

Ana explained, "It's a list of the top-performing students every quarter. Up until last year, Mr. Jergen did not allow students from the EPIC room to be eligible for honor roll. Celia fought that battle and finally won." "Yeah," Jaz said, "but no one expected an EPIC kid to top the list. Charity, this would send shockwaves through the whole school. I can already picture Darcy's parents turning blue in the face."

I was surprised that Darcy was first on the honor roll. Then I felt bad for judging her the way people judge me.

THIS TRADITION SEEMS UNFAIR. WHY PRAISE ONLY FOR GRADES?

I thought about years of failed tests that only left me feeling worthless.

"I know it's stupid," Jaz said. "But think about it, Charity.

An EPIC kid at number one on the honor roll? I mean, that might even get you an article in the paper."

I typed to Ana.

DO YOU THINK I HAVE A CHANCE?

"More than a chance, Charity. But don't worry about lists. Just focus on doing your best."

I thought about Sassygirl72 and her hunger to get me kicked out of advanced classes.

I nudged Ana so I could type more.

I WANT PEOPLE TO KNOW I AM CAPABLE. TO SHOW THERE ARE GOOGOLPLEX WAYS OF BEING SMART.

Sassygirl and I were both on a mission. I had to make sure that mine won.

Least Valuable Player

For years, I felt like life was a party, and I was not invited.

Breathe in: I belong.

Breathe out: I belong.

I repeated these words to myself to drown out my loud doubts as I sat courtside next to Dad in my new yellow uniform.

Cheerleaders shouted and danced to jolt the crowd with their bouncy energy.

> *People in the middle: Shake it just a little!*
> *People in the back: Show us where you're at!*
> *People in the stands: Jump up and clap your hands!*

I dug my fingernails into my arm and scratched.

I am a Hornet. I am a Hornet.

Scratch, scratch, scratch.

"Here, Cherry Girl," Dad said. "Hold onto this for me." He handed me my lucky sea glass, and I cupped it in my palm.

Jaz raced and twirled her wheelchair around the gymnasium. Ever since her nomination on the Princess Court, she loved shaking her pom-poms at pep rallies and games as an unofficial cheerleader. The whole crowd of students clapped and hooted for her. She did not do it just to annoy the cheerleaders anymore. In fact, she admitted that a few of them were actually *nice*.

Stuart marched by, playing his trombone with the band. He nodded as he passed.

At me?

"Go, chipmunk!" Pops hollered from the bleachers.

Gram, Mom, and Aunt Kiki yelled, but loudest of all was Aunt Elvi. "You got this, girl! Wooohooo!"

Who wears a black velvet cape? To a junior high basketball game?

Mason sat behind them, devouring a bag of popcorn and two hot dogs. When he spilled a drop of catsup on his mom's white blouse, she shot off the bleacher like bread from a toaster. He could not help smiling in spite of all her fussing.

I smiled inside too.

I had my own embarrassing cheering section. Embarrassing because I would not likely touch my sneaker to the court during this, my first-ever basketball game.

Dad pulled me to stand. "Let's warm up our cheering arms," he said, punching his fists in the air. "Go Hornets, go!"

I followed his lead, leaping and throwing my arms in the air.

Jump, punch, jump, punch.

"Go number twelve!" Gram screamed. That was the number on my uniform.

Twelve. What an amazing number. Could I live up to

its awesomeness? In math, it's called a superior highly composite number. Also, twelve months in a year, twelve zodiac signs, twelve Olympians from Greek mythology, twelve days of Christmas.

I could go on and on.

Jump, punch, jump, punch.

Coach suggested—and I agreed—that I cheer the team on for the first few games. Especially since I still could not dribble or pass or run in the right direction half the time.

I could shoot, but what good was that if my stubborn legs led me to the hallway instead of the hoop? I was happy to be included as a Hornet, even if only on the bench.

Jump, punch, jump, punch.

"Here, my little buttercups. You need to keep your energy up." Darcy's mother, who volunteered as team mom, handed out sports drinks to all the girls.

All the girls except me.

I must be invisible again.

She wore a black designer track suit with a pearl necklace and several large rings on her fingers. Her long, blonde hair seemed salon styled. How could anyone look that good in sweats? All the girls called her Mrs. Bling-Bling.

Not to her face, of course.

Before the game, Mrs. Bling-Bling pulled Darcy toward her and stroked her blonde ponytail. "Win this one for Mommy and Father, honeybun. You missed a few easy shots in practice. You want to win that MVP trophy at the end of the season, don't you?" I noted Darcy's frown.

I understand you better now, Darcy.

Enthusiastic parents—Darcy and I had that in common. I totaled her score—top of the honor roll, cheerleader, star basketball player. She had to be smart, beautiful, and athletic at all times to please her parents. I remembered feeling for so many years like I had let my mom down every time I could not hold a pencil or draw a letter or pull on my own socks. I wondered if Darcy felt the same sadness every time she missed a basket. Or scored second-best on a math test.

Bullies sprout from sadness. Hurting others is how they get their own hurts out.

Grace waved for me to join the opening huddle. Then she put an arm around me and whispered, "Don't sweat it, Charity. You'll do fine."

She was right. I did do fine. A fine job of sitting on the bench next to Dad. A fine job calculating each player's performance based on points scored, assists, blocks, steals, rebounds, missed shots, and fouls.

They did not need my help though. They were winning by six points going into the fourth quarter, with Darcy as top scorer.

Each time Darcy made a basket, Mrs. Bling-Bling screamed, "That's my superstar!"

Grace joined me on the bench when Coach subbed her out for a break. She wiped her sweaty face with a towel. "Hey, you didn't play yet, did you?" She turned to coach. "Coach, how about putting Charity in for a few minutes?"

Lilly, sitting next to Grace, gave her a *don't-even-think-about-it* stare.

Coach did not hear—or pretended not to—as he shouted, "Keep the ball alive, girls! Take it to the hole!"

Darcy swished another basket. Up by eight now.

Grace softly chanted, "Cha-ri-ty, Cha-ri-ty."

Dad grinned big.

Two other girls joined in. "Cha-ri-ty, Cha-ri-ty."

Finally, Coach George turned and asked, "Whaddya think, kid? Wanna get in there for a few minutes? Test the waters?"

My brain hollered *Nooooooo*! But my dumb legs sprang me right up.

Jump, punch, jump, punch.

"You go, Super Cherry!" Dad yelled.

Seeing me walk on the court, my cheering section went nuts. Aunt Kiki hollered, "You can do it, sweetie!" while making tiny hops in her high heels and clapping her manicured hands.

Hypothesis: Disaster.

When the ref blew the whistle, chaos erupted. In my body.

Ready, set, embarrass yourself.

Jump. Run. Turn. Hop.

Follow the bouncing ball. Follow the bouncing ball.

The orange ball flew from player to player. My eyes told my legs to go, but as soon as I ran in one direction, the ball bounced the opposite way.

Sprint. Swivel. Spin?

Page 17: A herd of bison can run up to 40 miles an hour.

My head could not turn fast enough for my eyes to keep up. And my legs—forget about it.

Swivel. Prance?

Pause.

My feet froze to the floor. My hands flapped frustration.

I spied Mom with her hands over her eyes as if she was watching a horror movie.

Get me out of here!

A few laughs from some kids in the stands shot directly to my ear.

Is this what you had in mind, Grace?

Almost on cue, I felt a hand in my hand. It pulled me down the court one way, then back the other way, following the ball. The bobbing honey-colored ponytail in front of my face belonged to Grace. She guided me same as Dad did during our practices.

Run. Run. Run. Turn. Run. Run. Turn. Run. Run. Run.

We stopped a few yards from the net. Grace let go of my hand and hollered to Darcy, "I'm open!"

When Darcy passed the ball, Grace handed it to me.

Darcy's perfect face turned ugly. "What the . . ."

"Shoot, Charity!" yelled Grace.

My hands automatically hurled the ball toward the hoop. It hit the backboard.

And dropped into the net.

The crowd clapped and screamed. "Way to go, Chipmunk!" Pops howled. Gram—her petite body perched on top of the bleacher—stood with both hands in the air. Mom, Kiki and Elvi joined in a jumping hug.

She shoots, she scores. For real!

Coach George flashed a toothy grin. "That's what I'm talkin' about."

My lungs filled with relief as I trotted back to the bench.

No such luck.

"Hey, where ya going?" Grace grabbed my hand again.

Run. Run. Run. Turn. Run. Run. Turn. Run. Run. Run.

We stopped in front of the basket, and my hands grabbed the ball from a player. A player with a blue shirt.

Grace screamed, "No, don't shoot!" But my arms launched the ball automatically.

What have I done?

This time the ball did not hit the backboard.

Nothing but net.

She shoots, she scores . . . for the other team.

A collective "Awwwwwwwww" came from the crowd. I could not look at my cheering section.

"You idiot!" Darcy spit words at me under her breath, and yelled, "Get her outta here, Coach!"

Coach's cheeks puffed up. "Darcy, you take orders from *me*, not the other way around. I'm keeping her in."

Oh, no. He cannot be serious.

The ref blew the whistle again. Grace grabbed my hand.

Run. Run. Run. Turn. Run. Run. Turn. Run. Run. Run.

In front of the basket, Grace got the ball and handed it to me. "Shoot, Charity."

Do not screw this up.

Throw and a miss.

Darcy caught the rebound and aimed for a shot. She tossed the ball toward the net.

I cannot explain why, but all of Dad's lessons on lay-ups popped into my head at that moment.

Page 17: Bison can jump six feet high.

Run. Jump. Reach.

I charged the net and jumped, right as Darcy's ball floated above it—perfectly timed to knock her shot away.

The other team grabbed the ball and scored a three-pointer in less than five seconds.

Darcy's mom howled. "Get that girl *off* the court!"

Thank goodness Coach let me return to the bench. My three minutes of play felt like three hours.

I sat next to Dad for the final minutes of the game chewing my knuckles and avoiding the evil stare of Mrs. Bling-Bling.

We lost by two points.

Least valuable player—Charity-Case Wood.

Darcy wiped her wet face then flung her towel on the floor. "We *had* this game till she came out and wrecked it for us."

"Hey!" shouted Coach. "You need to work on your sportsmanship, young lady, or I will be happy to bench you for an entire game."

Jaz rolled up to me. "Don't stress about it, Charity. I mean, you did score two baskets in your first game."

"Yeah, it's just game one," Grace said. "We have a whole season to get into our groove."

Dad helped me respond.

WILL TRY NOT TO SCORE FOR OTHER TEAM NEXT TIME.

A bald man in a dark suit charged up to Coach George, his whole face inflated with anger. Darcy's mom stood next to him with folded arms: She nodded at everything the man said.

Grace whispered, "Darcy's parents are pretty extreme. They

shelled out some serious coin to the school. Sometimes they act as if they own us."

Watching her parents have a meltdown over a basketball game, I felt sorry for Darcy.

From Coach's expression—kind of like my dog, Hero, when Mom catches him chewing her shoe—I could tell he was losing the argument.

Would I get to play in another game?

Probability: low.

Hornet Sting to the Head

"To deny education to any people is one of the greatest crimes against human nature." These words, written by Frederick Douglass, filled me with courage as I sat in English class waiting to begin our weekly reading quiz.

Frederick Douglass was the subject of the quiz, and I had been preparing all week. I did not tell Mom about my dream of reaching the honor roll. I kept it my secret wish.

Facts from the readings floated in my head.

Douglass was born a slave in 1818. He was not allowed to learn to read, so he had to learn in secret. After years of abuse, he escaped and then fought hard to gain freedom for other slaves. He understood how important education was to freedom.

Frederick Douglass was officially my new hero.

I jumped a little when Mason slipped into the chair beside me. He pointed to his phone, which he held in his lap so no one could see.

"It's that dumb gossip app again," he whispered. "Something's going down, so watch your back."

How could I watch my back when I could barely walk a straight line?

He angled his screen so I could see. Sassygirl72 wrote, "No retards playing basketball" in one post. In another, Sassygirl wrote, "11 am fetch rover."

"I have no idea what that second one means, but it's almost 11."

I glanced up at the clock—10:50. What was coming?

Mason returned to his seat. I stared down at my puzzle pieces, my hands too shaky to pick one up.

Ana sat next to me. "Are you okay, Charity?" She held up the keyboard, but I sat frozen. "Do not be nervous about the quiz. You know this material."

Sassygirl had to be Darcy. I glanced over at her. She sat at her desk, skimming the textbook.

Was she messing with me so I would fail?

What would happen at eleven? I scanned the room. No one was looking at me, no one whispering. A few students were sneaking texts as usual.

My body rocked back and forth, back and forth as Ms. Beckett passed back last week's homework.

The clock ticked forward . . . 55 . . . 56 . . . 57.

Finally, Ms. Beckett handed out the quiz—five simple multiple-choice questions. Easy-peasy, as Dad would say.

Ana steadied my arm to begin typing. The clock ticked to eleven, and I held my breath.

Nothing happened. I was jittery for nothing.

Then it hit.

EEEEEEEEEEEEEEEEEEEEEEEEEEEEEEEEEEEEEEEE

A hornet sting to my head. The same piercing noise I heard before. This time twice as loud! I slapped my ears.

Smack, smack, smack, smack.

I screamed.

AHHHHHHHHHHHHHHHHHHH!

Ms. Beckett ran over. Ana knelt beside me.

I hit my forehead on the table.

Bang. Bang.

Someone gripped my shoulders. I wiggled away.

AHHHHHHHHHHHHHHHHHHH!

Then silence. It stopped.

I opened my eyes to see Ana's worried face. I could not hear her voice. Her lips asked, "Are you okay, Charity?"

The class had gathered around me.

I could predict what was coming next as clearly as if I had a crystal ball. Ms. Beckett would send me to the nurse's office. Mom would take me to the doctor to get examined. Celia would call to say that someone complained about the disruption. And on and on until Jergen pulled me out of regular classes for interfering with learning.

Ana supported me to stand.

"Come, Charity. Let's get you to the nurse's office," she said.

And so it begins.

"Wait a minute." Mason stood up. His face was red and stretched as if he was in pain. Then I realized . . . these were the first words he ever spoke in front of the class.

His voice cracked a little. "I think someone's got an app on their phone that plays a dog whistle. Really high-pitched so we can't hear it. But I think Charity can."

I could hardly believe it. Mason was breaking his *keep-your-head-low* rule.

"Someone is doing this to her on purpose."

Mason was risking lifelong outcast status . . . for me?

Ms. Beckett wrinkled her eyebrows. "Such a thing exists?"

"Yeah. I just looked it up. It's a dog whistle app called Fetch Rover." Mason pulled out his phone and showed her.

"What makes you think this, Mason?" she asked.

He looked down at the floor and shrugged his shoulders.

Ms. Beckett nodded with determination. "Class, we will postpone the quiz until tomorrow. Right now, I want all of you to place your phones on my desk," she ordered. "Mason, can you check them for this application?"

"Hey, don't you need a search warrant for that?" demanded Rachel.

"No, I do not. If you'd like to wait for Mr. Jergen to confirm that for you, you're welcome to. I will not put up with bullying. At our school, bullying is an offense resulting in suspension and possible expulsion. And if I find out that someone has been purposely bullying Charity, I will personally recommend expulsion *unless* everyone cooperates here."

One by one, cell phones were placed on desks and Mason checked them as Ms. Beckett launched into a lecture on Frederick Douglass and the thirteenth amendment.

Before Mason got to her, Rachel broke down and confessed. Teary-eyed, she went to Ms. Beckett and spoke in fast whispers. Two other boys I hardly knew had the app on their phone too. All three made a trip to Jergen's office.

Darcy's phone was innocent.

How could that be?

At the end of class, Ms. Beckett came over to check on me. "I'm so sorry, Charity. The students claimed to have no idea the sound would hurt you. They said it was a prank. Rumor had it that the noise would cause the windows in the classroom to crack. Why anyone would believe *that* is beyond me, but junior high students are full of surprises."

Ana helped me respond.

I BELIEVE THEM. I AM GLAD IT WAS NOT IN MY HEAD.

I typed to Mason—Mason, who risked total school humiliation to protect me:

YOUR HEART IS FULL OF COURAGE.

He shrugged. "I was bullied at my last school. It's rough out there if no one's got your back."

"Who started this ridiculous rumor?" asked Ana.

Mason shrugged again.

I am sure he had a hypothesis. And so did I.

Basketball Savant

"We got the ball, get outta the way. C'mon, Charity, let's score today!" My whole cheering section chanted for me during warm-ups.

Grace and I had really improved our teamwork. She held my hand to lead me up and down the court. She handed me the ball and yelled, "Shoot." Most times I swooshed it right in.

Can I finally redeem myself in this game?

Darcy's mom, Mrs. Bling-Bling, paced the sidelines, her phone glued to her cheek. Today she was wearing a dark business suit and spiky heels, as if she had come straight from work. Her fingers fiddled with her diamond necklace. She marched up to Coach and handed him the phone with a big smile glued to her lips.

I had a bad feeling about this.

"By the way, Grace," Darcy dribbled around us. "Don't tell me to pass you the ball if you're not going to shoot it yourself."

"Chill out, Darcy," she said. "You're still the superstar."

"Dang right I am, girl." They high-fived.

Coach blew his whistle and motioned us over for the opening huddle. The other team, in green, seemed a half foot taller than us.

"The Green Giants look hungry tonight," Grace said.

Our huddle broke with "*Go Hornets!*" and Coach called out the girls' positions.

"Charity," he cleared his throat and put a hand on my shoulder. "Sorry, kid, but I think we're gonna have you cheer us on tonight."

"C'mon, George," Dad protested. "You saw her out there. She made eight baskets just in warm-ups."

"Sorry, Steve. It's kind of outta my hands right now."

When was Mrs. Bling-Bling promoted to head coach?

I sat on the bench, shuffling my feet and watching Darcy hog the ball while Dad fumed next to me.

"There is no *I* in *team*," he grumbled.

I answered him in my head.

But there is an I *in* win.

Life is a party. And I am not invited.

Pity filled my throat and made me feel like throwing up. I hate pity. I remembered Celia's words: *You have a voice now. Use it to lead.*

I tried to concentrate on the game. The Green Giants were squashing us like mashed potatoes. Most of Darcy's shots were missing. She was off her game tonight. My mind went into deep focus. Bodies on the court became masses moving through space. I observed the thrust of the arms, the arc of the ball toward the net, the speed of the throw.

I tugged on Dad's arm for my iPad, and he helped me type. I observed and typed, observed and typed.

At the end of the third quarter, the Hornets were down by twelve points. Dad called Coach over and showed him what I wrote.

"Can you really see all this, kid?"

"If she typed it, George, she saw it," Dad said.

Coach called the girls over for a huddle.

"Listen up. Ella, you were called twice for fouls because you stick out your elbows. Sierra, you tend to miss short. We need to work on distance control. Darcy, you need to shoot at the top of your jump. You're shooting late. You also twist when you shoot. Align your feet when you set up the shot. And this is for all of you—increase the arc of your shot to 45 degrees. That will give you a wider margin of error. Now get out there and fight!"

"Thanks for the great tips, Coach," Grace said. "You have a good eye."

"Not me," he said. "Charity's made some genius observations here from the bench."

Girls nodded and clapped. "Way to go, coach Charity!" "Cool bananas!" "Crush it, sister!"

Dad helped me answer.

I FINALLY FOUND A WAY TO BE INCLUDED WITHOUT GIVING POINTS TO THE OTHER TEAM.

A bunch of the girls patted me on the back or gave me a fist bump as they headed back on the court.

The girls shot a lot better in the fourth quarter, including

Darcy. We still ended up losing, but only by two points instead of twelve.

Would my suggestions convince Darcy I was a valuable member of the team? My heart hoped for it. My sixth sense told me the truth.

Probability: zero.

A Place Pity-Free

A big yellow bus pulled up to the front of the school, and we filed on. For my very first field trip, we were headed to a photography museum to see an exhibit celebrating Black History Month. I would finally look into the eyes of Frederick Douglass and tell him *thank you*.

Celia and Ms. Beckett had to convince Jergen to let me go. I imagined his argument. "Her unpredictable behavior puts her and others at risk. What will happen if she acts out or runs away like she has done at school?"

My hope was to prove him wrong. If only my body would cooperate.

Ana led me up the steps of the bus and sat me in the front seat. "Your friend has asked to sit next to you. I will sit in the next row if you need me."

A friend?

At that moment, Grace stepped on board and slid in the seat beside me.

She actually asked to sit with me?

Breathe in: I belong.

Breathe out: I belong.

I tried to believe these words. Never mind what Sassygirl said.

"Hey, Charity," Grace said, "ready to have some fun today? The exhibit will be cool, but the picnic we get to have in the park afterward is even more fun. Say cheese!" She held up her phone and clicked a picture of me.

At the museum, we saw so many hope-filled photos— there was Frederick Douglass with his haunting, dark eyes; also Martin Luther King, Jr. in front of the Lincoln Memorial; Rosa Parks with her kind smile; and Mae Jemison, the first African-American woman astronaut, who flew into space on the space shuttle.

My favorite was a photo of a lunch counter sit-in. Grace took my picture standing next to it. The tour guide, a woman with glowing dark skin and eyes rimmed with what Gram calls "character lines," described the scene. On February 1, 1960, four hopeful African-American college students, dressed in suits and ties, sat down at a lunch counter in Greensboro, North Carolina, and politely asked for a cup of coffee. Here's the problem—the store said only white people were allowed to eat there.

I thought about my own sit-ins on the Borden blacktop, my legs refusing to move.

The tour guide's voice was deep and musical. "When the students were denied service, they refused to leave, sitting there for hours until the store closed," she said. "Over the next few days, they were joined by dozens of other people, who all sat peacefully while angry citizens cursed and threatened and spilled food on them."

I stared at the black-and-white photo. Three of the four young men stared back at me, all of them serious and maybe a little scared.

Stuart raised his hand. "Did they ever get their orders?"

The tour guide smiled. "Yes, after about five months of protests."

"Five months for a dumb cup of coffee?" Lilly said. "What for? Hashtag pointless."

Ana helped me type, and Ms. Beckett signaled the tour guide that I had something to say.

THEY WANTED TO BE INCLUDED IN SOCIETY. PEOPLE LIKE ME STILL FIGHT FOR THAT.

Lilly rolled her eyes.

"You are so right, young lady," the tour guide said. "Everyone deserves a seat at the table."

I smiled inside, thinking of our welcome table in the cafeteria.

When the tour ended, we walked through a beautiful park with gushing fountains and a pond filled with blooming lily pads and giant fish called koi. I knelt down to feed them a crust of bread from my sandwich.

"Don't get too close, Charity," Ana said. "It's a little chilly for swimming."

"I'll help her out."

I turned to see Stuart. Ever since we became science lab partners, he has been very patient when including me in assignments, giving me extra time to type my comments. He did not try to finish lab assignments as fast as possible, like other kids in the class. I could sense that he really enjoyed observing and learning, just like I did.

Stuart knelt beside me. "Did you know that koi can grow up to three feet long?" We watched as a white-and-orange-spotted fish reached its lips out of the water to suck up my bread.

"In Japan, people believe that koi bring good luck and wealth," Stuart said.

Stuart loved animal facts like me? I sat back on the grass and breathed in happiness.

He pulled a package of sour gummy fish from his pocket and held it out to me. "Have one. I remember you like these."

He chuckled.

"This is the first time I've talked to you without your aide listening in."

We sat quietly for a few seconds, watching kids take selfies in front of the pond.

"Anyhow . . . I wanted to tell you that I really like being with you, you know, here and in class. I mean, the things you say, your ideas, they're not what normal people would say."

He shook his head and ran a hand through his sandy hair.

"No, I'm sorry. I didn't mean to say you're not normal. Or maybe yeah, you aren't normal . . . but in a good way."

I stared at the water, blinking about a hundred times a minute. I wished I could type something to him, but I was glad Ana was not there listening.

"Anyhow . . . I wanted you to know."

I peeked over at him. Without thinking, my hand grabbed his.

Chances of him pulling his hand away . . . pulling his hand away . . .

He did not pull it away. We sat in the cool grass holding hands and watching koi until the big yellow bus blew its horn to signal it was time to leave.

Grace sat next to me again on the bus and gave my arm a squeeze. "Nice going, Charity," she whispered. "Stu is a sweetheart. I took a picture of you two. I can print it out for you if you want."

I smiled inside. This is what it felt like to be included. I never wanted this feeling to end.

When I got home from school, Mom brought over the keyboard to hear about my day.

"Was the field trip fun? What was your favorite part?"

She supported my arm to type.

I FELT PITY-FREE TODAY.

Mom nodded and put her hand on her mouth like she might cry.

Mom's ringing phone jolted us both. It was Mason. She put him on speaker.

"Hi, Mason. How are you and your mom, honey?"

"Uh . . . hi, Aunt Gail. Is Charity there with you?"

"Yes, of course. She's right here."

Something in his voice told me he was not calling with happy news. And I was royally right. Apparently, the gossip app was buzzing again. Mason explained to Mom how to pull up the site on my iPad so we could see.

Sassygirl72 had posted pictures of me on the field trip—one with me drooling on the bus and one of me standing next to a photograph at the museum—the lunch-counter photograph—my lips pressed into a duck face. The captions read, "First-class embarrassment!!!" and "Is this the way we want Lincoln represented???"

I felt the knife plunge into my back.

Grace is Sassygirl?

It was more painful than anything I experienced at Borden. Why was I so stupid to think she was my friend?

Mom's eyes were shiny. Her voice screeched. "I don't understand. Who would betray you like this?"

Pity poured back into my heart and filled it with hopelessness.

Principal Pointless

My logical brain could add 2 + 2. Based on glaring evidence, Grace posted those photos. Grace was Sassygirl, probably scheming with Darcy this whole time.

My bulldog impulse wanted me to crawl into a hole.

"You want some OJ with your eggs, Cherry Girl?" Dad could not disguise his sad voice. Mom had told him all about it.

Mom and Dad sat silently for a few minutes. No one had an appetite for Dad's sunrise scramble.

"I made an appointment with Mr. Jergen today," Mom announced.

I looked at her with big eyes. I wanted to scream.

I told you NOT to.

"I'm going to tell him you're being bullied online. Mason agreed to come with us." She wiped the corner of her eye with a napkin.

This is pointless. Jergen will not care about teenage gossip.

"Remember all you've accomplished, Cherry." Dad stroked my French braid and then tickled my ear with it.

I was not in a laughing mood.

"This nonsense doesn't diminish any of your achievements." Dad sighed. "I know it stinks, princess. I wish I could take away the pain."

An hour later, there we were, sitting in Jergen's office. I was not the only one fidgeting. Mason, Mom, and I all nervously tapped fingers and feet waiting for him to arrive.

I noted Mason's sweaty forehead, as if he had jogged a mile to get there.

I nudged Mom so I could type a message to Mason.

SORRY FOR GETTING YOU SENT TO THE PRINCIPAL.

Mason shrugged. "I'm neck-deep as it is. Might as well dive all the way in."

A memory replayed in my mind. Mason and me, four years old, swimming with floaties in our backyard pool.

YOU ARE NOT KEEPING YOUR HEAD LOW ANYMORE.

He laughed. "Yeah, well, I have a new motto—do what's right. You're the one who taught me that, Cuz." He looked at Mom. "Any idea who took the pictures?"

"Yes, Charity says it was Grace. How she could turn on Charity like this, I just don't understand."

"Well, wait a sec," Mason said. "Grace might still be innocent."

What?

I pounded on the desk.

"How could that be?" asked Mom.

"Well, she could've posted them online. At that point, Sassygirl could've snagged them."

Oh my gosh. Why did I not think of that?

I prayed he was right.

"Are we in trouble?"

I jumped seeing Grace at the door. Literally—I jumped out of my chair.

Mom helped me sit back down.

"Hello, Grace, dear," Mom said. "Have a seat, and Mason can fill you in on the situation."

"Well, to start," Mason said, "I guess we were wondering if you posted any of your pictures from the field trip on social media."

"Heck no. I hate those sites."

Mom and Mason looked at each other.

"Soooo, no one had access to your photos?" he asked.

"No." She paused. "Well, except for . . . I don't have a ton of space on my phone, so I uploaded a bunch of my photos to the online yearbook album after school. I'm on the committee. I figured we'd include a few of them in this year's issue."

I breathed out relief.

"Good to know," Mason said, nodding at me. "And . . . out of curiosity, is Darcy Warner on the yearbook committee?"

"Yeah. Why do you ask? What's going on?"

I watched Grace's expression as Mason showed her the posts about me. Her face filled with disgust.

"This is totally sickening! You don't think Darcy is Sassygirl, do you?"

Mom helped me speak out.

SHE HAS NEVER LIKED ME.

"Well . . . I won't deny that. But honestly, this is not

something she would do. I've known her a long time, and . . ." Grace shook her head. "There's just no way . . ."

WHO THEN?

Grace bit her lip.

"Sorry to keep you waiting." Mr. Jergen looked more stressed than usual. "I received your email, Mrs. Wood. Can you show me evidence of this cyber-bullying?"

He scanned the posts on Mason's phone.

"This is indeed disturbing. Any idea who might be behind it?"

Grace looked down.

"We have no evidence," Mom said. "Mason tells us that users are anonymous. Impossible to track."

Mr. Jergen shifted in his chair and then looked me in the eye. "Miss Wood, I am very sorry you have had to endure this treatment. I am frankly shocked that any of our students would stoop so low. The sad reality is that unless we have proof that this bullying was committed on school grounds, it is out of our jurisdiction."

Mom's voice got squeaky again. "Are you *serious*? There's nothing you can do?"

Jergen shook his head. "Unless you find more evidence, my hands are tied."

He shooed us out of his office with a "Have a good day," and Grace walked away without a word.

I wanted so bad to tell Mom *I TOLD you so*, but I did not want to rub it in. She already looked like a kid whose dog just got flattened by a bus.

Voice Thief

Back in the EPIC room, Celia led me into her office and sat me down. "Your mom told me the bad news. I am so sorry about what has happened to you, *querida*. How are you feeling today?"

How was I supposed to answer her with no keyboard?

I peeked through her office windows to see if Ana was in the classroom.

"I am afraid Ana is not here today." She paused and cupped my hand in hers. "Actually, Ana will not be back for several weeks, maybe longer. She has flown to France to be with her grandmother, who is very ill. Her grandmother raised her, and Ana had to go care for her."

My arms started shaking. My body rocked back and forth, back and forth.

"She felt miserable to leave you so suddenly, *querida*. She said to tell you that you are strong and that she has faith in you."

My legs jiggled apart-together as if they were on fire.

Apart-together-apart-together-apart-together.

Translation: I have no voice anymore.

Faster.

Apartogetherapartogetherapartogetherapartogether

No Ana = no voice.

My body rocked backandforthbackandforthbackandforth.

Celia moved her chair closer and squeezed my shoulders rhythmically like Ana did.

"No, *querida*, there is no need for you to worry. No, no, no. I have called human resources. They are sending a communication aide to work with you. I have requested someone trained to support your typing. She should be here any minute," Celia checked her watch. "She must be running a little late. But she will support you in all your classes. I am sure it will be fine."

Fine? How could this be fine? This is 100 percent the opposite of FINE!

Did Celia forget that my typing facilitator not only supported my arm, she had to support my spirit, my emotions? She had to encourage me to keep going. More than anything, she needed to be someone I *trusted*.

My fist pounded on Celia's desk.

Bang, bang, bang, bang, bang.

"What would Ana tell you? Take a deep breath. Breathe in peace. Let go of the bad feelings."

It only works when Ana says it.

"Knock-knock, sorry to interrupt."

A young woman with long, blonde hair and a gold nose ring appeared in the doorway. She had on a grape-colored top that showed her belly and faded jeans—the expensive kind that are torn on purpose.

"I'm Ivy. Is this Charity?"

She reached out her hand, a couple of rings on her thumb . . . and then pulled her hand away.

"Oh, sorry, autistic kids don't shake hands, do they?"

Celia opened her mouth, but no words came out.

"I'm the sub? I'm gonna facilitate for Charity?"

Why do her sentences sound like questions?

Celia asked me to step out so that she could fill Ivy in on my schedule. She would probably inform her about a few other things too—the school dress code for one. And not calling me an autistic kid when I am sitting *right there*.

After their meeting, Ivy sat down with me to practice typing. She knew the technique a little, but my fingers were not always making it to the right keys. And she was not asking, "Is that the letter you want?" like Ana always did.

After practicing for a few minutes, Celia said, "Math class has already started. Why don't you go, and I will check in with you ladies at lunch."

When we walked into class, kids were working in groups. Everyone stopped and eyed Ivy.

"Hey gang, s'up?" Ivy waved to the class.

Jazmine's eyes popped out of her head. I could only imagine the comments she would let fly at the lunch table.

Ivy gave a few high fives to some of girls who apparently dug her "super-glam jeans."

Mr. Byrd pointed to a group we could join. "Young Jedi Charity, I'm sure your friends could use your assistance."

Stuart smiled. "Hi, Charity. We're working on this problem." He showed me the handout. Rachel and Lilly were also in our group.

Amy bought Sweater A on sale for 30 percent off the original price and Sweater B, which was 25 percent cheaper than the discounted price of Sweater A. She is using a credit card that gives her an additional 5 percent off her entire purchase. If the original price of Sweater A was $93, what was her final cost?

"Whoa, talk about overpriced sweaters," Ivy said. "Is she shopping at Abercrombie for that?"

Lilly and Rachel laughed.

Stu ignored the comment and continued to scribble numbers on scratch paper.

"Hey, I think I remember how to do this," Ivy said. "Don't you like minus the 30 from the 93 or something?"

Stu raised an eyebrow and shook his head at me as if to say, "Poor you."

The girls loved Ivy, though. Rachel asked her where she shopped, and they got into an intense discussion about whether skinny jeans were "totally over."

I sat there feeling useless as Stu scribbled out a few sample equations. Finally, he spoke up to Ivy, "Um, can you help Charity join the discussion?"

I owed him big time.

"Oh, yeah. Oops! I need to help you type, don't I?"

Ivy sat at a weird angle and grabbed my wrist. A lot of my letters were misfires. She kept forgetting to ask if that was the letter I wanted, so my sentence came out as

GGURSTMULTOLPYTHHE OTIFONAL PEICE BY ,330.

I was trying to say "First, multiply the original price by .3," but it was so far off, no one had any clue what I meant.

Rachel giggled. "Sorry, Charity, we don't speak Chinese."

Lilly rolled her eyes. "Hashtag confuzzled."

Ivy giggled. "Uh, Charity, maybe we should try that again? That was a lot of no comprendo nonsense."

What's the use?

I turned my body away and pointed to my puzzle. She turned to the rest of the group.

"Sorry gang, Charity's taking a time-out to play with her puzzle."

Time-out? Play with my puzzle? Where does she think I am, in kindergarten?

I tried hard to focus on the puzzle and keep my body under control as I listened to Ivy chat with Rachel and Lilly for the next twenty minutes about celebrity gossip. When class was over, a few more people high-fived Ivy and told me I was lucky to have such a fun aide.

Right. Lucky me.

"Ready for lunch, girlfriend?" Ivy asked. "I'm actually craving some gross cafeteria food. Maybe they'll have those little Jell-O bowls with canned grapes in it," she said, laughing.

She grabbed my backpack and walked out the door without me at first, then turned around. "Oops, almost forgot my sidekick."

After loading a cafeteria tray with food—not even asking me what I wanted—Ivy plunked the tray onto an empty cafeteria table and pulled out her phone. I looked over at my friends. Jaz shook her head. Julian motioned for me to come over to the welcome table.

As Jaz would say, Ivy was clueless as a jock at a comic book convention.

Celia found us a few minutes later and sat down.

"How are we doing, ladies?"

How could I tell her if I had no one to help me type? I took one of Ana's cleansing breaths and stared at my beefaroni, which Ivy kept calling "barfaroni."

"We're great," Ivy said, putting down her phone. "It'll take a while for us to get our flow going. But we'll soon be BFFs. Don't worry."

Ivy went back to checking her phone.

"Ivy, dear," Celia said, "unless you have an urgent call to make, you shouldn't be on your phone during school hours. It sets a bad example for the students. And your focus should be on Charity."

"Oh!" She sounded surprised. As if she were allowed to text friends all day at her previous jobs. Did she even have any previous jobs? She stuck her phone in her back pocket.

"It's cool. We're cool."

She glanced at my tray.

"Done with the barfaroni? Don't blame you, girlfriend."

She picked up my tray, but Celia put her hand on Ivy's arm.

"Ivy, dear, you need to actually *ask* Charity. That is what the keyboard is for. Don't assume you know what she is thinking."

"Oh yeah. Here, girl. All done with lunch?" She sat down and got in position to help me type.

I typed "Y."

"What do you mean why? It's almost time for science. Gotta eat quick and go, girl."

"The Y stands for yes," Celia said. A big sigh escaped her lips.

"Oh, right. That's what I mean about flow. We'll get there. Let's get rid of these trays and get your booty to class."

When Ivy left with the tray, Celia leaned in and whispered, "I will find you another aide, *querida. Pronto!*"

The next day, Celia said a new communication aide could not start until the following week. "Maybe we could ask your mother to help you communicate at school while we wait."

That was the last thing I wanted. Mom already caused enough trouble for the week.

I did not complain. I figured a bad helper was better than none at all. At least sometimes I got a sort-of readable sentence out.

One advantage—I was getting a taste of how it felt to be popular. Every time we walked into a classroom, kids came up to us and gabbed with Ivy about school gossip or fashion or music.

For an adult, she fit in pretty well with the junior high crowd, with her "Up top" high fives and *girlfriend* this, *girlfriend* that.

She was gabbing with the girls that afternoon in science lab while I sat staring at a snakeskin, trying to identify the species by its markings.

Darcy walked up to us. She glared at me for a second then turned to Ivy. "How come ever since Ana left, Charity basically speaks gobbledygook?"

"Huh?" Ivy had no idea what she meant. But I could hypothesize where Darcy was headed. Ripples of fear shot up my spine.

"Well, a few of us have noticed that without her aide, Charity isn't such a brainiac anymore. She's back to being, how shall I say it . . . STU-PI-DO."

She said that last word slowly, as if she were talking to someone who was hard of hearing.

My breathing sped up. My body shook.

"Get out of here, Darcy." Stuart jumped to my defense. "You're jealous she gets better grades than you."

"Well, think about it, Stuart," she said, pointing in his face. "This girl has not said one smart thing since Ana left. It was Ana's words that made her look smart. It was probably a scheme so they could get more money for all the retarded students and give them the privileges that we're supposed to have so that everyone in town could be all like *Aren't we so great, even our dumb kids are really smart!*"

Darcy spoke fast, getting louder with every word. Stuart looked confused. His head turned between me and Ivy.

"Hey, hey, hey, Missy," Ivy said. "Don't go trashing my girlfriend here. We're still working on our flow. We're getting better and better. Let's show them, girlfriend. What do you have to say?"

She whipped out the keyboard, but I was too agitated to type. My hands flapped, my feet tapped.

Flap-tap-flap-tap-flap-tap-flap-tap.

Ivy grabbed my wrist. I pulled it away.

I wanted to scream. *Stop!*

She grabbed it again and held on tight.

Stop! Do not do this!

Ivy was using my finger to type her own message. I tried to pull away. I did not even want to look at the words on the screen. I turned my head, hoping Mr. Harding would see the panic in my eyes.

Help me!

Finally, Ivy let go. "Here's what my girl had to say to you, Miss Thing. She typed, 'Go to hell, you loser in cheap jeans.'"

Ivy laughed and nodded at me. "Yeah, girl. Tell it like it is."

Ivy spoke loud enough for the whole class to hear, including Mr. Harding. Everyone stared in silence.

"Charity!" Mr. Harding said. "Go to the principal's office immediately and discuss this inappropriate language with him. I expect better from you."

Ivy rolled her eyes and grabbed my hand to lead me out the door.

Darcy roared, half laughing, half yelling. "Did everyone see that? She wasn't even looking at the keyboard. Those weren't her words. She was never the one typing anything. It's all a big fake-out!"

A few minutes later, I sat in Jergen's office, Celia and Ivy arguing with each other. Mr. Jergen held up his hands. "One person at a time. Tell me what's going on here."

Ivy jumped in first. "My girl Charity had a few choice

words for that uppity witch who dissed her in front of everyone. Girlfriend has a right to speak her mind."

"And what were those words?" asked Jergen.

Ivy hesitated and then pressed the speak button on the iPad. The insult sounded worse read in a robot voice.

Celia jumped in. "I don't understand. That is *not* something Charity would say. She has never said anything like this before."

Jergen frowned. "Do not make excuses for your students, Ms. Diaz. Charity must accept responsibility for her mistakes."

"But first we need to let Charity tell us what happened," Celia said. "Let her defend herself."

"Sure thing." Ivy sat next to me.

My arms started to shake again. What would she make me say now? In front of Jergen?

"Wait a minute," Celia said. "Just give me two minutes."

Celia flew out the door and returned two minutes and thirty seconds later. With Mason.

"Charity's cousin has been working with Ana to help Charity type. I think in this case it would be best if he supports Charity."

She turned to Mason. "Do you think you can do it?"

Mason took a deep breath. "I can give it a try if Charity is up for it."

Mason sat next to me and held my elbow. Celia sat on the other side with her hand on my back.

"Ready?" Mason asked.

We typed slowly for about five minutes. Just as Ana had taught him, he asked, "Is that the letter you want? . . . Keep

going . . . Eyes on the keyboard . . . Here's what you have so far
. . . What's next?" Then he read my words. *My words.*

IVY STOLE MY VOICE. I WOULD NEVER WASTE PRECIOUS
WORDS TO FLING TRASH AT UNKIND PEOPLE. IT GOES AGAINST MY
MISSION.

Ivy crossed her arms.

"Whatever. I may have thrown in a few burns, but I knew
that's what my girl wanted to say if she could. I mean, how
do you expect an autistic kid to make it in school if they don't
stand up to jerks calling them names?"

I lifted my hand, and Mason supported me to type more.

DO NOT CALL ME YOUR GIRL. AND PLEASE STAY AWAY FROM
KIDS LIKE ME. YOU BULLY US BY STEALING OUR VOICE.

"Well," Mr. Jergen said, "It seems that she can stand up for
herself just fine."

Ivy was fired from the district that afternoon.

•••

I was not in the mood for a basketball game that evening,
but Dad insisted. "C'mon, Cherry. Your team needs you. You
can't let 'em down."

I dragged myself upstairs to pull on the bright yellow
Hornets jersey. What a miserable day.

One thing I knew for sure—as much as I wanted to, I
never died of embarrassment. So far.

On the court, I noted other girls staring as we did a few
warm-up drills. Then Coach pulled me aside to watch the girls

form for free throws. Dad helped me type so I could give a few tips to Grace and Ella.

Mrs. Bling-Bling paced on the sidelines, sneering in my direction like a tiger ready to pounce.

"You're up, Darcy," Coach said.

"Um, I don't think so." The other girls stopped chatting and looked at Coach. He did not put up with backtalk.

"Listen, girls," he said, "Mr. Wood filled me in on what happened at school today, and he told me that Charity's aide typed words on her behalf. That incident has been settled."

"Yeah, okay, but how do you know that Charity is actually typing now?"

"Give it a rest, Darcy," Grace said.

"Charity can speak for herself," Dad said, and he held the keyboard for me to type. But my arms were quivering, and I pulled away from Dad.

Darcy glared at Dad. "No offense, Mr. Wood, but Coach said you used to be some big-shot basketball star back in the day. You could be using her to type your own words, and, no offense, but it's kind of pathetic to manipulate your daughter to make her look like she's a pro."

Darcy was fearless now.

Coach was not taking it. "You wanna be benched for the entire game, Darcy?"

"Why? For stating the obvious? The other girls agree with me, am I right?"

Darcy turned to the team for support. Most of the girls gazed down at the floor.

The damage Ivy did might never be reversed. She was still stealing my voice.

Coach George clenched his teeth. "On the bench, young lady."

That's when Mrs. Bling-Bling pounced. "How dare you speak to my daughter that way! You should be more concerned about your job, Coach, than about defending a questionable student." She hissed those last words and narrowed her eyes at me. Then she put her arm around her daughter. "Come on, sweet pea. We can discuss this matter with Mr. Jergen."

They both strutted out of the gym.

Dad made me stay for the game, but I told him I could not play or coach the girls. My body wiggled and jiggled and shuffled on the bench. At halftime, when Dad saw I was about to burst, he took me home.

Coach George called to apologize and also deliver the news that we won 42–36.

All I could see in my mind was Darcy spreading seeds of doubt.

I felt like Pinocchio turning back into wood.

Attack of the
Purple Elephants

Mom insisted on helping me type at school until Ana returned. I felt relieved, but also a little queasy at the thought of my mom following me to all my classes.

In English class, Ms. Beckett explained how to do research by finding articles in the library database. Mom was not really comfortable with computers, so she asked a ton of questions.

She kept saying, "I'm sure Charity understands this, but for my own clarity . . ."

Every time she said this, I heard snickers behind me. Of course, Darcy and friends were probably saying that Mom did the homework for me.

It got worse when Ms. Beckett talked about plagiarism.

"Who can tell me what plagiarism is?" she asked.

"Ask Charity," Lilly whispered loud enough for me to hear. "Hashtag faker."

"Plagiarism is using other people's words or ideas as your own," Grace said. She shot an annoyed look at Lilly.

"And does everyone know what our school handbook

says about the consequences for committing plagiarism?" Ms. Beckett asked.

Darcy raised her hand. "It says you will get expelled. Kicked to the curb. Tossed out with the trash. Jettisoned with the junk." She turned toward me with an evil grin.

"Admirable alliteration, Darcy, but that will be enough," Ms. Beckett said.

I held up my hand to the keyboard and Mom helped me. When I was done, Mom raised her hand. "Charity would like to add a comment."

"Go ahead, Charity."

THE OPPORTUNITY TO SPEAK IS PRECIOUS TO ALL. I WANT TO DO MY RESEARCH ON THOSE WITH NO VOICE.

"That's a great topic," Ms. Beckett said. "There have been so many groups throughout our history who had to fight to make their voices heard: women seeking the vote, African Americans, Native Americans . . . which group did you have in mind?"

CHILDREN. THEY HAVE NO POWER IN THE WORLD, ESPECIALLY IF THEY ARE DIFFERENT AND IF THEY CANNOT COMMUNICATE LIKE OTHERS.

"You're right, Charity. Children are the most vulnerable members of our society. They need strong advocates. I look forward to reading your research paper."

Ms. Beckett went around the classroom reviewing everyone's topics. When she skimmed my outline, she whistled. "Charity, you're proposing a genuine investigative report. Are you sure you're up for this?"

Mom steadied me at the keyboard as I typed.

YES. IT IS TIME.

"Well, keep me posted on your progress."

I had the sickening feeling that my days at Lincoln might be coming to an end. I had one last shot to help Isabella.

After class, Mom asked Ms. Beckett more questions while I finished my puzzle.

That's when Darcy breezed by and whispered, "If you really are the one typing, then how about this, genius. Say . . . purple elephants. Yeah, the next time you type in class, type *purple elephants*. Then I'll know you're really the one talking."

I did not want to follow Darcy's order. But then I thought if I could show her that it *was* me talking, she'd back off.

The next class was science. Mr. Harding lectured on plant cells while Mom scribbled notes a mile a minute. My heartbeat raced at the same speed as I tried to decide.

Should I?

My feet tapped the floor.

Tap-tap-tap-tap-tap-tap.

I do not need to prove anything to her.

Tap-tap-tap-tap-tap-tap.

Page 62: Elephants have the largest brain of any animal.

They are definitely not purple, though.

"Does anyone have any questions?" Mr. Harding asked. He turned to me. "Charity, do you have any insights on our discussion?"

I took a deep inhale, and Mom helped me as I typed, letter by painful letter, Darcy's silly words. I saw Darcy smiling at me from across the room with hope in her eyes. Maybe this would finally convince her I was real.

Mom looked at the screen and shook her head. "Is that what you meant to say?" she whispered.

I typed "Y."

"You want to say this to the class?"

Y

"Go ahead," Mr. Harding said.

"Well, Charity would like to say . . . I mean, I'm not sure what it means . . ."

"Mrs. Wood, your daughter often makes comments that challenge us to ponder the topic from a new angle." He smiled and nodded at me. "Please share her thoughts."

Oh no! Do not do it, Mom!

I buried my face in my hands.

Mom cleared her throat. "Purple elephants."

The class burst out laughing. Even Stuart.

"Is this some kind of joke, Mrs. Wood?" Harding asked in his *I-mean-business* voice.

Mom supported my arm to type more, but I pulled away.

I glared across the room. Darcy was laughing so hard she could hardly catch her breath. "Must have hit a few wrong keys there, Mrs. Wood," she gloated.

How stupid I was.

She tricked me. She only wanted to embarrass me.

Slam dunk.

Breadcrumbs of Truth

If I wanted to save Isabella, I had to expose Borden, so I made that the topic of my research paper. I told Ms. Beckett I would interview parents and collect evidence of kids being abused. The superintendent had my one complaint, but there must be other evidence out there of Borden's abuses. How to find it?

After school, Mom and I searched for complaints against Borden posted online. Every search came up empty. Every breadcrumb of a clue had been gobbled up by some hungry pigeon.

Finally, one crumb turned up on a business review website.

Only one?

Mom read it: "My daughter attended Borden Academy for two years. At the end of this period, she was despondent and depressed. Because she was nonverbal, she could not report any abuse, but she regularly came home with bruises on her arms. We finally removed her from the school. Our precious daughter suffered there."

Sounds like the work of Miss Marcia.

The review had a name: Veronica C.

"It was written two years ago. You probably knew this girl, Charity."

I searched my memory for another girl who could not talk. My mind flashed to an older girl named Abby Collins, probably about fourteen. She left Borden soon after I got there. I typed what I remembered.

SHE WAS USUALLY SILENT AND STILL. BUT A FEW TIMES A WEEK SHE BURST INTO RAGES. MISS MARCIA WOULD GRAB HER ARM AND DRAG HER TO THE TIME-OUT CLOSET. WHEN SHE LEFT, I GOT SENT THERE MORE OFTEN. MISS MARCIA DID NOT LET IT STAY EMPTY FOR LONG . . .

I could not type anymore. Mom put the keyboard down and held me. "I'm so sorry, sweetheart. Are you sure you want to continue with this project?"

I HAVE TO SAVE THE KIDS.

"Okay. Nothing left to do then but phone every Collins in the phone book."

Mom put the phone on speaker so I could hear and began dialing.

"Sorry to bother you, but did you have a daughter who went to Borden Academy?"

"Wrong number."

Click.

"Leave a message after the beep."

Click.

Click.

Eight people hung up on her.

Finally, one did not.

"Who is this?" a woman demanded.

"Mrs. Collins, my daughter Charity attended Borden Academy with your daughter Abby."

Silence on the other end of the line.

"Charity is investigating Borden Academy in order to end abuses there, maybe shut them down. She would like to interview you about your experience."

Click.

She hung up.

My one lead. Gone in an instant.

"I'm sorry, sweetheart," Mom said. "It must be unbearable for Mrs. Collins to relive those memories."

Hypothesis: This will be the shortest paper in history.

Brrrrrrrrrrrrring!

We both jumped.

A small voice spoke. "I'm sorry. I will try to help you. Where do you want to meet?"

•••

The next day after school, we went to Mrs. Collins' house. She was a round woman with a face wrinkled like a tortoise.

Mom introduced me. "This is my daughter, Charity."

I was surprised when Mrs. Collins gave me a hug.

"I didn't know any of Abby's classmates. I'm so happy to meet you, Charity."

When I did not reply, she turned to Mom. "My Abby wasn't able to talk either. I think these children are the most helpless. Anyone could do anything to them. A million and one hurts were done to my Abby until her gentle soul exploded in fear and anger."

Mrs. Collins took my hand and led us to the kitchen table. The chair had a red, plastic cushion ripped on the side. The plastic poked my leg when I sat down. She held up a bowl of mint candies. My hand wanted to reach for one, but the smell reminded me of Miss Marcia.

Mom pulled out the keyboard. With each word I typed, Mrs. Collins frowned harder.

I COULD FEEL ABBY'S STRUGGLE. I AM SORRY I COULD NOT HELP HER. I WANT TO HELP NOW BY SAVING OTHER KIDS.

"Amazing." Mrs. Collins ran her hands along the keyboard. "I tried typing with Abby so many times, but she couldn't do it."

PEOPLE LIKE ME NEED HELP TO TYPE. I CAN BE A VOICE FOR KIDS LIKE ABBY.

"But maybe she could have." Mrs. Collins put her hands over her eyes.

"How is Abby doing now that she's left Borden?" Mom asked with a hopeful smile.

Mrs. Collins held her head in her hands. She spoke in a crackly voice. "You have no idea how difficult it was. She couldn't control herself. Every outburst was more destructive than the last. I had no way to communicate with her, and I didn't know how to help her. I was terrified she would hurt herself or someone else."

She turned to Mom. "My husband and I divorced a decade ago. I had no one to support me."

She blew into a tissue then spoke in a quiet voice. "Abby is living at the Pine Valley Developmental Center. I pray so hard every day she is being treated well, but when I visit, she doesn't even seem to know I'm there."

Mom hugged Mrs. Collins a long time. After a few minutes, she was ready to answer the questions I prepared, and we recorded her answers. In two years at Borden, Abby transformed from gentle and cooperative to explosive and full of rage.

"I think she was depressed," Mrs. Collins said, "but the doctors would never call it that."

Mom helped me respond.

I FELT THE SAME WHEN I WAS THERE. THE THINKERS DO NOT BELIEVE WE ARE REAL PEOPLE WITH REAL HUMAN EMOTIONS.

"I keep wondering if I had had the courage to pull her out of there sooner, things would be different today."

Mom put a hand on Mrs. Collins' shoulder. "Based on what Charity has told us, we now know this was an abusive environment. I couldn't believe it myself. We kept Charity so well protected, so safe in every other aspect of her life, and here she was being mistreated by people we trusted to educate her."

Before we left, Mrs. Collins named two more parents she remembered. Their children also came home from Borden with bruises on their wrists or backs or faces. Over the next week, I spent hours interviewing them with Mom's help.

With the essay due in a week, we stayed up until midnight every night, typing letter by letter all I discovered. Typing and revising, typing and revising.

One.

Letter.

At.

A.

Reach, tap—T. Reach, tap—I. Reach, tap—M. Reach, tap—E.

"Keep your rhythm going." Mom supported not only my arm but also my jittery mind.

Reach. Tap.

"Is that the letter you want?"

Typing one letter at a time is S—L—O—W. A drowsy sloth might move faster. No one could hypothesize how much energy I used keeping my body in check and my racing mind focused on the next key.

Reach. Tap.

"Do you want punctuation here?"

Reach. Tap.

"Eyes on the keyboard."

Waiting for my thoughts to form drop by drop on the screen must be like watching paint dry on a humid day for Mom.

Patient as a monk on a mountaintop, Mom encouraged me with each tap, never judging.

Did it sound improbable for a thirteen-year-old to say she was on a mission? How could I say that without sounding like I was full of baloney, as Pops says?

After three days of typing, I told Mom,

DELETE EVERYTHING. I HAVE TO START AGAIN.

She did it, no questions asked.

I needed to get the words royally right. People's lives depended on it.

Then on Monday, I handed my report to Ms. Beckett.

She found me in math class later that day.

"Charity, I have a friend who is a journalist for the *Bay Tribune*. She covers articles on education. Would you mind if I mailed her your paper? She may want to investigate this further."

I was too excited to type. My body jumped and clapped.

"I think that means yes," Mom said.

Sounds like Torture

"You gonna finish your pizza?"

Mason held my arm and I typed:

GO FOR IT.

He reached over to grab my second slice. I was not feeling hungry these days. Sassygirl was on fire in the gossip app, accusing me of cheating on assignments. Kids looked at me differently now in class. No one asked me math questions anymore.

One bright spot in my day was usually the welcome table at lunch, which now included Grace and Stuart. But today, even there I felt alone.

I watched Stuart help Grace with a math problem and listened to her tease him about his taste in music.

Does he like her? Of course. Why wouldn't he?

My brain flashed to the field trip. We held hands for thirteen minutes. Was it a dream? Was he just too polite to pull away?

Fact: No boy would want to hang out with me.

The cafeteria was strung with turquoise and lavender streamers for the "Boogie Fever" spring dance. Jaz was already in complaint mode.

"Can you believe the money they blow on these stupid dances? I mean, do they really need a giant mirror ball in the middle of the cafeteria? Didn't they get the memo that disco is dead?"

Grace used her napkin to wipe a drop of sauce from Jazmine's check. "Lighten up, girl. I bet you can rock those disco moves in your turbo-powered chair."

Why did Grace have to be so sweet? She was making it tough for me to be annoyed with her.

"Everyone's going, right?" Grace asked.

Her question was answered with silence. Peter squinted at her as if she was kooky. Julian seemed to ponder the possibility.

Grace put her hands on her hips. "C'mon, guys. It's fun. You know what *fun* is, don't you?"

"I know what it is!" Skyler said, raising her hand.

Jaz rolled her eyes. "You're talking to the wrong crowd, Gracie. We would be clay pigeons for junior high target practice."

"Not if we all band together," Grace said, licking pizza sauce off her finger. "We can have a buddy system."

Oh no—who will she pick for her buddy?

"Peter, how about you be my buddy?" asked Grace.

I was floored, and so was Peter. His eyes got wide and he shook his head.

"No way! Fridays, I get to play Minecraft. I'm not wasting my game time on some stupid dance. No way!"

"O-kay." Grace scanned the table again.

Please do not say Stuart.

"Julian, you in?"

Julian typed a response, short and sweet and hit play. "In."

Grace smiled big. "Skyler, how about you?"

"I'll ask my mom and dad. Maybe they will let me come and dance." Skyler bounced up and down in her seat excitedly. She did not see the potential for disaster.

Mason was the next person to surprise everyone. "Jaz, I guess we should be buddies. I need someone to protect me from all those cheerleaders. I hear you're a pro at that."

The whole table burst out laughing.

The next few seconds of silence seemed to last hours. Peter slurped the last drops of chocolate milk through his straw. Stuart stared down at the table, chewing his pizza, not noticing Grace's burning stare. Finally, an elbow to his arm made him swallow hard and look at me. "Charity, I guess we could be buddies."

He did not sound too thrilled about it. I must have been delusional to think he had one nanogram of interest in me.

"Here, Charity, I got your voice here." Mason pulled out the keyboard so I could type.

SOUNDS LIKE FUN.

"Fun? Is that the word you wanted?" Mason asked. "Are you sure you don't mean torture? Sounds like torture? Yes, I think that's what Charity is trying to say."

Everyone laughed again.

"I think I'm with the right buddy," Jaz said.

"We'll stick together," Grace said. "Safety in numbers, you know—and have a blast dancing and being silly. Sound cool?"

Mason, who was now finishing *Jazmine's* second piece of pizza, mumbled, "As long as there's food, I'm ready to endure the torture."

He held up his hand for a fist bump and Jaz returned it.

What had Grace gotten us into?

Disco Drama Queen

"I think I got a case of boogie fever." Dad pointed his fingers in the air and shook his hips in the school hallway, determined to embarrass me before I set foot in my first-ever school dance.

I persuaded Mom to stay home because I thought that Dad would be a little cooler about the whole "first dance" thing.

I was wrong.

"C'mon, Cherry Girl. Let's get our feet moving in the right direction—I hear them playing our song."

I was not planning on moving yet. We had all agreed to meet at the gym entrance, and I did not want to go anywhere without the rest of the clay pigeons, as Jaz called us.

Jaz whizzed down the hall, wearing a tiara and blue sparkly shirt.

"Now there's someone with boogie fever," Dad said.

"Well, as a member of the Princess Court, I have a certain standard to uphold," Jaz said.

Dad gave her a high five.

Grace came next, wearing a shiny silver dress with white

boots that came up to her knee. "Right on, girls, you look fabulous. Jaz, you totally rock, and Charity, you're gorgeous."

I did not want to go overboard with the costume and make myself stand out any more than I normally do. I chose new jeans with violets painted all the way down the leg. Mom brushed my hair loose around my shoulders, and I picked out a purple headband. A little eye shadow and lip gloss, and I looked almost as cool as those girls in teen magazines.

"Get ready to get down," Grace said, bending her knees and moving her hips to the music booming inside the gym.

Within a few minutes our little group had assembled. Mason had slicked-back hair and was wearing star-shaped sunglasses. Julian wore a cool cowboy hat perched on his fuzzy afro.

Skyler, in a pretty tangerine party dress, sashayed down the hall with her dad, who was wearing his white navy uniform.

"You guys definitely win cutest couple," Grace said.

Her dad shook everyone's hand. "I never would have thought to take her, but when she said her friends wanted her to come . . ." He tapped his fist to his heart. "Well, we couldn't miss that, could we, honey?"

"Yes, we love to dance!" Skyler bounced, and her lacy dress floated up and down like a jellyfish.

We all stood there for what seemed like googolplex minutes waiting for the one missing person: Stuart.

Finally, Mason broke down. "I smell popcorn. Jaz, let's go check it out."

"Good idea," Grace said. "Let's all head in. I'm sure Stuart will be able to spot us. Who could miss Jazmine's electric shirt?"

The song "Dancing Queen" was blaring through the room, and the spinning mirror ball made the entire cafeteria twinkle like it was lit with diamonds. Dad hung out with Coach George to give me some space, but I only wanted to go home.

Grace tried to drag me onto the dance floor. I pulled my arm away and sat on a metal folding chair by the wall. The loud music vibrated through my body, but that was *not* why I was about to lose it. It's a strange fact that I can feel a lot lonelier in a crowd of people than sitting by myself in a room.

I stared down at the floor, and a plate of striped chocolate cookies appeared under my nose.

Mason sat down next to me. "Have one, Chare. Time to get your daily sugar requirement."

Jaz pulled up alongside. "You're the one who always says everyone should be included, and here you are being a wall-flower. What's up, girl?"

"I think she's waiting for Stuart." Grace came up out of breath. She and Julian had danced to the last three songs.

I felt everyone's eyes staring at me.

"Maybe he's not feeling well," Grace offered.

Translation: He is ashamed to be seen with me.

Dad came up with the keyboard. "Cherry, looks like you might wanna say something to your friends. Let me help you." I typed one word.

HOME.

"But we just got here, honey," Dad said. "Sure you don't want to hang out a few more minutes?"

My arm wanted to smack Mason's plate of cookies onto the floor to make my point, but I was stopped by a low voice.

"Uh, what's up, guys? Hi, Charity."

And there he was. Stuart . . . in an actual shirt and tie and combed hair, even.

Everyone patted him on the back, and Jaz teased him about his "lame costume."

"Okay, guys," Grace announced, as if she was our activity director, "everyone out on the dance floor."

Stuart swallowed hard. "I think I'll sit next to Charity for a minute. I'm not really in a dancing mood yet."

Everyone, including Dad, left us alone. Stuart ran his hand through his hair, messing it up so it looked more like normal. "Sorry I'm late, Charity. I actually never went to a dance before. I'm like the worst dancer in the world. I sure don't need one more thing for people to make fun of."

I could not believe it. How could he sit next to me and think that *he* was going to embarrass himself at the dance?

"You look great though," he muttered, his eyes glued to the floor.

I surprised myself by pulling him up and onto the dance floor. The song was "Boogie Fever," and my body started jumping to the rhythm. Stuart stood frozen for a minute. I guess everyone's body can get stuck sometimes.

Then Skyler took his hand and jumped to the beat with me. Jaz twirled her chair in circles and waved her hands. Stuart finally gave in, and our whole group was bouncing and spinning in the middle of the dance floor.

At that moment, I did not care if people cheered or jeered us. I finally realized it did not matter.

At a break in the music, we wandered over to the food table to grab some neon green lime punch. Grace dabbed my sweaty face with a napkin and said, "Let's go to the girls' room and brush our wild hair." I gladly followed, Jaz rolling behind.

In front of the mirror, Grace smeared some cherry lip gloss on me, and Jaz adjusted her crooked tiara. That's when I spotted Darcy behind us, smiling with her arms crossed as if she were sitting on the juiciest gossip in Hollywood.

Jaz spun around, ready for battle.

Grace looked at Darcy in the mirror and said, "How's it going, girl?"

"You all look so pretty tonight," Darcy said in a sugary voice. "So super you girls are having a final celebration before Charity gets kicked out."

"Cut the drama, Darcy," Grace said. "You never liked Charity, and honestly I think that's pretty disgusting."

Darcy raised her hand. "Don't even," she hissed. "That girl cheats on all her assignments. Probably planning to cheat her way to the top of the honor roll."

Darcy focused her squinty eyes on me. "What you don't know is that my mom got a copy of her research paper for English class and uploaded it to a website that checks for plagiarism. It's *full* of stolen sentences." She pointed her finger in Grace's face. "Plus, my dad got a statement from her so-called aide admitting she typed words for Charity. She is sooooo going to be expelled for this."

"Lay off, you cheerleader nightmare," Jaz yelled. "You give all us cheerleaders a bad name."

"Puh-leeze! Shaking your pom-poms with a dumb tiara on your head does *not* make you a cheerleader."

Jaz grabbed the punch from her cup holder and tossed it on Darcy's sparkly mini-dress.

"Eeeeew!" Darcy blotted the sticky mess with paper towels. "Stay away from me, you loser!" She half-smiled, half-grimaced in my direction and danced out the door to the sound of "Boogie Oogie."

Godzilla's Revenge

I knew we were in serious trouble when I saw Celia's face. "*Querida*, I don't know what to make of this. Tell us what this is."

She handed Mom and Dad a copy of my English paper with plagiarized sentences highlighted in yellow. For once, Dad seemed tense. His nervous knee bounced up and down.

Faces of passing students and teachers peeked at us through the window of Celia's office. Mom's panicky expression, along with the rumors Darcy had spread made this the gossip of the day.

"I know you have such a wonderful memory, *querida*. Is it possible that you quoted from other sources accidentally?"

I stared at the pages. It looked like my paper. Same title, same structure, lots of the same sentences. I read it quickly and blew out a puff of air. Mom helped me respond.

NO. NOT MY ESSAY. SOMEBODY ADDED WORDS.

"*Gracias a Dios*," Celia said, "but here's the problem. Ms. Beckett says she mailed your original paper to a reporter, but the reporter never received it. It was lost in transit somehow."

Dad grabbed the essay and stood up. "Lost, or stolen? Somebody obviously messed with Charity's words so they could accuse her of cheating. What maniac would do this?" He slapped the essay with the back of his hand. "Where did they get this copy?"

Skyler stood outside in the hallway, pressing her face to the office window. Her smushed nose fogged up the glass. Jaz pulled her away.

Celia frowned. "Jergen will not tell me who gave it to him or how he acquired it. Ms. Beckett mailed it from the school. All I can think is that someone in the office took it before it was sent out."

"Well, Charity, show them your copy of the paper on the computer." Mom spoke in her high panicky voice.

I thought for a minute. My accuser could say that I deleted the copied sentences.

Mom held up the keyboard. I was losing control with each letter.

MY WORD AGAINST THEIRS. THIS IS T . . .

I pushed away her arm.

We sat in silence for a few minutes.

"What's next?" Mom asked, blinking quickly.

"They have scheduled an investigation hearing for next week. The district superintendent will be there to hear evidence and make her decision."

Dad's voice lowered. "They couldn't expel her for this nonsense, could they?"

"If the committee determines this is not related to her

disability, then she is subject to the same disciplinary measures as any other student. We must prove our case."

Why do I always have to fight? First to come to Lincoln, now to stay? It is not fair. So many bullies bulldozing my path to peace. Not fair. Not fair. Not. Not. Not.

Celia and my parents talked for a while. My body rocked back and forth.

Rock-rock-rock-rock-rock-rock-rock-rock-rock.

Pity venom stung my entire body. The world zoned out. I was alone in the unfair universe.

Page 101: Vespa mandarinia . . .

A hand on my shoulder pulled me back to reality.

Mom tugged on my arm. "We'd better get you to math. You have your quiz today. Remember the formulas we reviewed at breakfast?"

I wanted to scream.

Have you lost your mind? What part of expelled *don't you understand?*

I pulled away. She tried again. I buried my face in my hands.

Page 101: Vespa mandarinia . . . the Asian giant hornet . . .

"I know how frustrated you must feel." Dad put his arm around me. "But our fight isn't over. The best thing to do is continue as usual." He knelt down. "Don't let the turkeys get you down, Cherry Girl."

Rock-rock-rock-rock-rock-rock-rock-rock-rock.

Mom held up the keyboard for me to type.

My mind was dark.

My heart was hard.

My soul was shattered.

> Page 101: Vespa mandarinia . . . the Asian giant
> hornet . . . as large as a human thumb . . .

Rock-rock-rock-rock-rock-rock-rock-rock-rock.
I felt numb. Hopeless.
I was . . . a nonperson. Just like everyone thought.
I did not exist anymore.

> Page 101: Vespa mandarinia . . . the Asian
> giant hornet . . . as large as a human thumb . . .
> can massacre a colony of bees, ripping their
> heads off . . . twenty heads per minute . . .

Rock-rock-rock-rock-rock-rock-rock-rock-rock.
A drumbeat inside my chest hammered louder and louder
as adults kept chattering at me.

> Their stings release a massive amount of
> venom . . . breaking down flesh . . . like
> being stabbed with a searing-hot . . .

Air moved in and out of my lungs until a chokehold slowly
gripped my throat, squeezing lightly at first and then increas-
ing pressure on my neck, until my breath strained and a dust
storm of fear gathered in my belly. Each breath became harder.

> Like being stabbed with a searing-hot sword.

Three sets of panicked eyes crowded around my face, urg-
ing me with words I could not understand. The storm in my
gut became a hurricane. With no warning . . . no countdown,
my body exploded in full fury.
Worse than a KETTLE EXPLOSION.
Diagnosis: Hurricane Charity.
Throat screaming. Arms thrashing.

The keyboard was my first target. I whacked it out of Mom's hand.

CRASH

It hit the wall. Keys broke off and scattered across the carpet.

More faces pressed against the glass. I was a zoo animal on display for gawking tourists. A freak in a sideshow.

I kicked the desk.

BANG. BANG. BANG.

I twirled and hit anyone and anything in my way.

More faces in the window. Peter. Julian. Mason.

The hurricane inside me could destroy you all.

Skyler now in tears.

Cry for the beast. Stay away or I will hurt you.

Mom screeched. "Charity, try to control yourself! You're going to get hurt!"

Control myself? CONTROL MYSELF?

You've lived with me for thirteen years. You know that I AM NOT ALWAYS IN CONTROL!

I swung my arms. Crashing. Thrashing.

It felt so good to give in to my body.

Not *think* anymore.

Not *try so hard.*

More shouts and hands trying to pin my arms down.

I was strong. I kept going.

I am Godzilla, stomping out Tokyo.

My eyes opened, blind to the terror in Mom's face. Deaf to her words. I only wanted to crush and destroy and release my anger into the universe. My body knocked over a lamp. Books flew to the floor. Each hit and whack painted my arms and legs with bruises.

I felt nothing.

The door burst open.

It was Jergen, Jergen with his smooth hair and starched shirt, his nose wrinkled with disgust. Like I was some radio-active swamp monster.

My hand reacted without thought.

Grabbing Celia's snow globe.

Whipping it toward him like a major league pitcher.

CRASH!

It smacked the wall an inch from his head. A splat of water marked the yellow concrete. Plastic snowflakes dribbled down and melted into the carpet.

My arms fell to my side, and Dad grabbed me in a tight bear hug. My body sweat and bled and burned.

We both panted.

No one spoke.

The office was in shambles.

Celia's face flushed and wet.

Jergen's white.

All my muscles shook, and Dad tightened his grip, probably expecting another explosion. Instead, I did something I had not done since I was five. The day Mason moved away.

I cried.

My body sank to the floor and wet tears ran from my eyes.

I gasped through the sobs. Water flooded my face and soaked Dad's shirt. Mom and Dad sat on the floor holding me from both sides, their chests heaving.

I cannot say how long we sat there.

Time had stopped.

Over and Out

I opened my eyes, and I was in my bed. Maybe it had all been a bad dream, a terrible nightmare. No one else was in the room, but I heard whispers outside the door. I could not tell who was there. I closed my eyes, hoping to escape back into the nothingness of sleep.

And I did.

"Charity . . . Charity . . . we're here. Everything will be okay."

I woke again to see Mom stroking my hair. I tried to shake off the sleep, but everything seemed foggy.

"Charity, we're worried about you, honey."

It was Dad's voice now. He pulled me up a little and propped my body into sitting position.

"You've been in bed an awful long time. You need to wake up and eat and drink something. I've got a tofu scramble ready." He smiled. "Or maybe you wanna go right for the strawberry shake?"

The thought of food made me want to barf.

Mom inserted a straw into my mouth. "Let's start with a little sip, honey. You must be dehydrated."

I managed to sip from the straw. It was a sweet, fruity flavor. "That's it. Keep going."

I blinked my eyes, and the room came into focus. It was dark outside. Gram was sitting in a chair beside my bed, reading.

"Well, if it isn't Sleeping Beauty," she said, smiling.

Mom snuggled next to me and held up the keyboard. I remembered what I had done to the one at school.

My soul is shattered. I will fight no more. Why did I struggle for so long?

I pushed her arm away and curled into a ball. The world became dark again.

I woke again to Mom's high voice. With frantic eyes, she put a straw to my lips. I took a long sip. Dad's face smiled and nodded. I could not understand their words. Did we speak the same language?

I am a shadow in this world.

I do not belong here.

I wanted to escape to a world where *all* people were valued. A world where I was accepted and supported to be my real self, where I was no monster. Would that world ever exist?

Chances of me fitting in anywhere, ever: zero.

Dad picked me up and brought me to the sofa in the living room. Aunt Elvi and Aunt Kiki were in the kitchen making soup—standard operating procedure whenever anyone was sick.

"Hey, kiddo." Elvi knelt down by the sofa. "You gotta hang in there, ya hear? I mean, we all have to wade through the trashy days to get to the sunny days. I can tell you that from first-hand experience." She planted a kiss on my cheek.

Aunt Kiki hovered next to her. "Sweetie. You're going to be fine, just fine." She bit her red lip and caressed my forehead.

I squinted at the bright sunlight. It burned my eyes. I melted into the cushions and buried my head.

The world became dark again.

When I woke, I was in bed wearing new pajamas.

A dull light peeked through the windows. Sunrise or sunset? I had no idea.

Hero snored at my feet.

A warm body pressed against my back. I did not have to turn my head to know it was Mom.

I sat up.

Mom shook off her sleep and put her arms around me. Then she reached for the keyboard. I pushed her arm away.

Hero nudged his graying snout under my arm. I lay my cheek on his pudgy neck.

Mom and Dad made me drink again, a gross chocolate shake this time.

"This will give you energy to get back on your feet," Dad said. "You need a few more of these before your stomach can handle a strawberry shake. But I've got extra whip on hand when you're ready."

They got me dressed and tried to get me to walk, but my legs did not cooperate. I only wanted to lie in bed. After a few more tries, they finally let me be.

I imagined my life locked in an institution.

All of us throwaway kids wasting our lives together.

Dark thoughts floated in and out of my brain.

I heard Mom whisper out in the hallway. "She's barely eaten in three days. She refuses to type. She's . . . she's given up."

More whispers. I closed my eyes and put my hand on Hero's head. He was laying across my legs. His stubby tail wagged, tickling my knee.

I could pretend I was asleep until they went away. I put the pillow over my head.

The door creaked open.

"Charity, there are a few friendly faces here to see you, sweetheart."

I did not move.

Mom lifted my hand and gently moved the pillow to the side. I stayed limp, praying they would leave.

Mom let go of my hand.

Thank goodness.

Then another hand was on mine, this one cool with long, slender fingers. I knew this hand. I opened my eyes.

"My Charity. I came as soon as I could, but you know, France is quite far away." I stared into Ana's beautiful green eyes. She put a hand on my chest and breathed deeply, a long inhale and exhale, and my body followed her lead. We sat silently breathing for a long time. I felt some of the darkness leave with each exhale.

"*Querida*, tell us what you're feeling." It was Celia. She stroked my hair.

Ana held the keyboard and supported my arm. My hand felt limp. I did not have the energy to do this anymore.

"You have worked too long and too hard on your words to give them up," Ana said.

"Please, Cherry Girl." Dad looked as if he might cry.

I turned away.

Ana squeezed my shoulder. "I will never forget the first day you communicated with us. I felt your spirit trapped inside you. But even with all you'd suffered, you were electrified with hope and determination. I prayed your voice would break through all the obstacles standing in your way: the ignorance and pity of other people, the sadness of separation, the loneliness of silence. When you typed your first words, I imagined the spirits of countless children rising in jubilation, and a warm wind blew through my soul. I know it is difficult for you to see this sometimes, Charity, but you are one of the lucky ones. Your voice speaks for a million voices."

She held the keyboard and supported my arm.

"Talk to us, *querida*," Celia urged. "We're listening."

My finger reached out to tap the letter *I*. Ana nodded. "Keep going." Letter by letter, I typed my shame onto the keyboard. It felt like a scab being pulled from my skin. She read my words.

I AM A MONSTER. THEY DID RIGHT TO KICK ME OUT.

Celia held up her hand. "You have to accept that you are *not* your body. Your spirit is struggling with a body that often betrays you. I am not surprised that you exploded in anger, *querida*. I am amazed that you do not do it every hour of every day."

Ana nodded. "You *know* the kids at Lincoln are better off with you there."

I HAVE LOST THE BATTLE. I AM TOO WEAK TO KEEP FIGHTING.

Celia shook her head. "You may have lost a battle, but not the war." She shook a finger at me. "You know what, Charity?

I will be the first to tell you that life is not always fair. You were born with a disobedient body in a world that often treats you like a disease. But consider the many blessings you have. A brilliant mind and a courageous, giving soul. Two devoted parents. And a team of cheerleaders standing behind you, everyone from me and Ana to all your teachers and your friends at school. We are all part of Team Charity. You are setting an example for so many children. Your mission is to change the world, and I believe you can do it."

HOW CAN I HELP OTHERS WHEN I AM A CHARITY CASE?

Mom shivered when she heard this. "Charity, darling, is that how you see yourself, as a charity case? Don't you know what your name really means?"

I hung my head.

Mom held my chin and lifted my eyes toward hers. "The definition of *charity* is 'benevolent *love* of humanity.' From the moment you were born, I sensed your beautiful, open heart." She laid her hand on my chest. "Your name does not mean that others should pity you. *You* are the one opening your heart to the world." Mom hugged me tight.

"You can't let setbacks bench you, Cherry Girl," Dad said. "That's not the Charity I know."

I AM SORRY FOR LETTING YOU ALL DOWN.

"But Charity, do you realize that was the *first* meltdown you had in over a month?" Mom said.

"And under the circumstances, I'd say you had a good reason to blow your top," Celia laughed. "We just need to work on your technique."

Mom kissed me on the cheek. "There's no point looking backward with regret. We can only look forward. Celia said your teachers and friends have been asking about you. They want to know if you're all right."

DID SHE TELL THEM I WAS KICKED OUT?

"You have *not* been kicked out, *querida*. Tomorrow evening is the investigation hearing. We will make your case in front of the committee. You do not have to be there."

I breathed out pity and thought about how my life had changed since that day on the pier . . . when my foot dangled over the wild water's edge . . . when my guardian angel saw me as valuable and saved me.

Was I worth saving?

Memories played in my mind like a high-def IMAX film— Mason finding his courage, Julian and the welcome table, Jaz cheering at pep rallies, Skyler twirling at the dance. Did I play a part in these small miracles? Maybe I can make a difference.

Fact: I have a mission.

I tugged on Mom's arm. I needed to type more.

I NEED TO GO TO THE HEARING.

"No, sweetheart," Mom said. "You're in no condition . . ."
I pounded my hand on my leg.

THEY HAVE TO SEE ME TO UNDERSTAND MY STRUGGLE.

Ana nodded. "Actually, I agree."
Mom let out a big sigh. "Then I suppose we have some work to do."

Final Words

Thoughts swam through my head as Mom and Dad led me through the school parking lot to where Celia and Ana were waiting. Mom smoothed my hair and tucked my shirt into my pants, which were a little loose after the last three days.

No matter how well-dressed I was, my shaking, rocking, twitching body would show I was different. The superintendent never met me, but she would have no problem picking me out in a crowd.

We were surprised to see Celia dressed like Jergen, in a lawyerly suit with her cinnamon hair in a tight bun.

"I want to look respectable in front of the committee," she laughed.

"Me too," Dad said. "That's why I ditched my shorts and put on actual pants." He spun around to show off his khakis and button-down shirt.

"Steve, this is serious." Mom frowned. "Charity's future hangs on what happens in the next thirty minutes."

He kissed her on the cheek and turned to Celia, dead serious. "So, what's the plan?"

"I'm not certain what they will accuse her of," Celia said. "But we can testify that the essay they have is different from the one she submitted."

"In the end though, it's our word against theirs," he said. "And since Darcy's dad controls the purse strings, something tells me his word's worth twice as much."

Even Dad's sunny viewpoint was turning dark.

I knew he was royally right.

"The investigation committee is made up of three district staff members from other schools," Celia explained. "They have never met Charity, so our hope is that they will be neutral judges."

Dad pulled open the heavy door, and our determined group filed into the hallway, dim and empty. Mom and Dad clutched my hands. All of us had sweaty palms.

I stumbled forward, feeling a little like Dorothy approaching the Wizard of Oz.

Voices echoed from the auditorium.

My feet stopped in front of the door.

Ana turned to me. "Charity, may I be your helper in the meeting?"

Mom supported me. I typed, **YES PLEASE**.

"Thank you, Ana," Mom said. "I would probably make her more nervous."

Ana squeezed my shoulders and peered into my eyes for what seemed like forever. She whispered, her voice ever calm, "Now is the time, Charity. You are ready."

I felt her peaceful energy surge through me, and my hands shook a little less.

Mom checked her watch. "Now or never."

Celia gave me a thumbs-up. "All will be well, *querida*." Then she swung open the door. About a hundred people sat in the audience facing the committee members, who were sitting at a table on the stage. I sensed a simmering anger in the room. Three frowning adults sat at the front table next to Mr. Jergen.

My mind flashed to the snow globe nearly smashing his skull.

Oh no.

As we stepped forward, the auditorium erupted in chatter.

"Quiet, please," Mr. Jergen said, holding up his hand. He motioned to the front row. "Please have a seat."

I marched down the aisle holding Dad's hand, my eyes focused down on the pigeon-gray carpet to avoid the angry eyes around me. I could not let them break Ana's bubble of calm. Then my mind flashed to the disaster of Elvi's wedding.

I thought that was the most embarrassing moment of my life. Maybe that was only a warm-up act.

I sat in a cold plastic seat, Dad still holding my hand and Ana on my other side.

Darcy and her parents, a few seats down, did not even look at us. Mr. Warner wore his usual grumpy frown. Mrs. Bling-Bling spread her lips wide like a hyena ready to sink its teeth into a rotting corpse.

Ana kept breathing deeply, loud enough so I could hear.

I closed my eyes, and my breath fell in line with hers.

Inhale hope. Exhale fear.

Hearing my name, I peeked one eye open and saw Celia talking to the three committee members. Her hands held my progress reports, sample assignments, and statements from teachers.

After a few minutes, my restless body started to jiggle. No puzzle to work on. No fidget to twist.

I shifted in my seat. My shoulders started shrugging.

Shrug. Shrug. Shrug. Shrug.

If I had a kettle explosion in front of the committee, that would be the end of it. My feet shuffled on the floor.

Shuffle. Shrug. Shuffle. Shrug.

Ana squeezed my hand in a slow, even rhythm.

Jergen shook his head at Celia and pointed to a chair.

He stepped up to the podium and spoke into the microphone. "Quiet, please as we begin this hearing."

Celia sank into her seat next to Mom, and the room fell silent.

Jergen smiled at an older woman wearing a mint-green jacket and heavy wooden bracelets. She wore reading glasses and took notes on a yellow pad.

"That woman is the district superintendent," Ana whispered. "She doesn't usually participate in investigation committees."

I tried to judge the superintendent's mood, but I could not read her at all. My sixth sense was not working. Friend or enemy? I had no evidence for a hypothesis.

Jergen clenched the podium with both hands as if it might float away. His lips turned down, and he spoke in a deep voice. "The committee is here to address the claim that Miss Charity Wood and/or her aides have violated the school's policy on academic honesty. Additionally, she is accused of disruptive behavior that puts other students at risk. Ultimately, this committee must determine whether Miss Wood should be removed from Lincoln Junior High and placed in a school better equipped to handle her . . . special needs."

He turned to Darcy's mom. "We invite the first witness, Mrs. Mitzy Warner."

Mrs. Bling-Bling smoothed her flamingo-pink skirt and walked up to the podium. She turned to the committee members and flashed a glamorous grin.

"In the course of this school year, Miss Wood has disrupted classes and assaulted several students, including my daughter *and* her own cousin."

"What is she talking about?" Celia whispered to Mom and Dad.

Mrs. Bling-Bling picked up a remote control and pointed it at the screen behind her. "I present you with Exhibit A."

Five seconds of security video played on a repeating loop— Mason grabbing me by the jacket. Me hitting him in the face. Blood draining from his nose.

The audience inhaled a gasp.

"Shocking, isn't it?" she said.

Where did she get this? How did she know?

"Hey!" Brave Mason stood up from his chair in the row behind me. "She couldn't help that. It wasn't her fault."

Mrs. Bling-Bling snapped at him. "Sit down and be quiet, young man. Has no one taught you respect?"

Aunt Kiki pulled Mason back down into his seat.

So far . . . so bad.

Mrs. Bling-Bling smiled again to the committee. "It has also been determined by the board that Miss Wood's assistants have been completing work on her behalf, leaving the school open to accusations of fraud."

My head, my shoulder, my neck, and my arm jerked as if I was being hit by stones.

Mrs. Bling-Bling continued. "This is particularly disturbing in the case of Miss Wood's research paper for English class, which was found to contain several plagiarized passages. In spite of all this, she is eligible to compete for a spot on the school's honor roll and on their basketball team. She is, frankly, a first-class embarrassment for the school. Is this the way we want Lincoln represented?"

"I object. That is not true!"

I turned to see Stuart pointing his finger at her. The room hissed, but my mind focused on her words.

First-class embarrassment . . . Is this the way we want Lincoln represented?

Could it be her?

I looked over at Darcy. Her face frowned. I saw her reach into her mom's purse and pull out a sparkly phone. Darcy scrolled and tapped, scrolled and tapped her mom's phone.

Was it *her* all along?

Mason poked me from behind.

"Those are the same lines. The exact same lines from the gossip app!"

Fear leaked sweat through every pore. Bright lights pierced my closed eyelids.

If Darcy's mom was Sassygirl72, there was no way for me to prove it.

My body rocked hard.

Rockrockrockrockrock.

I let out a moan.

Ahhhhhhh . . .

But my cry was drowned out.

"Boooooooo. Boooooo."

Shouts came from the back of the auditorium.

My mouth closed. My head turned to look at the spectators behind me.

Why hadn't I seen them on my way in? The audience was angry, but not at *me*. Dozens of classmates and teachers held posters—some decorated with Skyler's cherry trees and bunnies. They all said, "*Let Her Stay!*"

I spotted Grace, Stuart, Skyler, Jaz, and Julian. There was Mr. Harding, Ms. Beckett, Coach George.

On the other side, my usual cheering section—Gram and Pops, Aunt Kiki, and there was Elvi standing, holding a poster over her head—"SHAME ON YOU LINCOLN!"

It took my breath away.

Mr. Jergen rushed up to the podium.

"Anyone who cannot maintain a respectful tone will be promptly removed." He nodded to a security guard, who stepped forward as proof of his threat.

Grace stood on top of her chair and shouted, "We stand with Charity. C'mon, girls!"

She raised her hands and voices began chanting.

> *She got the ball (clap)*
> *Get outta the way (stomp)*
> *C'mon, Charity! (clap)*
> *LET'S SCORE TODAY! (stomp)*

The Lincoln Hornets made an uproar, waving their arms for other students to join in.

And they did.

Teachers too.

Jergen motioned to the guard, who pulled Grace by the arm down from her seat to the sound of more boos.

"Silence! Silence, students!" Jergen shouted.

Shouts faded to whispers.

"Those of you who think you are helping Miss Wood's case are seriously misguided," Jergen said. "I insist that you allow Mrs. Warner to continue her statement."

"*No!*" a voice shouted out.

It was Darcy.

She held up her mom's phone. "I think you're done speaking, Sassygirl."

Darcy flung the phone onto the stage and stormed out.

Mrs. Bling-Bling turned pale. She shook her jittery head. "No, angel. You don't understand . . ."

She scanned the crowd. Kids whispered and pointed.

"No, no, no . . . it's not what you think . . ."

Translation: Sassygirl revealed!

Mrs. Bling-Bling kept shaking her head as her strappy sandals sprinted her off the stage and out the door after her daughter.

Jergen returned to the podium, looking like he had been stung by a jellyfish.

Page 131: Jellyfish tentacles release
toxins to stun prey before eating it.

"Ahem. It would seem that Mrs. Warner has concluded her statement."

The superintendent raised her hand to speak, and Jergen nodded.

"I am indeed impressed by the support for Miss Wood tonight," she said. "However, the facts of the case are troubling. The idea of a student handing in plagiarized work, along with testimony to that effect from a former aide, Ms. Ivy Thornton. How does the student respond to these accusations?"

Jergen turned his gaze toward me. His intense blue eyes drilled into me. He smiled. I guess he was happy. He would finally get his wish. "Good point, Dr. Schwartz," Jergen said. "I want to give Miss Wood the opportunity to speak for herself."

He nodded at Ana, who took my hand and led me to the stage.

What's going on here?

Jergen turned to the committee members. "I feel it is important for those of you who never met Miss Wood to see her for yourself and listen to her words. I could only say that the first time I witnessed it, my mind opened to the realization of my own ignorance. Miss Wood taught me something about myself, as I believe she has done for many of the people here tonight."

"Come, Charity," Ana said, "it is time for you to be heard."

I wanted to resist, but my body followed her up the four steps and onto the brightly lit stage.

Darcy's father bolted in front of us toward the podium. He put his hand over the microphone as he and Jergen began a battle of whispers.

A voice from the audience began to chant, "Let her speak! Let her speak!" It was Jaz leading the cheer, shaking her pompoms.

Dozens of others joined in.

Dr. Schwartz stood and joined the whispered conversation at the podium. After a few seconds, all of them sat down, and Dr. Schwartz nodded to us.

Ana led me to the podium. "Charity has prepared her own statement, which I will read to you." She looked at Mr. Warner, who huffed a big sigh and waved his hand, as if to say, "Whatever."

Ana rested her hand on my shoulder, and I closed my eyes, praying to stay still for these few minutes. She cleared her throat and spoke each of my words with care.

FOR 13 YEARS I HAD NO VOICE. NO WAY TO SAY I LOVE YOU OR I AM HUNGRY OR I WANT A STRAWBERRY MILKSHAKE.

Some people chuckled.

NO WAY TO SCREAM FOR HELP. I SPENT YEARS NOT AT A SCHOOL BUT AT A PRISON WHERE NO ONE THOUGHT OF ME AS A REAL PERSON WITH A BRAIN. HUNGRY TO LEARN, I WAS WELCOMED HERE BY CARING TEACHERS AND STUDENTS WHO GAVE ME A CHANCE TO BE ONE OF THEM. EVERY PERSON HAS A RIGHT TO BE INCLUDED. AS FREDERICK DOUGLASS SAID, "THE RIGHTS OF THE HUMBLEST CITIZEN ARE AS WORTHY OF PROTECTION AS ARE THOSE OF THE HIGHEST." THAT IS A QUOTATION. I KNOW THE DIFFERENCE BETWEEN QUOTING AND PLAGIARIZING.

A few more people laughed.

I REGRET ANY TROUBLE I HAVE CAUSED WITH MY BODY THAT I STRUGGLE TO COMMAND. YOU AND I FEAR NOTHING IN LIFE WHEN WE ARE ACCEPTED FOR WHO WE ARE.

The audience started to clap, but Ana put up her hand to quiet them.

"I believe Charity wishes to add something else." Ana nodded at me and placed the iPad and the keyboard on the podium. She pulled me closer and whispered, "Remember what we were practicing before I left? I know you can do it. Speak your truth, Charity."

The room became pin-drop silent.

My mission came down to this moment. I looked out at the crowd—hundreds of eyeballs staring at me, including Mason right up front. But these stares did not make me feel puny. An army of supporters sat in front of me. The love I sensed from each one of them superglued my broken heart together and filled it with helium.

Ana steadied the keyboard, but she did *not* hold my elbow. Instead, she put her hand on my shoulder. I heard her breathing and my lungs inhaled as much hope as they could.

I felt my finger reach for the keyboard. As I did, every creature in the *Amazing Kids' Animal Encyclopedia* filled the stage with me, from aardvarks to zebras.

Page 210: Amazon parrots.
Page 23: Black bears.
Page 311: Warthogs.

I tapped one key. Then another.

"Keep going," Ana said. "Is that the letter you want?" "What comes next?"

Page 30: Chameleons.
Page 89: Goats.
Page 212: Pelicans.

She did not hold my arm, but her spirit guided me with faith in my ability.

I do not know how much time passed.

I do not know if the audience was noisy or quiet.

Page 301: Wallabies.
Page 29: Bobcats.
Page 176: Moose.

All the world faded away. Only me and my animals facing the keyboard, tapping letter by letter, word by word until my arm lowered.

"Are you done?" Ana asked. I reached over to type one more letter: Y.

She read my words. Not perfect, but hopefully clear.

I WANT A RREAL EDUCATION SO I CANNN SAVE OTHER CHILDREN WHO ARE HURTING LIKE I WAS. I AM A VVVOICE OF NEVER HEARD VOICES.

No one in the audience moved or spoke. Then Mr. Jergen stood and started to clap. He was joined by other board members and audience members, until the whole auditorium vibrated with cheers and applause. Celia came up and kissed me on the cheek. Grace ran up to us too, along with Skyler and Stuart.

Mom and Dad sat frozen in the front row with teary smiles.

Dr. Schwartz approached the podium.

"I want to thank Miss Wood for her wise words."

She turned to Mr. Warner. "I believe some of the information I was provided on Miss Wood was incorrect. Given her statement and the tremendous support in this room, I recommend that we dismiss this complaint."

More cheers and applause filled the room. My lips smiled—at least I think they did—and my helium heart soared to the sky.

Like Pinocchio, being loved made me real.

Mission Possible

Mom rushed to get my clothes ready for the presentation. This was our second trip to the state university. Dr. Peterman asked me to speak at a teachers' conference about being included in regular junior high classes. No pink dresses—that was my rule. Instead, I chose black pants and a peacock blue sweater with cool leather boots. I even got dressed today with almost no help from Mom, except for sticking the earrings into my newly pierced ears—silver starfish that Stuart got me for my birthday. Actually, not fish at all, but sea stars, according to page 254.

"Here," Mom said, "take a look at yourself, Charity." She encouraged me over to the full-length mirror, and I stared into the looking glass.

For a decade, my own reflection made me sad. I saw myself the way the world saw me—worthless.

Today, I am beginning to like me. The real me. Okay just as I am.

Celia says anger is a prison we lock ourselves into. I am still trying to bail myself out as I forgive Darcy and Miss Marcia and everyone who caused me pain over the years. Let's just say it's a process.

I entered the auditorium, and Dr. Peterman gave me a warm hug. "Good to see you again, Charity. I heard your science fair project got second place. Bravo! By the way, I visited Abby at Pine Valley again last week, and she's started typing some words now. Her mom is so grateful to you."

Best news ever.

Because the presentation would be streamed live through the internet, I waved into the camera. I knew Skyler, Jaz, and Julian would be gathered around the big computer screen in Celia's classroom . . . along with Isabella. Once her mom saw my picture in the local paper for topping the honor roll, she requested a transfer for Isabella. Celia, with the help of Mr. Jergen, sped up the process as a favor to me. Every morning, I got to see Isabella's bouncing red curls in homeroom. I could not believe how far she'd come in only two months. Skyler was showing her how to draw with pastels, and the girl was a natural.

Jaz would probably be wearing her cheerleading uniform today. After Darcy left, the girls on the squad all begged Jaz to join. Jaz agreed right away, but she drew the line when Rachel invited her to sit at the cool kids' table. "I have standards, you know," she joked.

We did not have to worry about Darcy teasing us. She transferred to an expensive private school that overlooks the ocean. I hoped she was doing well. I really did.

As for Borden, Mom emailed the reporter a copy of my paper, and the reporter dug up even more evidence against them.

Borden's enrollment tanked after her article came out in the newspaper. Then the state suspended their license, "pending investigation."

Will the school finally be shut down?

Probability: hopeful.

When it was time for me to present, Mom led me to the podium and squeezed my hand as she read my prepared statement. Once she was finished, I took questions. Today, there was a woman in a canary-yellow jacket who raised her hand.

"Charity, I am very moved by your story. People assumed for years that you could not learn. Then you scored in the top tier on your school's assessment test. Do you think there are other kids like you who are left behind by being labeled with low expectations?"

Mom held my iPad so I could type. She encouraged me with each letter and word, but today, as on many days, I did not need her to support my arm. The tablet helped too by using predictive text to complete some of my words faster. My dependable pointing speed today made me feel less like a typing snail and more like a powerful punching kangaroo.

Mom read my response.

IT DOES NOT MATTER IF A TEST SAYS THEY ARE SMART. IT MATTERS THAT THEY ARE HUMAN. BELIEVE THAT TREASURES ARE IN ALL. BELIEVE THAT ALL KIDS CAN LEARN. EVERYONE DESERVES TO BE INCLUDED.

The woman nodded her head. "I understand. You're right, Charity. Thank you for showing me that."

A man in a striped shirt raised his hand.

"Charity, can you describe what it's like to have your challenges?"

I SEE THE WORLD DIFFERENTLY. OFTEN I CANNOT CONTROL MY BODY. I CANNOT DO MANY THINGS THAT OTHER PEOPLE DO. BUT I CAN OPEN MY HEART. CAN YOU?

The man smiled and nodded.

I am Charity. Tomorrow is my fourteenth birthday. I still love sour gummies and pepperoni pizza. And like my name says, my heart is open to all the world.

Afterword by Carol Cujec

This book was inspired by the wisest, most courageous person I know, my friend Peyton Goddard. Peyton could not speak and did not have full control over her body when she was young, so the experts (she called them the Thinkers) labeled her "severely mentally challenged." They could not see her brilliant mind trapped inside. Here is how she describes it:

PERSONALLY, I SAW A LIFE I'LL NEVER WANT ANYONE TO TEACH AS ACCEPTABLE FOR ANY HUMAN BEING. UNDERSTATERS UTTER I'M NO ONE. I'M BROKEN, NOTHING WORTHY, MOLDY BREAD, THROW-AWAY TRASH.

She was removed from public school and sent to a school like Borden Academy, where she was often left sitting alone on the blacktop of the playground or locked in a seclusion room.

I DAILY WENT NOT TO SCHOOL, BUT TO VARIOUS INSTITU-TIONS, DEFINED BY ME AS ANY PLACE THAT ALL PEOPLE ARE NOT INCLUDED. SEGREGATION IS THE BEAST WHOSE BITE CHEATS US ALL. THE ISOLATION OF PEOPLE DIFFERENT RENDERS YOU AND ME

STRANGERS. REALITY IS THAT YOU ARE ME AND I AM YOU. DIFFER-
ENCE IS IN ALL OF US. FEAR IT WE DO NOT NEED.

Peyton became severely depressed. When her parents realized the abuse she was suffering, they fought to get her into
a public-school classroom with the support she needed. Right
away, they saw improvements in Peyton's ability to control her
body and in her overall well-being.

When Peyton was twenty-two years old, her mom learned
about supported typing and arranged for Peyton to be evalu-
ated. Her mom did not expect much to come of it, though.
She had tried, unsuccessfully, typing with Peyton at home
many times.

In her very first typing session, Peyton amazed everyone
when she typed a sentence she hoped would forever change the
way people treated her: I AM INTLGENT.

Finally able to communicate, Peyton asked for the one
thing she always wanted—a real education. And that's what
she got. With the support of teachers and administrators at
Cuyamaca College in San Diego, Peyton became the first person using supported typing to graduate valedictorian from a
US college.

Today, she is working on speaking words with her lips and
continuing to fight for the millions of kids who deserve to be
included in our classrooms and communities. She would like
all readers to understand the value of friendship, especially for
kids who are different.

TO HAVE FRIENDS IS THE MOST IMPORTANT THING FOR ALL
PEOPLE. WITHOUT FRIENDS, A PERSON CANNOT HAVE FUN. IT IS

HARD TO LIVE. THERE IS NO JOY, JUST SADNESS. I HAVE FELT THIS, BECAUSE I LOOK DIFFERENT AND I AM LABELED AUTISTIC. I CANNOT ALWAYS CONTROL MY BODY. IT DOES NOT DO WHAT MY MIND TELLS IT. MY FACE CANNOT SHOW MY FEELINGS. FOR MOST OF MY LIFE, I HAD TO SPEAK THROUGH BEHAVIORS AND MOST PEOPLE MISUNDERSTOOD. I NEED HELP TO DO MOST THINGS. BUT I CAN OPEN MY HEART. CAN YOU?

THERE IS JOY FOR ALL KIDS TO GREATLY CONTRIBUTE TO THE NECESSARY IMPROVEMENT OF HUMANITY BY PARTICIPATING AND BELONGING AND CONTRIBUTING AND HAVING DIVERSE FRIENDS.

THIS IS MY WISH FOR ALL OF YOU.

Acknowledgments

FROM CAROL AND PEYTON:

Dear readers, thank YOU for picking up our book. Like Charity, we're on a mission to spread kindness and include all people. We're tossing the ball to you now. Will you pass it forward for us? We want to hear your stories. Find us on social media and let us know what you're up to.

Teachers and librarians, thank YOU for seeing every child as capable. We would love to meet with your students, virtually or in person.

With endless gratitude to our agent, Stacey Glick, who never stopped believing our story needed to be told.

We loudly love the creative minds at Shadow Mountain Publishing, who embraced our story with open hearts, crafted our beautiful cover art, masterfully edited it, and helped us launch kindness into the universe.

Deep appreciation to our beta readers in the beloved community of inclusionists, who read and cheered us on—Caren Sax, Emma van der Klift, Norm Kunc, Diana Pastora Carson, Beth Gallagher, Jacque Thousand, and Rich Villa. And Anne

Donnellan, trailblazing pioneer exploring sensory-movement differences in autism, who encouraged us along the way. To all non-speakers, whose writings lifted and advised *REAL,* keep telling the world your stories so we can understand each other better.

FROM CAROL:

With everlasting love to my family. Anton, I am heartened by your kind heart. Noah, I am uplifted by your keen wit. Ella, thank goodness you were my first reader, with highlighter in hand, telling me you never wanted the story to end. To my wonderful husband, Tom, I am forever grateful for your love and support. Hugs also to my eight siblings and their sweet families for their encouragement and never-ending supply of bad jokes.

To my beta readers: Anne Marie, my SCBWI critique group (Jeanne, Danielle, Alyssa, Jessica, Fran, Ruth), and David Larson's writing meet-up. Googolplex thanks for your precious feedback and firm nudges forward.

Finally, to my many students over the years—you have also been my teachers. Thank you.

FROM PEYTON:

I loudly thank all persons who hearted help lift up my living. Each of your kindnesses hurry my healing and rest me as real.

To my family, your love saturates me, fueling my IOU quest to teach "treasure all, great is each." Murray and Lincoln, each dawning day your caring betters me and my writing. I am jellybeans happy you are my nephews.

To all who type to talk, your voices seed my feathers of hope for a better world where all are valued and welcome.

To those still waiting to be seen as real, know I will never stop advocating until all voices can be heard.

Discussion Questions

1. In the beginning of the book, why do people like Elvi and Miss Marcia assume Charity can't learn? What evidence do they have? Can we make assumptions about how a person's mind works based on the way their body moves? Is it okay to think that because someone cannot speak, they cannot understand?

2. Why do you think Charity's dad can teach her to surf and ride a bike, when doctors said she could never do these things? What makes him such a good teacher, according to Charity? Is there something you learned to do (or want to learn) even though someone told you that you can't?

3. How does Charity define pity? Why do you think she feels puny when people pity her? What makes you feel puny? What makes you feel real?

4. Why does Charity feel hopeless at the beginning of the book? What is her life like? What does she want more than anything?

5. When Charity feels overwhelmed by emotions, she often

thinks of her animals to help calm her. How do you stay in control when you feel overwhelmed?

6. Describe the changes in Mason from beginning to end. How does he think about Charity in the beginning of the book? Why? What makes him change his opinion? Why does he take a risk and stand up for her at school? Tell us about a time you stood up for a friend even if you felt scared.

7. Charity's first typed sentence was "I am intelligent." Why do you think she typed that first? If you were in Charity's place, what would your first sentence be? Why?

8. Charity says, "Believe that treasures are in all." What treasures might exist in characters like Skyler or Jazmine that can't be measured? What treasures exist in you that can't be measured?

9. Charity also says, "Believe that all kids can learn." How does this attitude—*Every Person Is Capable*—affect the way we treat people like Charity who can't talk or who communicate differently?

10. Once Charity is able to communicate, she discovers her true mission. What is it? Share ideas about your possible mission.

11. Charity tells us that kids like her rarely have friends. Why do you think that is? What are some ways to bring kids together instead of keeping them apart? Can you think of ideas for your school or community?

12. Try not speaking for one day (or half a day) and only communicating by typing on a tablet or writing in a notebook. How did it feel? What did you learn?